Body & Soul

By

Terri Molina

Body & Soul
Copyright 2019 by Terri Molina
ISBN: 978-1-68361-331-2

Cover art by Fantasia Frog Designs

Published by Decadent Publishing Company, LLC
Look for us online at:
www.decadentpublishing.com

Spiritualist Sylvia Chavez is well-known in the Rio Grande Valley as a gifted clairvoyant who has been helping the families in her community since she was a child. When she learns one of her clients is the latest victim in a series of ritual killings, she inserts herself into the investigation with the man who broke her heart ten years earlier. But what Sylvia doesn't tell him is that the killer is much more dangerous than he knows, and he wants revenge on her family.

Agent Steven Gonzales with the Texas Department of Public Safety's Criminal Investigations Division believes the murders are connected to a South Texas drug lord rumored to be involved in black magic sacrifices. Although Steven doesn't believe in the hocus-pocus, he allows Sylvia to consult on the case, as long as she keeps her theories of witches and black magic to herself.

Sylvia accepts she will always love Steven, but she won't risk giving him her heart if he has no faith in her. But when the spirits abandon her and all signs point toward death, can she put the past behind her and help him find the killer before it's too late?

When readers began to ask for Sylvia's book, I wasn't sure she had a story to tell. As a native Texan of Mexican descent, I am always anxious to delve into the history and superstition of my ancestry, and I realized, that is who Sylvia is too. It took a lot of fighting with her to get it all on paper, but the results were worth the headaches. I hope you enjoy her story and I would love to hear from you. You can catch me at Facebook, Twitter or email me at TerriMo2@yahoo.com

Body and Soul

Thank you for reading!

Chapter One

Six years working homicide with the Texas Department of Public Safety's Criminal Investigations Division and Steven Gonzales still wasn't prepared for the overwhelming stench of death coming from the mutilated body left to rot in the south Texas heat. He stooped under the yellow crime scene tape and made his way across the desert floor to his partner, David Sanchez.

"Is it our guy?"

"Can't say for sure," David said, meeting him halfway. "But from what I can tell, it's pretty close."

Steven followed him to the partially decomposed body spread-eagled over a bed of rocks. The victim was nude and female, barely in her twenties. Her hands and feet were bound with twine and tied to wooden spikes nailed into the ground. Dried blood and dirt was smeared over most of her body as if the killer had used her as a canvas. Flat stones encircled the area, the surfaces covered with fat black candle stubs and melted wax. Burned into the center of the woman's forehead was a five-point star within in a circle.

"We've just started canvassing the area. The sheriff's deputies wouldn't go near the body until the area had been neutralized."

"Neutralized?" Steven glanced around and noticed strings of garlic and peppers hanging in the mesquite trees and from the prickly ears of cacti. White candles had been placed intermittently inside the crime scene tape, leaving a wide enough berth to pass through without kicking one over. He shook his head and scowled. "You've got to be kidding me."

David shrugged. "Ritual killing. They don't want the bad magic turning on them."

Steven grabbed a pair of latex gloves from his pocket and moved toward the body. "I guess it's too much to ask if we have an ID on this one?"

"You're in luck. Her name is Caridad Angelica Salazar. So far, all we know is she's from up near Mathis. Couple kids' dirt-biking found her, called it in." He motioned toward a burly dark-skinned man in faded jeans and a thin denim jacket, speaking Spanish to two deputies. "San Patricio County Sheriff was able to identify her. Said she worked at a secondhand clothing store in downtown Mathis. Her boss reported her missing about a week ago after the impound lot called and said her car had been towed there. Apparently, she sold her old VW to Ms. Salazar but never had the title switched over.

"The ME has already been here," he continued before Steven could ask. "He went back up to the road to wait on his team. He couldn't say how long she's been dead. We'll have to wait until after the autopsy to verify. With the warm weather we've been having lately, I'd guess at least a couple days."

Steven pulled on the gloves and crouched down to examine the body. A pool of blood had gathered at the base of the woman's skull. He carefully turned the head and inspected the open wound. A section of her skull had been sawed off. The brain was missing.

"Pretty gory. You ever see anything like that before?" David asked. "Someone taking a brain for a token?"

Steven exhaled heavily and continued to inspect the body. "No. And I really don't care to imagine what he wants it for."

David sent him a brittle laugh and shook his head. "Maybe he's building his own Frankenstein's monster."

Steven didn't comment, but a part of him wondered if he had a point. Over the past five months, three bodies had been found in what appeared to be ritualistic killings, and each had been missing a vital organ. Their original theory had been black market organ donation, but with the inclusion of the brain, it was no longer a viable assumption. "You said she's been here at least two days? Why haven't the animals haven gotten to her yet?"

"Sheriff mentioned there was some sort of chemical about ten feet out, encircling the area. The smell probably kept them away. He also said the candles were still lit when she was found. He thinks our killer spent the two days with her, finishing up whatever ritual he was doing. Those kids who found her were lucky he was gone when they came across the body."

If the killer is who I think it is, they were damn lucky. Steven shifted his attention to the woman's hand. He carefully pried the fingers open and lifted a palm-sized black flannel bag from her grip.

David peered over Steven's shoulder. "What's that?"

"I don't know." He straightened and carefully stepped to the edge of the yellow tape enclosing the crime scene. He opened the bag and sprinkled the contents onto his gloved hand. Several dried twigs and a silver coin spilled out.

"It's a *bolso del mojo*." The sheriff moved forward and tipped his head at the bag.

David raised a brow. "A mojo bag?"

"It holds an *amparo* made by a witch or *curandera*. They are sometimes used for protection."

Steven knew he was going to regret asking, but he did anyway. "Protection from what?"

The sheriff shrugged. "Whatever or whoever the person felt they were in danger from." He glanced at the body and frowned. "'Doesn't look like it did her much good, though, does it?"

"You don't happen to know who she went to for this, do you?"

The sheriff raised his brow at the hard tone in Steven's voice. He hesitated as if he wasn't sure he wanted to give out the information. "No. But there's a woman in Edmondville, about two hours south of here. Her name's Chavez. She might be able to help you."

Steven went still. "Chavez? Sylvia Chavez?"

"*Si*, that's her."

"You know her?" David asked.

"Yeah. Her brother and I were college roommates. She and I were sort of...uh...friends." Regret punched him in the gut as soon as he said the words. He and Sylvia had been more than friends, but he'd betrayed her the night she gave him her innocence.

David turned toward the sheriff. "So, what? Is Ms. Chavez some sort of a witch?"

The sheriff snorted. "You'd better not let Ms. Chavez hear you call her that. She's a spiritualist. Does only the white magic."

The words jarred Steven from his thoughts. "What did you say?"

"*Si*. She has *clientelas* from all over the valley go to her for help. Ms. Salazar might have been one of them. But, unless she knows you, she isn't going to see you. You're going to need a referral."

"A referral? Are you serious?" David asked.

The sheriff shrugged. "She keeps a pretty low profile to avoid trouble. I suggest you don't go in guns blazing," he added, with a pointed look at Steven.

Steven returned the contents to the bag and scowled. *Terrific. Sylvia is another self-proclaimed witch filling desperate women with false hope and getting them killed.*

4

"Well, let's hope Ms. Chavez remembers you," David said.

***

Sylvia could tolerate a lot of things. Being called a witch was not one of them. She was a spiritualist, dammit. She didn't cast spells or worship the devil or do any of those other idiotic things people thought witches did. Okay, so maybe she *did* cast a spell or two once in a while, but they were basic protection spells to ward off evil, not curse an enemy or keep a loved one from straying. It didn't seem to matter how often she argued the distinction, there was always someone labeling her.

She tucked her cell phone against her shoulder and pulled out the magazine hidden under the counter. Her brother's name and address were on the label. She shook her head and set the magazine down.

A woman's nasally voice piped through the cell phone. "*Señora* Chavez, I love him so much. I need him to stay with me. I'd die without my José. Please."

"Carla, I told you, I'm not a witch. I don't do spells, and I don't make love potions." Sylvia tried to keep the annoyance from her voice, but she'd been on the phone with Carla Dominguez for nearly fifteen minutes and was starting to get a headache.

"I just need to know if he loves me. I'll pay you. Whatever you want. I can pay you."

Sylvia dropped her head back and held her breath with a mental count to five. It wasn't about the money; she made plenty as the acting postmaster at the Edmondville post office, but again, it was another one of those distinctions her clients looked past.

She eased out a resigned sigh. "Look, I can come by after work and do the cards again. But, that's all I can do." Although she couldn't guarantee *that* would even work since, for the past month, neither the cards nor her spirit board had been very forthcoming.

"Oh, *si*, thank you, thank you, thank you. I'll see you then."

Sylvia disconnected the call and groaned. God, if she ever became that obsessed with a man, someone better shoot her.

She stole a look at the clock mounted on the wall behind her. Only half an hour and she could lock up the substation, go home, and soak in a hot tub.

"I can close up for you if you want." Gabriel Mendoza, a fixture in the post office for the past twenty-five years, hobbled into the lobby carrying a white plastic tub. Stenciled on the side were the words US MAIL. "I still owe you for the half day you gave me last week."

She waved him off. "You don't owe me anything. You deserved to be at the birth of your granddaughter, especially since she's number twelve. That's a lucky number."

The man grinned, the creases deepening around his eyes. "She's a special one, all right." He placed the tub on the counter. "You look tired, boss. At least take a break, and I'll watch the front for you."

She considered the request. "Okay, you talked me into it. Thanks, Gabe." She took the bucket from him and moved toward a set of swinging doors as he settled behind the counter. "Oh, and try not to crinkle those pages. I don't think Ray will appreciate you reading his magazine before he does."

Gabe's gold tooth gleamed with his grin as he flipped open the *Sports Illustrated* she'd left on the counter.

Sylvia chuckled and shook her head as she continued toward the rear of the building. She flipped the tub onto a small worktable and spilled out a mound of envelopes. She sorted through them, making sure they were each facing the same way, then stacked them upside down on the postmarking machine. She pressed the green start button, and the machine hummed to life, whisking each envelope through to cancel the stamp. When it finished, she restacked the envelopes, placed them in a cardboard tray, and slid it into a metal rack tucked against the wall.

She took a minute to stretch out her tired muscles before heading across the floor to the locker room, which also doubled as a break room. Her heart nearly stopped when she spotted her future sister-in-law doubled over on a chair.

"Lexie!" Sylvia rushed forward and knelt in front of her, pressing her palm against Lexie's forehead. Clammy but not hot. "Are you okay? What happened?" She glanced around the room, tuning her senses to the empty space. There was no one there except her and Lexie.

"I'm fine." Lexie straightened in the seat. "I was just feeling a little dizzy. No big deal."

Sylvia dropped onto a vacant chair. "Jeez, you scared the hell out me."

Lexie sent her a benign smile. "Sorry. I guess I shouldn't have skipped lunch."

"You missed lunch? I thought you were going home for lunch."

"I did, but...." Her cheeks flushed pink. "Ray and I sort of got sidetracked."

Sylvia exhaled a disgusted breath. "Ugh, you guys are like a couple of horny rabbits." She rose and moved to the narrow refrigerator in the corner. She grabbed a bottle of water for herself and an orange juice, which she handed to Lexie. "You two need to get married already. I hear it really kills the sex life."

Lexie laughed. "God, I hope not."

Sylvia took a drink of the water, studying Lexie over the plastic. She looked okay, maybe a little flushed, but that could be from the afternoon delight with Ray. Maybe she should do the cards, find out if there was anything they should be worried about. Things had been quiet for the past ten months, but it could be the calm before the storm.

Lexie shook her head. "Would you stop doing that?"

Sylvia gave her a sheepish grin. "Sorry. I wasn't trying to read you. You sure you're okay?"

Her lips curved into a wry smile. "I'm wonderful." She rose to retrieve her purse from a box-sized cubicle. "But I do have to run. I told Ray I'd meet him at the grocery store. If I let him shop alone, we'll be eating macaroni for the rest of the month. I'll see you at your grandparents' later?"

"Yeah. But not for dinner. I have a date."

"Oh? Vincent, again? That's what? A month you've been dating?"

Sylvia sent her a wary look. "Six weeks. But don't read anything into it."

"I'm not. I'm just saying, I've never seen you date anyone seriously before."

"I don't do serious. I enjoy men so much better when there's no commitment," she added with a wink. After the call with Carla, she wasn't in the mood to talk about falling in love or happy-ever-after. Those dreams had died a long time ago.

Lexie pulled on a light jacket and turned to smile at her. "Well, I think it's great you're with someone, even if he's not *the one*. And, since I know you, you've probably already read *him*, which means he can't be all that bad."

Sylvia laughed. She'd been born with the gift of foresight and an uncanny ability to read people and sometimes know their thoughts. Over the years, it had become her own built-in relationship meter, and she used it to weed out the less-than-potential men who asked her out. It wasn't fair to the men, really, but it was her heart on the line, and she wasn't going to give it to just anyone. She'd done that once, and it had been thrown back at her, chopped into a million pieces. But, Vincent was different. She didn't sense anything harmful about him the first time they met. And when he'd asked her to dinner, the cards didn't have anything to say about him, good or bad. However, there was still a part of her reluctant to take the relationship further, that she couldn't quite explain.

"So, I guess I should add him to the guest list?" Lexie asked.

"Actually, I wasn't planning to bring him. He usually works weekends, plus I'll be so busy with my bridesmaid duties it didn't seem fair to ask him to sit with a bunch of strangers."

"Okay." Lexie sent her a commiserating smile. "Oh, I almost forgot. Ray heard from his old college roommate, Steven, and he's going to be able to make it to the wedding. I think he even agreed to fill in as a groomsman, so now you won't have to walk down the aisle alone."

"Steven?" Sylvia's heart did a triple backflip and landed like a hot stone in her stomach. She made an effort to loosen her fingers on the water bottle. "Steven Gonzales? I didn't know they still spoke."

"Ray said they hadn't spoken in a few years, but he heard from him the other day. Something about a case he's working on and that he was going to be in town. He's coming to your grandparents' house for dinner tonight. It's too bad you'll miss him. I think he asked about you."

"Really?" Sylvia said, managing to keep her voice even.

"I heard Ray tell him you worked for the post office." She pulled out her phone when it chimed and glanced at it. "Oh, Ray's waiting on me. I'd better go. I'll see you later."

Sylvia waited for Lexie to leave then pulled in a shallow breath to slow her racing heart. *Steven.* She hadn't seen him in what...ten years? Not since Ray's senior year in college when he'd spent the July 4th weekend at her grandparents' farm. She'd been head over heels in love with him, and they'd shared a night of passion she'd never experienced before or since. He'd been her first, and her foolish heart thought he'd be her only. But in the morning when she awoke, he was gone. No note, no phone call, nothing. And she never heard from him again.

She folded her arms on the table and rested her head on them. He'd be thirty-four now. Not that she remembered he was five years and six months older than her or that he'd been born on Valentine's Day.

She frowned as the memory of their night together broke through the crevices of her mind.

She'd spent the day with him and Ray on South Padre Island, swimming in the gulf and horseback riding. When they'd returned home, she took him for a walk in the cornfield, to the spot where she knew her ancestors' spirits were the strongest. Under a waxing moon, he'd pulled her into his arms and kissed her.

They'd made love right there in the fields, surrounded by six-feet tall stalks of corn. He'd been so gentle, touching her as if he were handling fine china. His kisses had sent a blaze of passion through her so fierce she didn't think she'd ever reach a normal body temperature again. Even now, the thought of his body on hers sent hot currents scorching through her veins. The memory still made her moan.

"Uh, Sylvia?"

She bolted upright, pulling in a lungful of air. *Shit! Was that out loud?*

Gabe peered around the door. He cleared his throat and took a hesitant step forward. "There are some men here to see you. They look important."

She sent him what she hoped was an easy smile. "Thanks, Gabe. I'll be right there."

She waited for him to leave then scrubbed her hands over her face. Damn that son of a bitch Steven for invading her mind! Why did he have to come back now? And how the hell was she supposed to look at him, stand with him at the church, like nothing had ever happened between them? *Because I'm doing it for Ray and Lexie. Nothing is going to mess up their big day. Not even that jerk.*

She pushed away from the table and headed to the lobby. Two men stood in the center of the room, facing the front door and speaking in low tones. They were dressed the same—dark suit jackets, Wrangler jeans, black cowboy boots, and cream-colored Stetsons. She gave herself a moment to admire the solid frame of their bodies, the narrow hips and long muscular legs. She loved a cowboy in formfitting jeans.

She cleared her throat to get their attention. "Gentlemen?"

In unison, the two men turned around.

Recognition punched her in the chest and took her breath away. He'd grown more into his body. His chest was broader, his face more rugged, but he was still the same drop-dead gorgeous man she remembered from ten years ago.

She swallowed hard, fighting against the giant butterflies battering her stomach. His smile was quick and sexy, and she nearly melted into a puddle of need. *Pinche cabron!*

Steven stepped forward, his arms rising as if he planned to greet her with a hug. "Sylvia." Her name sounded wistful on his breath.

She planted her feet and waited for him to move closer. Before he could touch her, she swung her arm back and punched him in the jaw.

The man standing beside him barely concealed his laugh. "Yeah, I'd say she remembers you all right."

Chapter Two

"A handshake would have sufficed," Steven growled, rubbing a palm over his chin. Although he hadn't been expecting the hit, he'd managed to stay on his feet. He touched his lip with his tongue and tasted blood. No one could ever accuse Sylvia Chavez of hitting like a girl.

She ignored him and turned to his partner with a refined smile. "I'm Sylvia Chavez. What can I help you with?"

David shot Steven an amused look before pulling out his badge. "I'm Special Agent David Sanchez with the Texas Department of Public Safety Criminal Investigations Division. You apparently already know my partner."

She swept a look at the silver star and nodded. "Why don't we talk in the break room?"

Steven watched her turn and saunter back into the room she'd come from. Ray had told him his sister was the postmaster of the small station, which was why she didn't wear the standard uniform. His gaze slid down to follow the sway of her hips, snug in the faded jeans. She was taller than he remembered, still slender but with fuller curves in all the right places. Longing shot through him like a surge of electricity as the image of her in his arms flashed through his mind. He could still feel the softness of her skin against his palm, taste her passion on his tongue, hear the throaty moan as she surrendered herself to him. He'd never had a woman leave such an ingrained impression on his senses, not before Sylvia and never since.

Although she'd greeted him with a right cross, all he wanted to do was take her to a hotel and make love to her until she forgot why she hated him.

David's not-so-subtle clearing of his throat jolted Steven from his thoughts. "Are you ready, or do you need a little time to roll your tongue back in your mouth?"

"Shut up," Steven growled, stepping past him to push through the swinging door.

Sylvia moved into the break room and waved the men to the folding chairs tucked under the card table as she continued to the mini refrigerator for an icepack. *Damn his hard-as-a-rock jaw. Probably sprained my wrist.* She sat in the seat across from the two men and placed the ice pack over her knuckles.

Steven sent her a sympathetic smile. "Is your hand okay?"

She spared him a glance. She'd felt his gaze on her ass earlier and hated that her body had reacted like a fifteen-year-old with her first crush. That bastard wasn't getting anywhere near her body again!

She turned to the other officer, David. "You want to talk to me about the ritual killings."

David's brow came up as he set his Stetson on the table. "How did you...?"

Sylvia shrugged. For the past six months, her client list had increased, with younger women wanting spells to protect them from the serial killer on the loose. But, she wasn't about to tell them that. "Word travels. So, how can I help you?"

The two men exchanged a look then Steven dug into his jacket and pulled out a five-by-seven photocopy of a driver license. He slid the picture across the table.

"Do you know this woman?"

She studied the photo a moment. An ache punched her chest. She frowned and nodded. "Angel. Angel Salazar. She's your latest victim?"

"How did you know Ms. Salazar?" Steven asked.

Sylvia set her attention on his partner. He was a few inches taller than Steven, but with a more slender build. High cheekbones and almond-shaped eyes verified his Native American ancestry. She guessed him to be in his mid-thirties. His black hair was coarser than Steven's and styled with product. He wore a gold band on his left hand and a patient, paternal expression on his face.

"I didn't know her," she said. "Not really. She came to me a few months ago to help her with a personal matter."

"What kind of personal matter?" Steven asked.

"Angel had recently ended a relationship, and she thought the guy was following her. She asked for my help, so I gave it to her."

"And what, exactly, did you do?" David asked.

Sylvia suppressed a sigh. She hated the twenty questions, and she already knew anything she told them about the *amparo* she'd given to Angel would be met with skepticism. And she really wasn't in the mood to deal with it today. "I talked to her."

"That's it? She drove two hours to see you, and all you did was talk?" Steven asked.

She glanced at him and cursed her jumping pulse. Why did he still have to be so damn sexy? "All we did was talk," she said, evenly. She didn't need the power to read minds to know they didn't believe her. She picked up the water bottle she'd left on the table. "Angel's ex was giving her a hard time. Maybe you should speak to him."

Steven gave her a dry look. "Thanks, we'll add him to our to-do list."

"Ms. Chavez—" David said.

"Sylvia."

"This was found with the body. Can you tell us what it is?" He put a Polaroid photo on the table and slid it next to Angel's picture.

She kept her expression passive, but her heart was racing. It was the bag she'd given to Angel the last time they'd met. A protection spell to ward off more than the evil Angel was hiding from. It was one of her strongest spells. If they found it on the body, that meant whomever killed Angel had been strong enough to break it. *This is so not good.*

"Ms. Chavez?" David cut into her thoughts. "Are you familiar with this item?"

She took a drink of her water then held the bottle between her hands. "It's called a mojo bag."

"Do you know what it's used for?"

She shrugged. "It depends. Witches will use them as hex bags to put a curse on someone. Others use them to hold protection spells."

"Which do you use them for?" Steven asked.

She glared at him. "I'm not a witch." Although, at the moment, she wished she was one. She'd certainly enjoy putting a curse on him. Not the garden-variety toad either. Something more damaging to his ego. Like permanent erectile dysfunction.

"Ms. Chavez...Sylvia, you wouldn't happen to know who gave this to her, would you?"

"No." *Dammit, I shouldn't have answered so fast.* Thankfully, her clerk peered around the door and interrupted the interview.

"Miss Sylvia, you have another visitor," he said.

She rose and nodded her apology. "Excuse me." She made her way through the distribution room as a man walked through the swinging door. Though cliché, tall, dark, and handsome was the only way to describe Vincent Rodriguez.

Built like an athlete with a broad chest and lean, muscular legs, his dark-blue eyes and perfect smile could melt any woman into a pool of lust. Unfortunately, they did nothing for Sylvia's libido. Not that she didn't enjoy his company or the attention he gave her, but she couldn't see happy-ever-after with this one, not like she once had with Steven.

She mentally kicked herself for thinking about him again and moved into Vincent's arms. Okay, maybe it was catty, but she wanted Steven to see men desired her, even if he didn't.

"Vincent, what a nice surprise," she said, giving him a peck on the cheek. If he noticed the overly perky tone in her voice, he didn't show it.

Vincent returned her kiss and smiled. "As they say, I was in the neighborhood and wanted to stop by and say hi." His smile wavered when his gaze shifted to the break room.

Sylvia stole a look over her shoulder and noticed Steven watching them from the doorway, his expression unreadable. His partner remained at the table, speaking on his cell phone.

Vincent glanced toward the room. "I'm not interrupting anything important, am I?"

"No, not at all. They're here to do a spot inspection on the routes," she said, with a wave of her hand. She didn't know why she felt the need to lie to him.

Vincent nodded then turned his smile back on her. "We're still on for tonight, right?"

"Yes, of course. But, can we make it seven? I have to swing by my brother's house for a bit."

"Seven is perfect. In fact, something came up with one of my vendors, so I have to put in a little overtime myself."

"Then I'll see you at seven." She leaned forward to give him a kiss. His hands came up and cupped her face, pulling her in. *Marking his territory.* Not that she minded, Vincent was a good kisser. Of course, he was no Steven.

The memory flashed through her mind before she could stop it. Steven's brown eyes focused on her. The gentle touch of his lips. The subtle taste of mint as his tongue caressed hers. Even now, she could feel his strong fingers as they slid around the nape of her neck, hear her name whisper from his lips as he kissed a hot trail over her skin, sending delicious tremors shuddering up from her toes. She wasn't one to swoon for a man, but....

"Maybe we should finish this later."

Vincent's voice slapped her back to reality. She blinked to clear the images of Steven's naked body from her mind. *Shit. I did not just swoon out loud.*

Forcing a smile, she hooked her arm around Vincent's and led him to the front room. "I'll see you at seven." She closed the door behind him and flipped the lock then rested her head against the glass to give herself a moment to steady her pulse.

Pushing away from the door, she walked behind the counter and began to total out the register. She caught Gabe staring at her as she cleared out the drawer.

"I can close up if you want to get out of here." She pulled the tray out and set it on the countertop.

"Uh, Sylvia...what about the gentlemen in the back?"

She stopped and gave herself a mental slap. What the hell was wrong with her today? "Right. Guess you're closing up for me."

Gabe laid his hand on her arm before she could leave. "Are you okay?"

She offered him a smile. "Just tired. I took care of distribution, so just total up sales and shove it all in the safe. I'll do the deposit in the morning."

She returned to the break room and found Steven waiting by the door, his expression impassive. She squared her shoulders and pushed past him.

"Sorry to keep you waiting, Officer Sanchez." She hesitated. Something felt off about the room.

She took a quick scan and noticed the table was cleared. She looked at the agent, but his expression was as blank as Steven's. It was almost as if they knew she could read them. Except, at the moment, she couldn't.

Officer Sanchez stood and smiled at her. "That's okay. I think we've taken up enough of your time. Thank you for speaking with us. We'll see ourselves out."

Steven nodded his goodbye then followed his partner to the front room. Once they were out of the building, Sylvia grabbed her cell phone and tapped in a number. Her brother answered on the first ring.

"Ray? I think we have a problem."

Chapter Three

"What do you mean we have a problem?" Ray's voice was low, but she heard the strain behind it. He didn't want Lexie to know she was calling.

Maybe he was right. She shouldn't worry either of them until she knew for sure what they were dealing with. Just because the police wanted to talk to her about Angel, didn't mean Jerry Kemp had come back into their lives.

Her mind shifted to Lexie's ex-boyfriend, a once very powerful *hechicero*. He'd been psychotically obsessed with her future sister-in-law and had used his dark powers to bind her to him. Although Lexie had found the courage and strength to get away from him, he'd still been able to use his power to terrorize her. If it hadn't been for Ray and the strength of his love for Lexie, they'd never have been able to break the hold Jerry had on her. During the battle with Jerry, Ray had absorbed the bastard's power which Sylvia took and hid away where only she could find it.

"Sylvia—"

"I don't want to talk about it on the phone. Wait for me at your house, I'll be by within the hour." She disconnected the call before he could respond, her thoughts going to the mojo bag. She should have asked what had been left inside it. But Steven was already suspicious of her.

She glanced at her watch and moved to her locker to gather her things. She needed to get her hands on that bag. If any of the charms were missing, then it meant whoever killed Angel knew what to take.

She frowned. Jerry Kemp was the only person she knew of with enough power to render the bag useless. But he couldn't. She'd made sure of it.

A thought froze in her mind. *Unless he found another source of power.*

***

Steven placed Sylvia's water bottle into an evidence bag and carried it to the rear of the SUV. With any luck, they'd get some decent prints off it, maybe even her DNA. The phone call David had gotten earlier was from the crime lab, letting them know they'd pulled a latent print off the silver coin in the mojo bag. Sylvia told them she didn't know where the bag came from, but he could tell she was lying. Of course, after the greeting she'd given him, he wasn't about to call her on it. Not yet anyway.

"Run this as soon as you can," he said, placing the bag in a black case.

"Wonder what kind of welcome she'll give you when she finds out you swiped her water bottle for prints."

"If it clears her as a suspect, she can swing at me all she wants." He pulled out a small carry-on bag before slamming the hatch shut and moved around to the driver's door where David waited.

"You want a lift to your friend's house?"

Steve glanced at the post office. The lights were off and the shades drawn. Sylvia would be leaving soon, heading to her brother's house according to what she'd told her *boyfriend*. Not that he'd been eavesdropping on their conversation.

The memory of their kiss played in his mind. He'd seen her initial surprise when the man pulled her into the embrace, and her shift to acquiesce as she melted into him. He couldn't tell if she was trying to make him jealous or make a point, but it had hit its mark.

He absently rubbed a hand over his chest. "No, I'll ask Sylvia for a ride. She's already heading that way."

David's lips curled with a smirk. "Sure, because that charming smile of yours worked so well earlier."

"Just see how fast you can run the prints and call me as soon as you know something."

"You got it." He climbed into the SUV and lowered the window. "Oh, one more thing. Don't forget to block."

Steven shook his head and waited for David to leave, then made his way to the other side of the post office building. He rubbed his palm over his chin. Hopefully, she'll be more receptive to him this time.

He turned the corner to the parking lot and froze. Sylvia was on her toes, leaning under the hood of an older model Jeep, her firm, heart-shaped bottom raised high in the air. Lust shot straight to his groin. He swallowed hard and dried his palm against his thighs before moving closer.

"Need some help?" He winced when she jumped and smacked her head on the hood.

"Dammit!" She rubbed a hand over her head and turned to glare at him.

"Sorry." He stepped closer, gripping two hands around the handle of the bag to keep from touching her. He wanted to rub more than her head. "Car trouble?"

She pushed a strand of hair from her face and scowled at him.

23

"No, I like crawling under the hood of my car for no reason."

He grinned at her and tossed his bag onto the back seat. "Why don't you get in, and I'll have a look."

She hesitated then, with a huff of resignation, yanked open the driver's side door and dropped onto the seat.

Steven studied the engine, checking the battery cables and spark plugs. He spotted the distributor cap and noticed the loose coils. He adjusted them then peeked over the side.

"Try her now."

The engine roared to life. He slammed the hood down then moved to the passenger side and climbed onto the seat. Sylvia threw him an icy stare.

"I just fixed your car. The least you can do is give me a lift to your brother's house," he said, before she could speak. He clipped on his seat belt and smiled. "I promise not to talk to you the whole drive."

"Fine." She turned on the radio, blaring Linkin Park through the speakers, and pulled out of the lot.

He settled into the seat, stretching his legs out as best he could. The canvas hood was rolled down and tucked behind the back seat, so he tossed his Stetson behind him on the floor beside his bag. He tried to watch the road in front of him, but Sylvia's long finger stroking the steering wheel to the rhythm of the radio kept distracting him. He caught sight of a speed limit sign as they flew past it and stole a look at the speedometer. She was going fifteen miles over the limit. She must be in a hurry to get rid of him.

After twenty minutes of ear-piercing music, he lowered the volume and shifted to look at her. "It's really good to see you again, Sylvia."

Her fingers tightened on the wheel. "I thought you weren't going to speak."

He shrugged and cocked a smile. "I lied."

"Gee, there's a shock," she murmured, her voice coated with sarcasm. She twisted the volume higher. Evanescence's soulful voice crooned "My Immortal" from the speakers. She stabbed the button and changed the station to a screaming heavy metal song.

He shook his head and reached over to lower the sound again, ignoring her glare. "So, Ray's getting married soon, huh? He sounded really happy when I spoke to him the other day." He frowned as the memory of another woman, another engagement, played in his mind. He'd been there for Ray when it fell apart, had drunk with him to oblivion for three nights, and gone two hours in a ring, letting him fight it out. "He's happy now, right?"

Sylvia visibly relaxed at his question. "He is. He's over the moon in love with Lexie."

"And her? Does she truly love him?"

She glanced at him, her lips curving. The warmth in her eyes made his heart stutter. "Yes. She's as much in love with him as he is with her. They complete each other. They're soul mates. I always knew he'd find her."

Steven grinned. "Always the romantic."

Her expression chilled, and she turned her attention to the road again. *Damn.* He grasped for something to say that would bring back her smile. "So, postmaster. Congratulations. I was surprised when Ray told me. I thought you were planning to go to the University of Texas, become a doctor or something. You always said you wanted to help people."

She glanced at him but didn't return his smile and didn't answer him. He swallowed his sigh. Maybe he should just address the elephant in the back seat. If he could explain to her why he left, why he dropped contact with her, maybe she wouldn't hate him so much. She needed to know he'd never intended to hurt her.

He only had himself to blame. If he had just stopped with the kiss, stopped when he'd realized she was a virgin, when he'd realized the depth of her feelings...but as they stood in the middle of her grandparents' field, the sounds of the night enveloping them in a warm cocoon, he'd been unable to resist her.

Making love to her had been like stepping into another world, one where nothing existed but the two of them. He'd never experienced anything like that before—or since, not even with his ex-wife. He'd become so lost inside Sylvia, as if he'd been waiting for that moment all his life. As if she'd been made for him. But then she'd uttered those three words in the heat of passion, and he panicked.

He forced the memory from his head and turned to look at the symmetrically aligned grooves in a newly plowed field. A large green tractor was pulling an elongated tiller over the ruts, kicking up brown clouds of dried earth. A woman stood near the center of the field. She lifted her head and fixed her gaze in his direction. Though he couldn't see her face clearly, he felt her fear as if it were his own. In an instant, a man appeared behind her. One hand snaked through the woman's dark hair, twisting it in his grip with a strong hold. He tugged hard and jerked her head back to expose her throat. Sunlight glimmered off the knife in his other hand. His lips curled into a fierce smile. He swiped the blade across her neck.

Steven's heart slammed against his breastbone, panic surging through his veins like a river of fire as dust kicked up by the tractor buried the field in a haze.

"Stop the Jeep!" He braced his hands on the dashboard when

Sylvia smashed on the brakes. The tires screamed against the road in protest, the Jeep shuddering as she fought to control the sudden action.

"What the hell?" she growled.

He unclipped his seat belt and stood. The field was clear except for the tractor. "What the—?"

"Are you insane?" she snapped. "You're lucky we didn't roll over!"

He stole a glance at her. *Damn, she's hot when she's pissed.* He cursed his libido's bad timing and dropped onto the seat. "Sorry, I thought I saw...something."

The anger dropped from Sylvia's face, replaced with a sudden unease. "What did you see?"

He huffed out a heavy breath and pushed a hand through his hair. "It was nothing. Probably just the light playing with my eyes. Sorry." He sent her a sidelong glance and tried a smile. "Maybe now you'll stop speeding."

Sylvia glanced at the field then at him, her expression grim. "Don't count on it," she murmured before shifting into drive and quickly merging onto the road.

Chapter Four

"Why did Sylvia say she needed to see you?" Lexie asked as she put the last of the groceries away.

Ray shrugged and took a drink from his water bottle. He should probably help her with the groceries, but he loved to watch her move. "She didn't say."

Lexie turned to stare at him. He knew that look, the one that said she thought he was hiding something from her. He offered her a reassuring smile and shrugged, lifting his hands in surrender. "I swear. She didn't say."

She nodded, a worried frown creasing her brow. "You don't think this has anything to do with Jer—?"

"No." He closed the distance between them and placed his hands on her shoulders, stopping her words. "You know how overdramatic Sylvia can be. I'm sure it's nothing to worry about." He placed a finger under her chin and tilted her head up, giving her a soft kiss. He didn't want her thinking about her ex, Jerry Kemp, not after everything she'd been through. The bastard had tried to kill them ten months ago and, because his father had deep pockets, only spent two weeks in jail. And, although they hadn't heard from him since, he knew Lexie was still afraid Jerry would come after her again.

Ray pushed down his anger, before it had a chance to settle, and sent her a playful frown. "So, soon-to-be Mrs. Chavez, are you really going to make me spend the last week before our wedding with my grandparents?"

"Yes. It was your grandmother's idea, and you know better than I not to argue with her." Lexie curled her arms around his neck and gave him a coy smile. "Besides, a week away from each other will make the wedding night that much more special."

He circled an arm around her waist and pulled her against him. "Our nights are always pretty damn special," he said before claiming her mouth. A soft sigh whispered from her lips and sent his pulse racing. He slid his hand up her shirt as he moved the other to cup her bottom and press her tighter against him.

She gripped his shirt and snapped open the buttons and grazed her fingers over his chest. Desire sparked hot inside him. She loosened his shirt over his shoulders as he moved to her neck. She moaned softly, her hands sliding to his hips to hook in the waistband of his jeans and edge him closer. Damn, he wanted her naked...now.

"Jesus, Lexie, what you do to me," he murmured, running kisses along her jaw as his hand snaked up to cup her breast.

"Whoa. Sorry."

The familiar male voice jolted Ray from the passion-induced fog filling his mind. He turned to see his longtime friend standing in the doorway, one hand covering his eyes.

"Oh, for crying out loud. Again?" Sylvia stepped into the room and rolled her eyes, casting a sardonic look at Steven. "If you're planning to stay here, you'd better get used to seeing them paw each other in the kitchen. You know, Ray, there *are* three bedrooms in this place."

Ray straightened, shifting to give Lexie a moment to gather herself, and shrugged his shirt on. "There's also a doorbell. You should learn how to use it," he replied, though there was no heat in the words. This was as much Sylvia's home as it was his.

"Why? I have a key." She smirked at him and moved to the

refrigerator, pulling out two water bottles.

Lexie moved around Ray and offered her hand to Steven. "They might be at this a while. Hi, I'm Lexie."

Steven grinned and took her hand. She was a few inches shy of his six-foot height, with wavy brown hair framing a lovely face. He guessed her to be in her mid twenties, a couple years younger than Sylvia. Her brown eyes sparkled with amusement, and her olive-colored skin was slightly flushed, which only added to her beauty.

"Steven. It's a pleasure."

Ray moved forward and pulled him into a hug. "Damn good to see you, buddy."

"You, too, big brother," he said, using the nickname Ray had been given as a child. Sylvia was given the name little sister, and everyone in town used the labels, but he could never bring himself to call her that because he never saw her that way. "And thanks for putting your clothes back on."

Ray laughed and leaned against the counter. "I see you found Sylvia."

Steven nodded his thanks to Sylvia when she handed him a water bottle. "Yeah, caught her at work. She was having car trouble, so I helped her out." He thought about how he'd' found her, leaning over her car, her sweet round ass up in the air. He remembered she had a little birthmark on the curve of her right hip in the shape of a tiny brown sunburst. He'd been so drawn to it he'd tattooed one on his left pectoral, with a few modifications.

Before he could stop them, images of their night together replayed in his mind. Her slender body straddling him as they lay in the cornfield, his fingers gripping her hips, guiding her into the seductive dance. The dark passion in her eyes as she reached the peak of her orgasm.

He took a deep drink of the water to extinguish the heat the memory shot through his system.

"You came with Sylvia?" Lexie asked.

Steven sputtered and choked on the water.

Ray hurried forward and slapped his hand against Steven's back. "Whoa, hey, you okay?"

"Sorry, drank too fast," he said, clearing his throat. "Uh, yeah, she gave me a ride...lift...uh, yeah." *Jesus, can I sound any more idiotic?* He stole a look at Sylvia. Her expression was unreadable, but he caught a hint of annoyance. He shifted his gaze to Ray. "I could use a ride back to town later if you don't mind?"

"You're welcome to stay here," Ray said.

"Thanks. But, I'm working a case, so I need to be closer to town. There's still a motel off the highway, right?"

"Yeah, but Sylvia has a place in town and an extra bedroom. You should stay with her," Lexie said.

Steven hid his amusement as, this time, it was Sylvia's turn to choke on the water.

"That would be great." He cast a grin at her. "How about it, roomie?"

Instead of commenting, she stepped around him and headed for the front door. "I gotta go."

"So, is that a yes?" he called after her.

Sylvia made it to her car before Ray caught up with her.

"Hey, what was that about?"

She turned and forced a smile. "Nothing. I just gotta go. I have a reading for Carla."

"So, you don't mind if Steven crashes at your place?"

She shrugged and tried for nonchalance. "Whatever. It's not like I'll be there." She resisted the urge to squirm at her brother's penetrating gaze. She'd never told him about her and Steven because she didn't want to come between them and ruin a wonderful friendship. Thankfully, Ray didn't have the same gift of reading people like she did.

"I thought you liked Steven," he said. "You used to be friends."

"He's your friend, not mine," she said, barely masking the venom in her voice. Before Ray could comment, she flicked her wrist and waved him off. "Never mind. He can stay at my place for the weekend. Just give him your key." She pulled open her door, but Ray placed his hand on her arm to stop her.

"What's going on? You're more tense than usual. When you called earlier, you said we had a problem. So, what is it?"

"It's nothing." She pulled her arm away. During the drive to his house, she'd decided it would be best to wait until she knew who really killed Angel before she told him her theory about Jerry. "I can handle it."

"Sylvia." Ray pinned her with a glare.

" Drop it, Ray. It's nothing to worry about. You're getting married in two weeks, so the only thing you should be focusing on is your wedding and my future little niece I'm going to be spoiling rotten."

He went still, and his face paled as if all the blood had been drained from him. His Adam's apple bobbed, and his expression became a mask of sheer panic.

Sylvia threw her head back and laughed. "Wow, that really had you rattled." She patted a hand on his shoulder. "Don't worry, big brother. Lexie isn't pregnant...yet. Besides, when it does happen, it's her news to share. Not mine." She climbed into the Jeep and turned the key in the ignition. "I'll see ya later."

She was still smiling as she pulled the Jeep to the rear of her grandparents' farm. It was a modest-sized ranch-style house, framed in white trim with a built-in log porch circling it. A fresh coat of stain had been added to the wood a week before in preparation for Ray and Lexie's wedding reception.

She fished her house key from her bag as she slid out of the Jeep. The house was quiet, and her grandfather's truck was gone, which meant he'd taken her grandmother to town. *Probably out buying the fatted calf for Steven's homecoming dinner*, she thought sourly. Her grandparents had always been fond of Steven, treating him like one of their own from the moment Ray brought him home. Of course, Sylvia had fallen in love with him the moment she'd laid eyes on him, too. But that was long before he broke her heart.

She scowled as she let herself into the house. Dammit, she was going to stop thinking about him. He was in her past, and he needed to stay there.

She continued through the kitchen and to her old bedroom. She and Ray spent every weekend with their grandparents, so the room hadn't changed much in the ten years since she'd moved out. The walls were still painted the light-green she'd chosen as a child. Her grandfather had stenciled ivy along the ceiling border, and her mother's ivory-colored linen curtains still hung on the window. Unlike most teenage girls, she'd never tacked posters of rock stars on her walls. Instead, they were covered with astrological charts and various landscape watercolors.

Above her bed hung a large dreamcatcher wrapped in dark-red

leather, with several earth-toned feathers draping from the ring. The desk her grandfather built was now in her own home, replaced with a sewing table and four-drawer chest her grandmother used to store her sewing supplies. Next to the full-sized bed set an end table that had once belonged to her mother.

Her parents had been killed when she was five. They'd been returning from a trip to Dallas and were caught in a storm that had spawned several large tornadoes. A twister swept their car off the road, tossing it into the air like a child's toy. She had watched the scene play out as she slept, felt the impact of the car as it hit the ground and burst into flames. She'd run out of the house, screaming, waking everyone inside. They found her curled into a ball in the middle of her grandparents' field an hour before the state highway patrol came to their house to give them the news.

Sylvia inhaled a breath to wash the memory away then pulled open the drawer to take out the tarot cards she kept there. She really wasn't in the mood to do a reading, but she'd already promised Carla.

She tucked the cards into her tote, her gaze landing on the long, white garment bag hanging on the closet door. She stepped to it and ran her fingers over the plastic cover with a wistful sigh. Her mother's wedding dress. Lexie would be wearing it when she walked down the aisle.

When Ray had first asked her if he could offer it to Lexie, Sylvia had been more than happy to agree. It made her proud that Lexie would honor their mother on her special day.

Her thoughts shifted to Steven again. She'd once dreamed she'd be wearing the dress and walking down the aisle to him. She'd seen it as a child, long before she understood what love and marriage meant. Long before she understood heartbreak. But, she'd been wrong.

35

Steven didn't love her then, and he wasn't going to love her now. It was her own damn problem that she still loved him. She shook off the ache and left the room, taking one last look at the dress then closing the door quietly behind her.

***

Sylvia frowned at the cards spread over Carla Dominguez's table. There were five cards laid out to form a diamond, with one card in the center. She'd dealt the cards based on Carla's concerns about her relationship with her boyfriend, Jose Rivera.

Starting with the top point of the diamond and moving clockwise, the outside cards represented Carla's present position, her present desires, the unexpected obstacles, the immediate future, and the center card showed the possible outcome. She always used the same five-card spread to give her clients what she knew they'd understand, but at the moment, she couldn't make any sense of the puzzle in front of her. They were just random cards that didn't answer the question Carla had asked.

"What do they say?"

Sylvia glanced up at the young woman perched on the edge of her chair, peering at the cards. She'd been working with Carla for three months, and the girl always had the same request, to find out if her boyfriend would stray. Sylvia would have dropped her as a client long ago, but Carla had been referred by another client, so she felt obligated to help her.

Carla chewed on her thumbnail, her expression a mix of dread and excitement as her gaze shifted from the cards to Sylvia. She was young, in her early twenties, at most. The ends of her brown hair were dyed blond and looked like the tips of a bird's feathers, fringing her

36

shoulders.

Sylvia focused back on the cards. It was the second spread she'd done in the past hour, and the second one that didn't make sense. Part of her wondered if Carla's concerns about her boyfriend were really what had her nervous.

"Miss Sylvia?"

Sylvia shook her head. Carla had given her twenty-five dollars for the reading; she had to tell her something. But she didn't want to lie. She took a drink of the iced tea Carla had poured her and resisted the urge to grimace at the bitter taste. The woman did not know how to make tea.

"I'm sorry," she said with a slight shrug. "The cards aren't making sense."

Carla frowned, and her eyes brightened as if she were on the verge of tears. Sylvia placed a hand on her arm with a gentle squeeze. "But that doesn't mean anything. They aren't saying anything bad, and I really don't think you have anything to worry about. I'm sure your boyfriend loves you. He wouldn't have moved in if he didn't, right?"

Carla wiped at her eyes. "But what if he changes his mind? What if he's planning to leave me?"

"Carla, he's not going anywhere." She gathered her cards and stood, trying to restrain her annoyance. This was why she didn't like to take on new clients, she thought sourly. "Look, you have to stop doing this. There are no guarantees in a relationship. You either trust your heart, and his, or you don't. I suggest you stop questioning his loyalty to you or you're going to drive him away." The woman gasped, and Sylvia mentally kicked herself for the brusque response. She quickly offered Carla a benign smile. "Carla, right now, the best advice

I can give you is to trust in your love. Your heart knows if he's truly the one."

Carla nodded but didn't look convinced. Sylvia glanced at the cards again and groaned inwardly. She didn't do love spells, but the only way she was going to end Carla's insecurity was to give her a little reassurance.

She dug into her bag and pulled out a blue quartz stone. It was about the size of a golf ball with both smooth and rough edges. She'd found it a few years ago when she'd taken a trip up to the Balcones Canyon Lands National Wildlife Refuge near the Hill Country. The stone didn't hold any power, didn't glow or emit any kind of light. She just thought it was pretty and liked to carry it around.

She held it up and let the light catch on the edges. "Okay, I don't like to do this because love should be natural and not coerced by magic, but I think you need this." She placed the stone in Carla's hand. Her face lit up as she studied the blue color. "It's a love stone," Sylvia said, mentally rolling her eyes. "As long as you hold on to it, keep it safe, Jose isn't going anywhere. But remember, you have to believe he loves you for the stone to work. Don't question it. And don't doubt it."

Carla lunged from her chair and threw her arms around Sylvia's neck, ramming her hip against the edge of the table. "Oh *gracias*, Miss Sylvia. I won't ever let it go."

Sylvia glanced at the Mickey Mouse clock above the kitchen sink. Shit. It was almost six o'clock. Vincent was picking her up at her house at seven. She didn't have much time.

She pulled herself out of Carla's grip and grabbed her bag. "I have to go. Don't forget what I told you. Don't lose that rock."

Carla nodded like a bobblehead. "I won't. Ever."

Sylvia pulled her Jeep away from the clapboard house, guilt worming its way around her conscience. Okay, so she'd lied. But she was only trying to help. If she'd tried to decipher what the cards were really saying, Carla would have gone into a full-blown panic and she'd have never gotten out of there. So, she used the stone like the proverbial Dumbo's feather. No big deal. Just a little white lie. What harm could it do?

Chapter Five

"You're sure?" Steven paced the deck of Sylvia's grandparents' house, his cell phone pressed to his ear. He stopped along the railing, facing the expanse of land. The sun had set two hours earlier, sending a cool breeze in its place. The smell of dirt and fertilizer wafted across the field.

He'd always loved visiting Ray's family, being a part of a real family. His father had left before he was born, leaving his mother to raise him on her own. She'd worked full-time in a tannery at one of the *maquiladoras* until he was fifteen. She had to leave the job when she'd developed lung cancer from working with the toxic chemicals used to dye the animal leather. A small settlement with the factory had been enough to cover her treatments, but his mother had refused traditional medicine, choosing to find her cure across the border.

He pushed aside his anger at the memory and focused on the phone call with David. "They're sure it was a positive match?"

"One hundred percent," David answered

"Shit."

"How do you want to handle it?"

"For now, all we know is that Sylvia gave her the coin. I'll speak to her again tomorrow. Maybe knowing we have her prints on the coin, she'll be a little more forthcoming."

"Something tells me you're in for a rude awakening," David said with a laugh.

Steven ignored the comment and glanced toward the house. "I'll call you later." He tapped the phone to end the call and dropped the phone in his pocket. "Dammit," he murmured, pinching two fingers to the bridge of his nose.

"Everything all right?" Ray stepped from the house, holding two water bottles, and handed one to Steven.

"Yeah, just the case I'm working on." He peered behind Ray. "Where's Lexie?"

"She went to bed. She has an early shift tomorrow."

"You're a lucky guy, Ray. She's a great girl," Steven said, leaning against the railing.

Ray grinned and sat on the swing hanging from the rafters. "Yeah, she is. So, what about you? You ever get married?"

Steven laughed half-heartedly. "Yeah, for about five minutes."

"What happened?"

Steven shrugged. "Wasn't meant." He frowned. He didn't believe in fate or meant-to-bes. He'd married Linda because it felt like the thing to do. She'd been a godsend for him, working as a home health nurse, caring for his mother during the last years of her battle with cancer.

He had been there for the end, sitting with his mother, helping to keep her comfortable. He'd found solace in Linda's bed, and, after convincing himself he loved her, they got married. It took less than three weeks for them both to realize they didn't belong together, so he'd filed for an annulment and moved to Austin to join the state police.

"Anyway, she's happier now. Married to my partner, actually. And they're expecting their first child in a few weeks."

"Your partner? That must be awkward."

"Not at all. I introduced them."

The sound of a motor pulled his attention to the side of the house. His heart nearly stopped as Sylvia climbed out of her Jeep. She wore a black, form-fitting dress with a plunging V-neck, which enhanced the shapely curve of her breasts. He took a large drink of water to help douse the fire burning in his gut.

She walked slowly up the steps, her expression guarded. As she reached the deck, she raked him with her gaze. The fire inside him turned into an inferno.

"Isn't that sweet? You waited up for me." A slight grin played along her lips as if she could sense his reaction to her.

"Yep, and the shotgun is locked and loaded," Ray said.

She cast her gaze up at Steven. "When I was younger, Ray would wait up for me with a shotgun across his lap. His way of making a statement to anyone I might bring home that he didn't approve of. Which is why I now keep them all to myself at my place," she said with a wink.

Steven glanced at his watch, so she wouldn't see his reaction. "I should get going. I have an early appointment tomorrow." He turned to Ray. "How about that ride?"

"I'll do you one better. You can use my truck."

"Are you sure? I'm not sure how long I'm in town."

Ray rose from the swing and headed toward the door. "Yeah, I can use Lexie's car or Grandpa's truck if I need to. I'll get the keys."

Steven took hold of Sylvia's arm before she could follow Ray into the house. "We need to talk."

She straightened her back and glared at him. "No. We don't. Now, let me go."

He dropped his hand and kept his voice low. "Your print was found on the coin belonging to Angel Salazar."

She lifted her shoulder with a noncommittal shrug. "So?"

"*So*? Why did you lie to me?"

Her brow cocked slightly, and she gave him a critical look. Then, she shuttered her expression and exhaled a resigned breath. "I didn't lie...exactly. Look, I'm not going to talk to you about this here."

"But, you are going to talk to me." It wasn't a question.

She hesitated, then said, "I get off work at three tomorrow. Meet me at the diner on Main."

She escaped into the house as Ray returned with his keys and a slip of paper.

"Here are the directions to Sylvia's place. It's pretty easy to find. Keep the truck as long as you need it. I can pick it up from her place when you leave."

Steven bit down on his annoyance and took the keys. "Thanks."

***

"Dammit," Sylvia huffed, leaning against the closed door of her bedroom. The last thing she wanted to do was spend any time with Steven.

She tossed her purse on the bed and kicked off her shoes. She should have known they'd find her prints on the bag items, and a part of her was relieved the coin was still intact. But, if the killer didn't take the coin, then what did he take?

She chewed her lip in thought then knelt beside the bed and pulled the Ouija board out from underneath. From the time she was twelve, she'd used the board to contact the spirit realm, seeking guidance for her path in life. Although she was destined to become a shaman, like her great-grandmother, she'd focused more on the spirituality of her gifts, most of all the clairvoyance.

She set the board on the bed then fished a lighter from the end table and lit the candle sitting on top. After chanting a prayer, she sat on the bed and placed the tips of her fingers on the planchette. She closed her eyes and focused on Angel and the previous ritual murders.

"Do these murders have anything to do with Jerry Kemp?" she murmured.

A soft tingling sensation shimmered along her fingers, and she could feel the pressure of the spirits in the room, but the planchette didn't move.

"Come on, I know you're there. What's going on? Why is someone killing these women, and does it have anything to do with Jerry?"

Her fingertips warmed and the pressure strengthened, but the planchette stayed in the center of the panel. She opened her eyes and stared at the board. Something was wrong. The spirits could be cryptic in their messages from time to time, but they'd never refused to answer. Why were they locking her out?

Beside her, the flame on the candle flared, sending shadows dancing across the wall. Muted whispers filled the room, but she couldn't make out the words. "Is someone there?"

She jolted when a knock sounded at the door. The candle blew out.

"What the hell?" she murmured.

"Hey, you decent?" Ray's voice sounded from the other side of the door.

"That would depend on your definition," she answered. "Come in."

Her brother opened the door and stuck his head inside. "You

okay?"

She scowled and shoved the board under the bed. "Peachy. What do you want?"

He raised his brow at her gruff tone. "Bad date?"

She took a calming breath and shook her head. "Sorry. No, it was fine. What's up?"

He moved inside and sat in the chair beside the sewing table. "Steven told me about Angelica Salazar. Isn't she the woman you were working with a few months ago?"

She frowned. "Yeah. Poor girl. Did he say what happened?"

"No, just that she was the fourth in a series of murders." He glanced at the board partially hidden under the bed then said, "Lexie's worried this might have something to do with Jerry. I told her it didn't. I'm not going to be called a liar, am I?"

"I wish I could say no, big brother, but I just don't know."

He bolted to his feet and paced. "Dammit. I thought we'd gotten rid of that son of a bitch for good."

"We did. But Jerry was powerful at one time, and he had a lot of friends." She stepped in front of him and placed a hand on his shoulder. The tension radiated off him like an electric current. "Look, it could be completely unrelated to him. Let's not stress about it until we know for sure. I'm going to meet with Steven tomorrow. Maybe I can find a way to insert myself into his investigation and get some answers."

"What makes you think he'll let you do that?"

She shrugged a shoulder. "The killings are ritualistic. I'm the best contact he has with the supernatural. If he doesn't agree, I'll just find a way to convince him."

Ray raised his brow. "I know how stubborn you can be, but

Steven is pretty dead set against anything having to do with magic."

She took the defiance in his voice as a challenge. "Yeah, well, so were you, once. But you came around. He will, too."

Ray gave her a short laugh and shook his head. "Just go easy on him."

"Of course," she answered. "And, don't worry. You and Lexie are going to be safe, and your wedding is going to happen without a hitch. I'll make sure of it." She turned him toward the door before he could question her further. "Now, get out. It's been a long day, and I need to get some sleep. I have to open the store tomorrow, and five o'clock comes fast."

Ray paused at the door and turned. "You'll let me know if there's anything I need to do, right?"

She offered him a smile which she hoped was convincing. "Yes, of course. But I don't think we'll need to worry about that. Now, good night."

She closed the door behind him, leaning against it when it clicked shut. Even if she did need his help, she wouldn't risk giving him back a power he had no idea how to handle. She would take care of the situation without putting him or Lexie in harm's way. Even if it meant working side by side with Steven.

Chapter Six

Sylvia's home was located north of town approximately thirty miles from her grandparents' farm. Steven parked the truck near the front entrance, the headlights giving him a glimpse of the house.

It was a single-story brick building set off the road in the middle of a half-acre plot of land. Various shrubs and flowers in a variety of shapes and colors bordered the windows on each side of the front door, as well as the narrow walkway leading to the wide front porch. A large, formidable oak tree loomed on one side of the house, its branches spread out like arms reaching for the heavens. Attached to the wall next to a bay window stood a ten-foot lattice wall. Thin stems of climbing ivy wove through several of the slats like a lifeline to the building.

Steven grabbed his overnight bag and climbed out of the truck, noting there were no security lights, even at the rear of the house. Not very smart when the backyard was nothing but trees. *Probably put a protection spell around it,* he thought bitterly.

The porch light flashed on as he walked up the stoop.

"Okay, a motion sensor. At least she's not completely clueless," he muttered as he let himself into the house.

He flipped the switch by the door and walked through an arched entryway and into a brightly lit living room. It was larger than he expected, with rust-colored walls adorned with various watercolor paintings. An oval-shaped mirror hung above a shelf built onto the wall. Several Native American statuettes were set on the ledge.

An overstuffed sofa draped with a multi-colored serape sat

against the far wall giving the room more space. Above the entryway hung a mahogany crucifix much like the one his mother had kept above her front door. Several candles in different sizes were positioned on a silver platter centered on a dark cherrywood coffee table.

Steven tossed his bag on the sofa and continued into the adjoining kitchen. It was a modest sized room with an L-shaped counter separating a quaint breakfast nook. The stucco walls were painted soft yellow, the floor laid with pale Saltillo tiles. Bright-white cupboards with fat yellow sunflowers stenciled on the doors, lined the walls. A half-melted candle sat on the windowsill and on the other side of the glass was a rectangular-shaped planter with several leafy plants sprouting from the soil.

Sylvia had made quite a home for herself. He couldn't help but feel proud of her.

Steven helped himself to a beer from the refrigerator and continued his tour of the house. A built-in bookshelf stood at the far side of the living room, each shelf packed with books. Some of the editions looked old, the bindings worn and frayed.

He cocked his head to read the titles and frowned. Books on Spiritualism, Taoism, and *Curanderismo* lined one shelf, while another held books titled *How to Read Tarot Cards, Working with a Ouija Board,* and *Magic by Numbers*.

"Give me a break," he murmured. He and Ray had been roommates and friends for nearly six years before they lost touch, and not once did he mention Sylvia played with magic, especially since he knew how Steven felt about it. Or maybe he didn't say anything because of it.

He grabbed his bag from the sofa and took a long pull from the beer as he continued into an extended hallway. There were three doors, the one in the center slightly ajar so that he could see it was a bathroom. Ray didn't tell him which room Sylvia slept in, but if he had to guess it would be the one on the east side of the house since she liked to wake up to the sunrise.

He stopped short. Why did he remember that?

Pushing the thought aside, he moved to the room at the end of the hall. He placed his bag on the bed and turned on the bedside lamp. The room was just as vibrant as the rest of the house. The walls were painted a light shade of green with the curly pattern of ivy stenciled along the ceiling. The only window in the room faced the backyard. Moonlight filtered in through the open drapes, glistening off the hardwood floor.

Though the house was empty, he felt Sylvia's presence in the room. He could almost smell the subtle scent of jasmine she always wore, and the familiarity surged a warm current through his veins.

Although he wasn't as angry at her as he'd been at the farm, he was still annoyed that she'd found it so easy to lie to him. She'd looked him straight in the eye and lied. And when he'd called her on it, she had the nerve to shrug that slender shoulder as if he were the fool.

He scowled and finished the beer.

History aside, he was not going to let her get under his skin. She was a person of interest in his investigation, and he wasn't about to jeopardize his career, no matter how much she churned his insides.

He shrugged out of his jacket and hung it in the closet then pulled an expandable folder from his bag and lounged on the bed. Inside the folder were several thick files, each containing his notes from the investigation. He'd been working this case since November after the first body had been found. They'd been lucky so far that the details of the investigation hadn't been leaked to the press. Of course, the public didn't much care when a "Jane Doe" was found in the desert since it was a common occurrence with immigrants trying to cross into Texas from Mexico.

The first case had landed on his desk because of the ritualistic nature of the deaths and the possible connection to Caesar Garza, a local drug kingpin he'd arrested on conspiracy to import and sell cocaine. Garza had been rumored to be involved in black magic, sacrificing animals because he believed doing so would keep him and his business "protected."

He shook his head at the absurdity. Garza's so-called magic didn't protect him this time. And if he could connect the scumbag to these four murders, he could put the son of a bitch away for good.

He pulled out the three files, each two inches thick, the pages inside bound with a butterfly clip, and set them on his lap. Each of the victims was Mexican, most likely indigents from across the border since they hadn't been able to find an ID on any of them.

He flipped open the folder for the first victim, Jane Doe #1. She was five foot six and approximately twenty-three years old. Time of death put her murder around Halloween, six months ago. She'd been dead about two weeks before her body was found, partially buried in the desert outside of Del Rio. The animals had gotten to her and much of her flesh had been ripped off, screwing up any traces of evidence left on the body.

According to the autopsy report cause of death was blunt force trauma. A crude symbol, like a star within a circle, had been carved so deep into her forehead that it nicked the bone. Toxicology showed a blood alcohol level of .5 and traces of cocaine. The trauma to her body concluded she'd been tortured before death. On her lower back were two incisions where the killer had removed her kidneys.

Jane Doe #2 was approximately twenty-seven years old. Time of death was the week of Christmas. Her injuries were much the same as Jane Doe #1: blunt force trauma, the same symbol carved into her forehead, signs of torture, and traces of cocaine. She was missing her liver.

Jane Doe # 3 had been killed New Year's Day. Her injuries and cause of death were much the same as the other two, and she was missing her intestines.

All three women were also missing half of their blood, but very little was at the crime scenes, so they concluded the bodies had been dumped at each site.

He pulled out the file they'd started on Angel Salazar. As much as he wanted to connect Garza to this victim, he wasn't sure he could make it fit. Aside from the condition of the body being different, she was the only victim they'd been able to identify by name. Why?

He scanned the information David had written up. They hadn't received the autopsy report yet, but from what he'd seen of the body, the injuries were pretty much the same, except for the marking. The first three victims had the symbol carved on their foreheads while Angel's mark had been burned into the skin. And, there was the *mojo* bag they'd found on her. As far as he knew, these weren't with the other victims.

He already knew Sylvia was the one to give Angel the bag since her prints were on the coin, but he was going to have to wait until he spoke with her tomorrow before he knew for sure if she was keeping something else from him. He was pretty good at reading people and would know if she was lying to him.

His lips quirked as he remembered how she'd greeted him that afternoon. He touched a hand to his chin where she had landed her punch. He had to hand it to her, she had a hell of a right cross. Were it anyone else, they'd be spending the night in a cell. He frowned. Of course, if it turns out she is involved in the murders of the four women, she could still end up behind bars. Not that he believed she had anything to do with their deaths, but she was involved somehow; otherwise, she wouldn't have lied to him.

Either way, he was going to make sure the unexpected turn in the investigation didn't affect his case against Garza.

Chapter Seven

Sylvia stepped into Johnny's fifties-style diner and scanned the room for Steven. She was ten minutes early, but something told her he'd be waiting.

Several of the booths were already packed with families out for the weekend, enjoying the warm spring day and the chocolate shake specials Johnny's offered. She spotted Steven at the other end of the store, sitting in a booth. He was leaning over the Formica topped table, his focus on an open folder. He wore a charcoal-colored polo shirt instead of the suit from the day before, the sleeves stopping slightly above the firm muscles of his biceps. His profile was strong and rigid, his olive colored complexion smooth over the elegant curve of his cheekbones. Straight black hair tapered neatly to his collar and several loose strands fringed his forehead. He hadn't shaved today, the dark shadow of growth giving him an edgy, sexy appeal.

She mentally cursed him and the quick jump in her pulse. Even in the crowded restaurant, his presence was compelling.

His brow furrowed as he read the file. He seemed pensive, not disturbed or angry. Which relieved her. She thought for sure he'd still be mad at her after the way she'd treated him. Sure, he deserved it, and more, but if she wanted in on his investigation, she was going to have to play nice.

A woman wearing a blue-checkered polyester waitress uniform came around the counter as Sylvia started toward the booth.

"Hi, little sister. Eating alone today?"

"Hi, Dena. No, I'm meeting someone." She gestured toward

Steven.

Dena flashed a smile. "Ooh, a date?"

"No. He's just a friend of Ray's. He's here for the wedding."

"Oh. He's gorgeous. And I didn't see a ring on his finger. Maybe I'll slip him my number with his bill." She winked.

Sylvia bit down on the stab of jealousy. Why should she care who Steven dated?

"Sure," she said with a careless lift of her shoulder. "But he's really not your type." She leaned in and lowered her voice. "Gay."

Dena sighed. "The hot ones usually are. Go ahead on. I'll bring you your usual."

"Just an iced tea, please. I'm not staying that long." She continued to the table, pressing her lips closed to keep from laughing.

Steven straightened in his seat, his brow rising as she slid onto the opposite seat.

"You look surprised to see me," she said with a laugh.

He closed the file. "I had no doubt you'd show, but I made a side bet with myself that you would be fashionably late."

His easy smile made her heart trip. He'd always had a great smile.

"And how much did you lose?"

He pulled a bill from his wallet and set it under the salt shaker. "Twenty bucks. It goes to the waitress now."

"Well then, I can't say I'm sorry you lost."

His eyes glittered with amusement. She picked up the tea Dena set on the table and took a drink to settle the flurry of butterflies in her stomach, while Dena took longer than necessary to refill his coffee cup. Why did she suddenly feel like she was on a first date?

She sat back in the booth and forced herself to settle down. "You wanted to discuss Angel," she said after Dena left.

The warmth left his eyes. With a curt nod, he pulled a small notepad from his jacket. "Let's start with why you lied about the bag."

Sylvia suppressed a sigh. She'd practiced exactly what she planned to say until she could convince him to let her in on the investigation, but the cool expression on his face told her she wasn't going to be able to evade his questions.

"It wasn't because of the bag. I knew Angel. We met about nine months ago through a friend. Her real name is Catalina Rubio. She's from Juarez and moved to Mathis about a year ago to start a new life." She paused. "But, you already know that, don't you?"

He nodded. "We got a hit on Ms. Rubio's prints this morning. They were on file with the El Paso PD. She'd been arrested for prostitution and possession and she was a known associate of a man they call *fantasma del diablo*."

"The Devil's Ghost?"

"It's the name given to him across the border because he lives in the shadows. And anyone who's met him face to face didn't live to tell about it. He's been on the *Federales* radar for about ten years, after the bodies of a cartel family were found burned to death in their own home. He became an interest to the states a few years ago during a human trafficking bust. One of the surviving detainees, a twelve-year-old girl, told us this ghost puts the younger children to work as mules and when they hit thirteen he turns them to prostitution. Once they've outlived their usefulness in that area..." His jaw clenched and he let the sentence hang.

"Well, whoever he was to Angel, she was terrified of him," Sylvia said. "She found a way to escape him and that life and she was working really hard to make a new life for herself in Mathis. She got herself clean, changed her name, found a decent job at a second-hand clothing store, even started taking classes at a college in Corpus. But even with all that, she was still afraid the *ghost* was going to find her and kill her. So, she came to me for help."

"For a protection spell."

The sarcasm in his voice kicked up her annoyance. *Play nice.* "Yes."

"Well if you haven't noticed, it didn't work."

She tried to ignore the unexpected ache his words caused. She was used to the doubts—her own brother used to scoff at her—but hearing it from Steven felt like a knife to her heart.

Instead of dwelling on it, she leaned on the table and fixed a firm gaze on him. "Because it wasn't the ghost who killed her."

"And you know this, why?"

"The spell was specific to him, so unless he knew she had it, and I highly doubt he did, there was no way for him to find her. The spell was like a cloak." She paused and scraped her teeth over her bottom lip. "What did you find in the bag?"

He blinked at her. "What?"

"When you poured out the contents, what were they?"

He hesitated then handed her a photo from the file. She pulled it forward to study. The items she'd placed in the bag were spread on a white cloth: the angelica root, the rosemary, the silver coin. All the items except one. "The hair."

"The hair?"

"A sprig of her hair tied with a piece of root called the Devil's Shoelace. It's missing." She frowned, furrowing her brow, and tapped her nails on the tabletop. The hair worked like a reagent, blending all of the items together to bound the spell. But how did the ghost, or whoever killed Angel, know what to take to break the spell?

Her gaze slid to the folder and landed on the photo peeking out from under the flap. She snatched the picture before Steven could stop her.

"Hey!" He reached for it, but she shifted farther back in her seat.

It was a full-length shot of Angel lying on the desert floor within a circle of stones, her arms and legs spread were apart and tied to stakes in the ground. A dark pool of blood was gathered at the base of her skull. On her forehead was a burn in the shape of a pentagram—a five-point star within a circle. Various markings were smeared on her flesh with blood and dirt.

"Oh God." Sylvia pressed a hand to her stomach and fought against the panic coiling its way to her chest.

Steven plucked the photo out of her hand. "Yeah. That's what your protection spell got her," he snapped. His expression turned to remorse when she looked at him. "I'm sorry. I shouldn't have said that."

"The blood...at the base of her skull...." she swallowed. "Her brain is missing, isn't it?"

Steven straightened in his seat, his eyes narrowed. "How do you know that?"

She shook her head and pulled some money from her bag, placing it on the table. "We should go," she said, skirting out of the seat.

Steven grabbed her arm before she could bolt. "Goddammit, Sylvia, where the hell do you think you're going?"

She jerked her arm from his hold. "Back to my place. We need to talk somewhere more private." *Somewhere more protected.* She headed toward the front exit and didn't check to see if he followed her.

***

Sylvia parked at the back of the house and let herself in through the kitchen. She pulled a bottle of Patrón Silver from the pantry along with two shot glasses.

"I need a drink. Want one?" she asked when Steven entered the room. He waved off the offer and leaned against the counter as she filled both glasses. "Right. On duty. That's okay, I'll take yours." She tossed the clear liquid back, hissing through her teeth as the burn slid down her throat.

"I'm sorry. I didn't mean for you to see that photo," Steven said.

"Thanks for putting *that* back in my head," she muttered before swallowing down the second glass. It wasn't the photo that had her on edge. She'd seen a dead body before, not quite like Angel, but dead was dead, and she wasn't squeamish. No, what bothered her were the markings. Whoever had killed Angel had used the marks to keep her from moving on, essentially tethering her to him and the spirit world. Taking the brain insured the magic would work. The fresher the brain, the stronger the magic.

Her great-grandmother had told her stories of spirit bindings and as far as she knew it took a very powerful *hechicero* to do it. Her throat went dry. Which meant, what she'd told Ray was a lie. Jerry was back.

"Are you okay?" Steven asked.

"Couldn't be better," she retorted, twisting the cap onto the bottle.

She felt the heat of his intense gaze as she moved to the refrigerator to pull out two water bottles. He wanted answers and she planned to give them to him, but gradually, and after he guaranteed she'd be part of his investigation. Because if Jerry was the person responsible for the murders, then it meant he'd found someone or something to help him uncover his power. And that would make him a much more dangerous man than before.

She handed Steven a water bottle, appalled that her hand was unsteady.

He pulled a chair out from the kitchen table. "Why don't you sit down?"

She cast a look at him. His eyes were soft again, his expression benign. He was treating her with kid gloves as if he thought she was going to become hysterical. She wanted to laugh at that but was afraid it would sound hysterical.

He took the seat opposite her when she sat and placed his hand over hers as if he thought it would calm her. "Now, talk to me. What do you know about Ms. Salazar's murder?"

She pulled her hand away and edged the chair back. She didn't need calming, she needed answers. "The other victims...were they killed the same way as Angel?"

He straightened in his chair, and, for a moment, she thought he wouldn't answer her.

"Pretty much, except for the brain. The other victims were missing different organs."

"Which is why you thought the killer was taking the organs to the black market," she murmured.

Surprise flickered in his eyes replaced with annoyance. "How do you know that?"

"And they had the same markings?"

"Yes," he said between clenched teeth. "Now, answer my questions. What do you know about these murders?"

Sylvia picked up her water bottle and took a sip. She wished she could take another shot of the Patrón, but she still had to drive to her grandparents' farm. She and Ray spent every weekend with them, and she hadn't missed one yet.

"I think the person killing them is looking for something. Something powerful. And he's using these women to get it."

"What are you talking about?"

"The marking on Angel's forehead is called a witches' mark. Hundreds of years ago witch hunters used them to keep a witch from rising from the dead. But I think the killer is using it, and the organs, as a tether to bind their spirits."

His jaw clenched. "You expect me to believe Ms. Salazar and the other women were witches?" he said with a contemptuous edge in his voice.

Sylvia stood up to pace. "No. As far as I know, Angel wasn't a witch. Otherwise, she could have made the spell herself." She scraped her teeth over her lip as she mulled over the thought. "Maybe I wasn't the only person she came to for help..." And if so, she would have another hex bag, she mused. She turned around to face Steven. "Do you think I can get a look at her home?"

He stared at her as if she'd sprouted two heads. "No."

She placed her hands on her hips and cocked her brow. "Why not? It's not a crime scene. And even if it was, you wouldn't know what to look for like I would."

His expression hardened. "You're not a part of this investigation."

Her lips quirked with a wry smile. "You consider me a person of interest, so doesn't that make me a part of this investigation?"

Steven's eyes flashed with anger. He rose from the chair and stepped to her. His voice was hard and exact when he spoke. "What it makes you is a suspect, and unless you give me some straight answers, I'm going to haul you into the nearest police station."

To her credit, she didn't flinch or step back, but the sexy heat in his eyes kicked her pulse into overdrive.

"I am giving you answers," she said in as firm a voice as she could manage. "You're not listening to what I'm saying."

"You expect me to believe I'm looking for a witch-hunter?"

She hated that he made her sound like a fool. "I expect you to believe there's more to these murders than a simple serial killer." She reined in her annoyance and stood tall. Before he could get any angrier with her, she placed her hand on his wrist. A shimmer sparked along the tips of her fingers and flooded her palm with warmth. She ignored the sensation and kept her hold. "Look, you know I had nothing to do with these murders, but I can help you find who did. Let me work with you on this. Angel was killed because of me. I need to know why. Please."

He glanced at her hand then swept his gaze up to hers. She could almost see the internal debate in his head. After a moment, he gave her a short nod.

"Fine. But the minute you start talking witchcraft and black magic, we're done."

Sylvia picked up her water bottle and took a deep drink to extinguish the fire kindling in her stomach from touching him. She'd gotten what she wanted, but it was going to be next to impossible to disprove that magic was involved.

***

"I can drive myself to the farm," Sylvia said as she climbed onto the passenger side of her Jeep.

"You've been drinking. You're not driving." Steven adjusted his seat back and started up the engine. He'd have preferred taking Ray's truck, but Sylvia was adamant about taking her Jeep to her grandparents' house.

"Two shots are nothing, lightweight," she muttered, crossing her arms like a petulant child.

He tossed her a steady look. "Put your seat belt on." She snarled at him but did as he told her then turned the volume up on the radio, blasting the latest rock sensation.

Fine by him. He was still annoyed with her and wasn't in the mood for another argument. Not to mention he was angry at himself for agreeing to let her work on the case with him. He still didn't know what possessed him to say yes. One minute he was going to say no, the next she was touching his arm and he was ready to agree to anything. It was as if she'd cast a spell over him.

His fingers clenched on the wheel. There was nothing mystical about it. It was his desire for her, plain and simple that made his pulse kick and his blood heat through his veins.

Besides, if he really thought about it, it wasn't a bad idea for her to stay close. If their killer was going after women because he believed they were witches, then Sylvia could be on his radar as well. And he'd die before he let anything happen to her.

They continued the trip in silence, so he used the time to take in the scenery of the small farming community. Several of the fields were starting to sprout green leaves. Some of them would be corn, some watermelon. Once harvesting started, vendors would begin setting up the little farmer's markets on the roadside, selling fresh fruit at a better price than the grocery stores.

His lips curved. He could see himself living here in a little two-bedroom house with a wood deck and a nice big kitchen with a breakfast nook. Maybe he'd get something with an acre of land that he could fence in for a couple of dogs. He'd always wanted a dog. He'd bet Sylvia would love a dog, maybe even a cat. Or both. She might even plant a garden, filling it with herbs instead of the flowers she nursed in her front yard. They could even build onto the house to accommodate their growing family—

He snapped to attention and gave himself a mental slap. What the hell was he thinking?

He stole a glance at her as he took the two-lane road to her grandparents' farm. She'd put on a pair of wide-lens sunglasses and had reclined her seat so she was lounging back. Her feet were propped on the dashboard, knees bent, one foot tapping to the song on the radio, so he knew she wasn't asleep. Knowing she could dismiss him so easily, while he was fantasizing happy-ever-after with her, kicked his annoyance up a notch.

His phone chirped on his belt. He freed his grip from the steering wheel and unclipped his phone, keeping his eyes on the road as he pressed Send. "What?"

"Uh-oh, you're in a mood," David said by way of a greeting. "I'm guessing your meet with the champ didn't go well?"

Steven glanced at Sylvia. "Not really."

David chuckled on the other end. "Did she clock you again?"

"Funny."

65

"Well, if it makes you feel any better, the background check came in on her, and it's clean. No legal troubles, not even a parking ticket. Her financials show a pretty hefty bank account for someone so young, and it all comes from her job with the postal service which she's been at for about nine years.

"She has great credit also, better than mine. And, for the past five years she'd been sending $2500 a month to her grandfather, Mr. Hector Chavez's, savings account."

Steven cast another glance at Sylvia. She looked relaxed, her body slightly swaying to the ballad currently playing on the radio. He couldn't stop the pride that welled inside him. Not many people would give half their paycheck to help their family. Nor make the forty-five-minute drive every weekend to spend time with them.

"For what it's worth," David continued, "I don't think she has anything to do with the murders."

"Yeah. Me either." He paused then lowered his voice. "I decided to let her consult."

"Really?" David said, the surprise raising his voice an octave. "So, you're getting on board with the whole magic thing?"

"No."

"Then, why?" When he didn't answer, David laughed. "She's right next to you, isn't she?"

"Yeah."

"Well, that explains your monosyllabic answers."

"Did you really call to annoy me?" Steven growled.

"Nah, it's just a perk. Actually, I wanted to let you know I need to work from home for a while."

"Is Linda okay?"

"Yeah, yeah...I think so. She's been having contractions, Toni

66

Braxton or something."

Steven laughed. "I don't think that's what it's called."

"Well, whatever it's called the doctor is a little concerned, so he wants her on bed rest until the baby is born. Her mom's coming to stay for a couple weeks, but she won't be in until Wednesday. So, I want to stay close by."

"No problem. I think I can handle things without you for a while."

"I doubt it," David said, the humor coloring his voice. "But thanks."

"Keep me posted. And give her my love." He disconnected the call and returned the phone to his belt.

"When's she due?" Sylvia asked, shifting in her seat to face at him.

He glanced at her, ready to say something snarky about her finally speaking to him after a half-hour drive but changed his mind. If they were going to work together, he was going to have to play nice. "Couple weeks, I think."

She nodded and resettled against her seat. "Twins during the spring equinox. They'll be very blessed."

Steven refrained from commenting and pulled the Jeep into the driveway of her grandparents' farm.

Lexie came onto the porch to greet them as they climbed from the vehicle. She wore a pair of faded jeans and a pink T-shirt. Her long hair fell in wet waves around her face.

"Hi," she said with a warm smile as Sylvia moved up the steps.

"Hey. Where's Ray?"

"Getting dressed. He just got out of the shower."

Sylvia tugged playfully on Lexie's hair and winked at her. "Looks like you just did, too."

Lexie flushed and slid her gaze to Steven. "Good to see you again, Steven. I thought Ray said he was meeting you at the house later."

"You, too," he answered. "And he did, but Sylvia needed a ride."

Lexie's brow furrowed with concern. "Are you okay?"

Sylvia rolled her eyes and gestured toward Steven. "I had a drink so Mr. Letter of the Law wouldn't let me drive."

Lexie gave her an amused smile. "Well, I guess he doesn't know about your ability to drink everyone under the table. Come on in, Steven, I'll get the keys for you."

Sylvia turned and held up her hand to stop him. "What keys?"

"For Ray's house. I'm staying there tonight," he said as Lexie returned to the house.

"Why?"

He didn't bother to hide his irritation. "Because we're hitting the road early tomorrow and I don't want to drive back and forth to town." He pinned her with a hard look. "You inserted yourself into my investigation, but if you keep questioning everything I do, we're going to have problems." He moved past her then stopped and turned to her with a hard stare. "And keep in mind, this lack-of-trust goes both ways."

Chapter Eight

A haze of dark clouds hid the morning sun as Sylvia made the mile walk across her grandparents' field to Ray's house. Steven had said he'd pick her up, but she wanted to save him the trouble and the questions about why she was going away with him.

She hated lying to her family, even though she was doing it to keep them safe. But, she would keep them in the dark until it was absolutely necessary to let them know Jerry was back in their lives. *If* he was back.

She'd left her laptop at her home, so she'd spent most of the night trying to remember everything she'd learned of Jerry Kemp. Since the first night Lexie told them about her ex, Sylvia had been gathering as much information on him as she could afford to buy off the Internet.

Over the past year, she learned Jerry Kemp came from a long line of *brujas* and *hechiceros*. His great-great-grandmother on his mother's side was a known descendent of a group called The Order of the Shadows—religious fanatics who used their powers to dominate, murder, or torture anyone they considered a threat to them. They were thought to be a very powerful cult a few hundred years ago, and many believed the sect had been wiped out during the Christos Rebellion. But, according to the records she'd found, Jerry's great-great-grandmother had managed to escape.

Unfortunately, she couldn't find anything else on Jerry that she didn't already know, which meant she had to find another way to get some answers. She wasn't about to allow Jerry Kemp to ruin Ray and Lexie's happiness. Their souls had spent an eternity trying to find each other. She would do whatever it took to make damn sure they stayed together.

She entered Ray's house through the front door and followed the aroma of fresh-brewed coffee to the kitchen. She found the room empty and tossed her keys onto the tile countertop before helping herself to a cup of coffee. She turned to stare out the kitchen window as she sipped. Although rain hadn't been predicted in the forecast, angry clouds were gathered in the distance. She'd noticed the change as she walked across the field to the house. But the acidic charge in the air wasn't just from the storm. Something else was coming. And her senses were telling her, it was something more dangerous than Jerry.

"Jesus Christ, Sylvia!"

Steven's voice jolted her from her thoughts and nearly had her dropping her coffee. She spun around to find him in the doorway, water dripping from his hair and spilling down his broad shoulders. He held a gun and wore only a pair of unfastened jeans.

She swallowed hard as she drank in him. His sculpted chest glistened under the kitchen light. Tattooed above his left pectoral muscle was a red-and-gold sunburst. Her gaze slid down to his well-toned abs. *Hot damn, he's ripped!*

"Are you trying to get yourself killed?" he fumed, lowering the gun to his side. "Why didn't you knock first? Or ring the doorbell?"

She swallowed again and lifted her chin to boldly meet his gaze. "Because I have a key and I didn't expect you to come out guns-blazing." She wheeled around to grab a mug from the tree next to the coffeemaker and filled it, using the time to steady herself. The race of her pulse had nothing to do with the gun or the fright he'd given her. "Sorry, I'm used to just coming right in."

He took the coffee she offered and scowled at her. "Then wear a bell."

She smiled, despite herself. "They don't go with of my outfits. You're getting water all over the floor, and I'm not cleaning it, so you should finish drying off."

He turned and stalked back to the bedroom, mumbling something she couldn't quite hear.

She pressed her hand to her stomach and blew out an unsteady breath. It was bad enough she had to pretend to like working with him, but now she had to do it with the image of his hard, wet body branded into her mind.

Steven returned to the kitchen ten minutes later, wearing the same clothes he'd worn the first day she saw him. He stopped short in the doorway and stared at her as she turned to greet him.

"What's that?" he asked, his brow raised at the plate of food in her hands.

She held the dish out to him. "In the valley, we call it breakfast." She shrugged, suddenly feeling foolish for making him breakfast. "I was hungry and figured you hadn't eaten yet, so I made us something." She threw him a dry look when he didn't take the plate. "For crying out loud, I didn't poison it." She picked up the burrito and bit into it. "See?"

He took the plate with an apologetic smile. "Thanks. I figured we'd grab something in town." He refilled his coffee cup then carried it, with the plate, to the table.

"Well, now we don't have to. And maybe we can consider this a peace offering."

He narrowed his eyes at her when she moved to the table. "Why are you being so nice?"

She feigned a hurt pout. "I'm always nice."

"I have a busted lip that says otherwise."

She pressed her lips together but didn't succeed in hiding her smile. "Yeah, sorry about that. I was having a bad day. Fresh start?"

He took the hand she held out and wrapped his fingers around hers with a warm grip. "I'd really like that."

"Great." She yanked her hand away and sat across from him at the table. His smile was warm and sincere, but she heard the double meaning in his voice. As much as she wanted to be more than friends, she'd be damned if she allowed herself to trust him with her heart again.

They left the house twenty minutes later, and Steven took the highway to Edmondville. He turned the radio volume down and shot her a firm look when she tried to turn it back up.

"It's a long drive, and I'm not going to try to talk to you over the radio the whole time," he said. "We need to swing by your place and pick up Ray's truck."

"Why? What's wrong with my Jeep?"

"No offense, but Ray's truck is newer and more reliable, which is why I wanted to take it last night. Also, you'll need to pack an overnight bag," he added before she could comment.

She bit down on the surge of anger. Did he think they were going to spend the night together? "Why do I need an overnight bag if we're just taking a short trip to Mathis?"

"Because, in my experience, short trips are never short. Plus, after we visit Ms. Salazar's home, I have to stop in Sinton to pick up some files from the San Patricio County Sheriff, and afterward, I want to detour to my place and grab some fresh clothes."

72

"And your place is, where?"

"Austin." He slid a glance at her. "Are you okay with that?"

She forced herself to relax and gave him a careless shrug. "Sure. No problem. I don't have work tomorrow, so I don't have to rush back."

"Good." Steven pulled out a binder with the thickness of a Stephen King novel and handed it to her. "This is for you."

"What is it?"

"Notes of the case, so far. If you're going to work on this, you might want to familiarize yourself with the investigation."

"Wow, that's a lot of notes."

"It's three cases, not counting Ms. Salazar's," he replied.

She flipped through the pages. "Shouldn't there be photos of the victims or crime scene?"

"I didn't include them. These are just preliminary notes. You'll get the gist of the condition of the bodies from the autopsy reports and I can answer whatever questions you have."

She nodded, then said, "Thank you for letting me come along."

"I'll have to pull some pretty tight strings to officially get you on this case. But, if anyone asks, you're consulting." He shrugged. "Besides, maybe you'll see something I don't."

"Maybe," she murmured. She'd already seen a lot of things he hadn't. But telling him what she knew about Jerry wasn't going to help if he didn't want to hear it.

***

It was almost noon when they finally reached Mathis. Since

Sylvia had buried her nose in the files, Steven spent the entirety of the trip with his own thoughts, and they hadn't all been about the case. He'd barely gotten any sleep during the night, which wasn't unusual when he worked a new case. But his mind hadn't been filled with thoughts about his victims or what they must have suffered through before their death. Instead, whenever he closed his eyes, he'd see Sylvia standing before him in all her golden glory, a thin silk gown pooled around her feet.

Within seconds she'd be in his arms and writhing beneath his body. He'd awaken hard and erect as a flagpole and unable to erase her image from his mind; which left him slightly disgusted with himself and very much irritated with her.

When he finally crawled out of bed, he took a long cold shower to freeze the dreams out of his mind and had succeeded in doing so until he found her standing in the kitchen wearing curve-hugging jeans with a form-fitting T-shirt and offering him breakfast and friendship!

He clenched his teeth and tried to keep his grip light on the wheel. *Friendship, hell.* He wanted more than that. He'd screwed it up before, but that didn't mean he couldn't get it back. One way or another, he was going to get her to fall in love with him again. Even if he had to beg.

He continued down a narrow dirt road bordered by thin cedar elm trees and dry shrubs. Sylvia closed the file and pressed a hand on the dashboard for balance as the truck bounced over several deep ruts left by a previous rain.

"You might want to go back, I think you missed a few," she said as he slowed the truck to maneuver around a deep groove.

"I think I'm going to owe Ray new shocks."

She lowered her window and took in the scenery. "Pretty

isolated."

"She was definitely hiding from someone," he said, as he moved onto a blacktop road that wasn't in any better condition than the street he'd been on.

The house was located at the end of the way, hidden among several large oak trees. It was a rectangular-shaped, single-story building built on cement piers and covered with dirty, pale yellow, vinyl siding. The roof dipped where part of the gutter had rusted off and several of the wood-shake shingles were missing. Someone had covered the windows with slats of wood and crisscrossed them like a six-pointed star, likely to keep trespassers out. He noted there weren't many neighbors within walking distance, which would have been preferable for someone wanting to stay hidden.

Sylvia jumped out of the truck as soon as he shifted into parked. She stood beside the door and scanned the area as if she were looking for something or someone.

"What are you doing?' Steven moved around the truck to join her.

She bypassed his question and gestured toward the house. "Can we go in or do we need to wait for a key or something?"

"No, it's open. The crime unit already processed the place and since the house sits so far off the road, and there was really nothing of value inside, they didn't bother to lock it."

He led her to the rickety front porch and opened the front door. A whiff of warm, stale air wafted from the building. Sylvia breathed in deeply, blowing the air out through pursed lips.

"Do you smell that?"

He breathed in the musky air. "Smell what?"

"Never mind." She took a step forward then stopped to look up at him. "Do you mind if I go in alone first?"

He started to ask why but changed his mind and stepped back, sweeping his arm out to motion her inside. Hazy beams of light filtered in from the un-boarded kitchen window, giving them enough light to see inside.

The room was shaped like an L with a kitchenette built at the smaller end. Several dishes were stacked in a plastic dish drainer beside the sink. In the larger room, tucked in the corner, set a twenty-inch television atop a wrought-iron stand that looked like it once housed a large fish tank. Opposite the makeshift entertainment unit set an overstuffed sofa that had seen better days and a faded-and-cracked green vinyl arm chair. A worn circular throw rug had been placed in the center of the room. Across the room an open door revealed a square bedroom.

"What exactly are you looking for?" he asked as Sylvia glided through the room, one hand hovering above the furniture, but not actually touching it. She reminded him of one of the so-called psychics he saw on TV. who convinced small town law-enforcement they could find missing people because they *saw it in a dream.*

She slid him a glance. "I'll know when I find it," she said before moving into the kitchen. She stopped beside the round glass table and took in the room as if memorizing the layout. After a few minutes, she returned to the living room and moved toward the bedroom. She stood in the entry a moment then moved inside.

Steven followed her and stopped at the threshold. He didn't have a problem letting her roam through the house as long as she stayed in his line of sight.

He crossed his arms and leaned a shoulder against the doorjamb as she wandered around the square room. A twin-sized bed and chest of drawers were the only pieces of furniture taking up space. Aside from a wood crucifix hanging above the bed, the yellowed walls were bare.

Like she had in the other two rooms, Sylvia kept her back to him and stood still. After a moment, she moved to the adjoining bathroom and peered inside. "Did they find anything?" She turned away from the room.

"According to the sheriff, nothing of importance. I'll get the notes from him later."

She nodded and looked around the bedroom again. "She might have known her killer. Whoever he was, I think she knew him."

"Why do you say that?"

She hesitated then shrugged. "A feeling. What time are we seeing the sheriff?" she asked before he could comment.

He glanced at his watch. "About half an hour. Why do you think she knew him?"

She hesitated then said, "Because she was getting ready for a date."

Tired of the twenty questions, he cocked his brow with a questioning look.

"Pre-date routine." She gestured toward the bathroom. "Razor and shaving cream are still on the tub, body lotion and makeup are on the sink, and there's a hanger on the back of the door."

"So, she was killed by a john."

Sylvia shook her head. "I don't think so. She was out of that life, doing something good for herself. She wouldn't have gone back to it, no matter what."

"She wouldn't be the first to go back to the streets if she were desperate enough."

She bypassed his comment and took another sweep around the

room, briefly inspecting the narrow closet. "What happens to all her things now that she's gone?"

"Unless she has family, the county will come in and haul it all out, donate most of it probably."

Sylvia frowned and nodded absently. After a moment she moved past him and headed out of the house to stand on the porch. He followed, closing the front door behind him.

She continued down the steps and wandered to the back as if she were doing an inspection of the building. "Do you have a flashlight?" she asked when he moved alongside her.

"Not unless Ray keeps one in his truck."

"He does. Front passenger seat. Would you mind?"

He hesitated, then moved to the truck for the light. He was trying to keep his irritation in check, but he could tell she was hiding something from him and he didn't like it.

Sylvia was down on her knees, her backside raised toward him, and staring under the house when he returned. His heart nearly stopped at the sight. Christ, she had a nice ass. She turned to look at him and her expression cooled. He felt like he'd just been caught spying on her naked.

Sitting back on her heels, she put her hand out for the flashlight. "There's something under here."

He knelt opposite her and followed the beam as she swept it under the house. Partly buried in the dirt was a small square container that looked like a music box.

"What is it?" he asked.

"A box," she said dryly. She rolled her eyes at him. "Pull it out and let's see."

He swept a look at the house. The concrete piers holding up the building were about two feet high. Water dripped from several rusted pipes, turning the dirt beneath the house into mud. He judged the box to be at least six feet away. With his height he would only have to go in about three feet. Either way, it was going to be a tight fit and a very muddy job.

With a resigned sigh, he sat back and took off his shirt then handed it to Sylvia. "Hold this." After pulling a handkerchief from his pocket, he stretched out flat on the ground and shimmied his upper body underneath the house.

The space was much tighter than he'd anticipated, thanks to the artery of pipes running under the house. Good thing he wasn't claustrophobic.

The smell of earth, mildew, and something foul he couldn't quite place assaulted his senses. He braced up on his arms to keep from sliding his chest in the slime and army-crawled six inches at a time. The edge of the vinyl siding scraped against his back when he moved forward but thankfully didn't take skin with it.

As he draped the handkerchief over the box, the floor above his head creaked heavily, sending particles of dust raining down on him. He went still, his heart slamming against his breastbone. Within seconds the noise stopped, and the house went quiet. He hissed out the breath he held. For a split second, he thought the house was going to drop on him.

Trying to keep his face from touching the wet ground, he stretched a hand out and grabbed the box then carefully eased out from under the house.

Sylvia greeted him with a towel as he stood. "Thought you might want this."

"Yeah. Thanks." Her fingers grazed his as he took the cloth, sending a spark of heat spiraling to his gut. She pulled her hand away quickly but not before he saw she'd been just as affected by the touch.

"There's a faucet and hose back here," she said, moving quickly to the rear of the house.

Steven used the water to wash the mud from his lower stomach and arms, splashing his face, just in case. Satisfied he was as clean as he was going to get, he glanced up and spotted Sylvia crouching next to a small planter that had been left against the wall of the house. Half-dead purple flowers sprouted from the soil. She adjusted his shirt, still draped over her shoulder and pulled out her phone. The shutter clicked several times as she photographed the plant.

"What are you doing?"

Instead of answering him, she tucked the phone in her pocket and gestured toward the box. "Let's look inside."

"I'll look in it after it's been processed," he snapped, scrunching the towel into a ball. He stepped to her and pulled his shirt from her shoulder, pinning her with his glare. "Then you're going to tell me exactly what the fuck you're hiding from me."

Chapter Nine

Sylvia raised her brow and sent him an icy glare. "What makes you think I'm hiding something?"

"Call it a *feeling*. I'm getting pretty damn tired of whatever game you think you're playing."

She straightened and kept her expression frosty. "You're the one who said you didn't want to hear anything about magic." She held up her hand when he scowled. "Let's just go see your sheriff and see what's in the box. Then we'll talk."

She moved past him before he could argue and headed back to Ray's truck. Steven stalked into the house and came out moments later with a brown paper bag.

He stayed quiet the whole drive to the sheriff's department, and she could feel the anger radiating off him in hot waves. She didn't care that he was angry with her. As long as he was mad, she didn't have to think about how much he affected her.

She stared out the window as he drove through town, following the verbal directions of the GPS on his phone to the sheriff's station. She used the silence to piece together the puzzle of Angel's house. She'd smelled death when she'd first entered the house and she'd felt the presence of spirits in the main room. Some bad, some not so bad, and all of them fearful. But what she didn't feel was Angel or the protection spell she'd given her.

She almost didn't need to open in the box from under the house to know what was inside. Because whatever was in there was the reason her protection spell didn't work.

***

They arrived in the rustic town of Sinton twenty minutes later and Steven pulled the truck into the parking area in front of a single-story building with a tinted plate-glass front. Stenciled on the glass was the name Hitt Law Enforcement Center. A handful of cars were parked in the lot. Sylvia started to climb out of the truck, but Steven stopped her with a glare.

"Wait here." He pulled the keys out of the ignition and stepped out of the cab.

"Yes, sir," she murmured as he shut the door and stalked straight to the entrance of the building. She stole a glance at the back seat and noticed he'd left the paper bag holding the box on the floor. Damn, he was really mad. Okay, so she wasn't being truthful with him, but she couldn't really tell him anything about Jerry or what had happened last year until she knew for sure what was happening now.

She tapped her nails on the armrest. Maybe she should read Steven. Figure out just how open he'd be to her story. She exhaled heavily and frowned. No. Looking into his head would also give her a glimpse of who was in his heart and she couldn't bear to see who that was since she already knew it wasn't her.

Steven put on his sunglasses as he exited the station, a folder clutched in his hand. She could tell by his rigid steps he was still angry. She'd never seen anyone so mad before, least of all at her. It was very unsettling.

He climbed into the truck and started the engine, keeping his attention in front of him.

"I thought we were going to look in the box," she said.

He slid her a glance, and she felt his fury through his sunglass lenses. She bit down on a sigh. She was going to have to wait until he calmed down before she could talk to him. And no telling how long that would take.

She put on her sunglasses and adjusted the seat to recline. Closing her eyes, she forced herself to relax, tuning her senses into the feel of the truck as it moved along the road and the soft hum of the engine. The smell of earth and aftershave mingled together drifted from Steven. She forced the scent from her mind and settled deeper into the seat, letting herself relax enough to fall asleep.

She ran through the woods, branches slapping at her arms and face, tearing flesh and clothes. The figure behind her closed in, his steps almost casual, as if he knew she couldn't outrun him. The wet mud on the ground made it difficult to move quickly. No, not mud. Blood.

Her heart hammered painfully in her chest, the heat of the globe clutched in her hand and burning into her palm. Tears blurred her vision and bled down her cheeks. She refused to die like this. She would find the way out. She had to.

A dip in the ground caused her to stumble, and her hands sank into the earth, scraping against the shards of bone littering the soil. She staggered to her feet and limped as quickly as she could toward a group of trees, falling against a large trunk for a moment's rest. Branches cracked behind her. She pulled her knees to her chest, trying to make herself as tiny as possible.

The sky above her faded to dark as the moon began its eclipse across the sun. A breeze carrying the smell of burning flesh fluttered the branches above her. She was running out of time.

Using the tree as a brace, she rose to her feet and peered around the trunk, scanning the woods for movement. The man was gone. She must have lost him.

Relief flooded through her with an icy rush to her veins. She took a step back and turned to run. In front of her stood the demon. The man who wanted her soul.

Before she could scream, he slammed her head against the tree. Spots danced behind her eyes and she felt her legs buckle.

The man grabbed the orb from her hand. "This belongs to me. And now, so do you," he said before the world around her went dark.

Sylvia shot awake, the scream caught in her throat. Her heart pummeled against her breastbone, her mind hazed from the darkness of her dream. It took her a moment to realize the truck had stopped and they were parked in front of a two-story apartment building. A glance at the dashboard clock told her she'd slept for nearly two hours.

She sat up and cast a look at Steven. His hand was on her knee, and he was staring at her, his face slightly pale and his brow furrowed with concern.

"You're awake," he said with a hint of relief in his voice.

She pushed out the breath from her lungs and pressed her hands over her face. "Yeah. Sorry, I guess I was tired."

He looked at her as if he wanted to say something but, instead, pulled the keys from the ignition and gestured toward the building. "Come on in."

She followed him up the stone stairwell to the second floor. After opening his door, he stepped aside to let her in.

Like most apartment complexes, it was a simple floor plan with a moderate-sized living room and an adjoining kitchen. Several framed landscape pictures were placed sporadically on the whitewashed walls above the sofa.

On the opposite wall stood a large media center housing a fifty-inch flat screen TV. Two bookshelves bordered the unit and were stocked with a variety of books, CDs, and DVDs, most of which were romantic comedies. *Weird.*

The furniture taking up the rest of the space looked fairly new and consisted of a black leather sofa and armchair, a rectangular coffee table and two matching end tables. She noted all the furniture was black, including the appliances and the small round dining table set off to the side of the kitchen.

"Nice place," she said, for lack of anything better.

Steven pulled two water bottles from the refrigerator. Although he didn't seem to be as angry with her as he had been earlier, she sensed his distance.

"Here." He handed her a water. "Make yourself at home." Before she could respond, he moved to his bedroom and closed the door behind him.

She huffed out a breath. *Could this trip get any better?* The sound of pulsing water penetrated the thin walls. Great, he was going to make her wait.

She moved to the sofa and noticed the silver urn on the end table. Embedded on the surface was a photo of a woman in her mid-forties. She saw the resemblance to Steven right away. The pang of grief touched her heart. She'd forgotten he had lost his mother, too.

She dropped onto the sofa and stretched out, resting her head on the arm. She placed the water bottle over her forehead to try and quell the headache starting to grow. Why did she feel like she had a hangover? She should probably see if Steven had any aspirin, but she didn't feel right snooping through his things.

When she closed her eyes, images pulsed across her mind like a discolored strobe light, but she couldn't make them out any more than she could remember what she'd dreamed about during the drive. The only thing she knew for sure was someone was going to die. And soon.

Sylvia bolted upright when the bedroom door opened, instantly regretting the quick movement when her head throbbed heavily. She swung her feet to the floor and placed her head in her hands, groaning softly.

"Here," Steven said.

She opened her eyes to his naked feet standing in front of her. Scanning her gaze up, she noted he wore a fresh pair of jeans and an unbuttoned blue linen shirt. Her gaze lingered a moment on his bronzed skin. A sprinkle of black hair traveled a line from his navel down to the inside of his jeans. More dark fuzz dusted the valley between his pecs. His hair was wet, and he smelled of soap. In the palm of his hand were two red-and-white capsules.

"Ibuprofen," he said.

She blinked at him before taking the pills. How did he know? "Thanks," she murmured, tossing them back with some water.

"Give me a minute to finish getting dressed, then we'll get some food."

The rumble in her stomach reminded her she hadn't eaten since breakfast. She wanted to believe hunger was the reason for her headache, but she knew better.

"You okay with Chinese?" His eyes stayed steady on hers and a delicious shimmer she hadn't felt in a very long time, fluttered in her stomach.

"Yeah."

He nodded then went into the bedroom. She rose and moved to the patio doors and closed her eyes, lifting her face to the sun heating the window, pulling in as much of the energy as she could.

Steven returned moments later, wearing his boots and buttoning his shirt. "Food will be here soon. Have a seat." His voice sounded oddly detached. "How's the head?" he asked once she settled back on the sofa.

"Still attached." She studied him as he sat opposite her in the armchair. His expression was impassive, giving nothing away.

"Good. Now start talking."

"Do you have a banana?"

He blinked at her, apparently taken aback by the question.

She suppressed her smile. "For my headache."

"Sorry, no."

She shrugged. "That's okay, maybe the pills will kick in."

Steven closed his eyes, his muscles contracting along his jaw line, and inhaled a deep breath. "Sylvia, I think I've been more than patient with you these past couple of days. But it's starting to wear thin."

She held her hands up in concession. "You're right. But I didn't want to say anything until I knew for sure what was going on."

"And what do you think is going on?"

She shrugged. "I don't know. But I have a pretty good suspicion of who's behind the murders." She hesitated then said, "His name is Jerry Kemp. And he's Lexie's ex-boyfriend."

Steven stared at her, bemused. "Explain."

"Long story short, Lexie was in an abusive relationship with the....him. When she left him, he didn't take it well and came after her, even kidnapped her. Ray found her, brought her home, and Jerry was arrested."

"Sentenced?"

She shook her head and scowled. "No. His father is an attorney and has a long reach. He had the charges lessened to aggravated assault, and Jerry was given probation and taken back to New York on the stipulation he never set foot in Edmondville again, much less Texas."

Steven's eyes narrowed. "Why does it feel like you're not telling me everything?"

"Because I'm not sure you really want to hear it," she mumbled.

He sat back and crossed his arms. "Try me."

She paused, skimming her tongue over her teeth. What was she supposed to say to that? She'd never had to explain her or her family's gifts to anyone before. For as long as she could remember, it had been a given. The people who came to see her and her grandmother for help with a curse or illness already knew of their abilities.

Ray told her to go easy on Steven because he didn't want anything to do with magic, but did that mean Steven believed in it? Or had once believed in it? How would he react if she told him about her gifts? Or Ray's gift?

The doorbell rang and saved her from having to respond. Steven rose to answer the door and handed money to the delivery boy then carried the large paper bag to the dining area. Sylvia stood and moved to the table as he pulled two plates from the cabinet. He'd ordered her favorites: fried rice, sweet and sour chicken, steamed vegetables, and egg rolls.

They served themselves and ate quietly at the table. She used the silence to run her thoughts through her head, but she could feel the impatience vibrating from Steven. His tension was making it difficult for her to enjoy the food, so she set her fork down and pushed the plate aside. Steven did the same and shifted in his seat, crossing his arms as his signal for her to continue their conversation.

She picked up the water bottle, picking at the label with her nail and spoke. "I told you about Jerry's father, but he wasn't the only one with power. Jerry had plenty of his own. He was an *hechicero*. A very powerful one." She continued quickly, before he could scoff. "He used his magic to control Lexie. Last year he imprisoned her on another plane. After we found her and brought her home, I stripped Jerry of his power and hid it away. But I think he's looking for a way to take it back, possibly by using the spirits of the women he killed.

"If we can't stop him, he's going to succeed in getting his power back and go after Lexie and Ray again. And, this time, he won't hesitate to kill them both." She stopped and stared expectantly at him. He'd watched her quietly as she spoke, with no trace of emotion, although she'd seen his jaw clench more than once.

Instead of speaking, he picked up his plate and rose to go into the kitchen, setting the dish in the sink. He pulled a bottle of Crown Royal from a cabinet above the refrigerator and poured himself a shot, drinking it in one hard swallow.

"Did that help?" she said when he hissed out a breath.

"Not even if I drink the whole thing." He poured another shot but held it, staring at the amber liquid. "What the hell do you expect me to do with that?"

"Find out if Jerry's still in New York or if he hopped a plane to town?"

"Easier said than done," he murmured. "But I'll see what I can do."

"So, you believe me?"

He turned to her, his expression sober. "Do I believe Lexie's ex-boyfriend was some kind of warlock? No. But I think he manipulated her enough to scare her...and you."

"Well, talk about not committing," she said dryly. Steven frowned and swallowed the second drink. "So, when do I get to look in the box we found at the house?" she asked to change the subject. She was not going to rehash their past. She was over it. Mostly.

Steven turned and rinsed his glass in the sink then set it in the drainer. "What do you expect to find in there?"

"A reversal spell or maybe something to cloak her. There was no presence of Angel in the house. Or no spiritual presence that I could feel, so he must have found a way to bind her before he killed her."

"Spiritual presence? What, are you psychic, now?"

She bristled at his cold inflection and tried to keep her expression passive. "Not exactly. But I *do* sense things. Spirits mostly. I can also speak to them when they let me."

Steven held up his hand, a scowl curling his lips. "I've heard enough."

Sylvia stood and stepped forward, resting her fists on her hips. "Why do you find it so hard to believe the magic is out there? You were born and raised in a border town. Hell, even your own mother believed the spirits could help her with—" She froze when his expression darkened.

He glared at her, his hand gripped at his side, his jaw clenched tight. "How do you know that?"

She swallowed, stealing a look at the urn. "I told you, I see things, and I speak to spirits."

"We're done," he said in a low growl. "Get your things. I'm taking you home."

Before she could answer, he stormed to his bedroom.

She pressed her hands to her eyes and mentally kicked herself. *Good job, Sylvia. I'd say you eased him into that pretty well.*

Chapter Ten

Sylvia rested her chin on her palm and stared out the window at the landscape as it blurred by, her fingers absently tapping on her leg to the song on the radio. Steven had turned it to a country station, playing it loudly as if to keep her from speaking to him. Not that she had plans to. She'd already figured out that when he was mad, it was best to let him ride it out.

She closed her eyes a moment and tuned her senses to him. His anger was like a thick wall of fire—blazing hot and difficult to penetrate. She frowned. Yeah, she would definitely get burned if she tried to talk to him now.

Her phone chirped, startling her. She pulled it out of her pocket to check the number, hoping it wasn't Carla again. She'd already ignored an earlier call.

Vincent's name flashed across the screen. *Oh shit.* They had a date tonight. How did she forget that?

She stole a glance at Steven. Since the sky was overcast, he'd removed his sunglasses. His was attention fixed on the road ahead, his lips pressed into a hard line.

She tapped the send button, keeping her voice low. "Vincent. I'm so sorry, something came up and I completely forgot about dinner."

"It's okay. I hope everything is all right."

"Yes, fine. Just some things I have to take care of before my brother's wedding next week. I'm so sorry." She chewed her lip. Why did she find it so easy to lie to him?

She sensed his smile on the other end. "It's okay, *bella*." His voice lowered sensually. "Maybe I can come by later? When you get home? You can make it up to me then."

She hesitated, her mind racing to find an excuse to tell him no. She didn't invite men into her home, much less her bed. Even after nearly two months of dating, Vincent hadn't made it past the front door.

"No. You're right," he said as if sensing her uncertainty. "We aren't quite there yet."

"I'm sorry." Although she wasn't quite sure why she was apologizing.

"It's refreshing to know you're not like other women. That you're saving yourself for someone special. It's very admirable."

It took a moment for his words to process in her brain. *Holy hell, does he think I'm a virgin?* Okay, so she hadn't had sex since...well, Steven, *damn him*, but it's not like her hymen would grow back.

"I know we've only been dating six weeks," Vincent continued, "but I hope when you're ready, it'll be me you're ready with."

Jeez, what the hell was she supposed to say to that? She knew she should tell him she wasn't a virgin, but as excuses went, it was a good one. She wasn't ready to go that far with him, especially since she didn't quite know what her feelings toward him were. She glanced at Steven. His fingers were gripped white around the steering wheel and his jaw looked clenched tight enough to crack his teeth.

"Uh...yeah. Sounds good. I'll call you later."

"Of course." There was a change in Vincent's voice, but she couldn't quite make it out. She disconnected the call and shoved the phone in her pocket, avoiding a glance in Steven's direction.

Why did she feel like she'd just been caught cheating? And which one of them was she actually cheating on?

Terri Molina

It was almost nine when they arrived at Sylvia's house. The sun had set an hour earlier, dark clouds closing in to shroud the moon and stars, spreading an ominous silence over the town.

Steven shifted the gear into Park but didn't shut off the engine. He wasn't as angry anymore, but she sensed he was still in a foul mood.

He'd turned the radio off during the last hour of the drive so she'd been left to sit quietly in the dark with her own thoughts and decided she was tired of his brooding. Angry or not, they needed to talk.

"You should come in," she said to break the silence.

He shook his head but didn't look at her. "It's late. I'm going to get a room in town."

"I have a room," she snapped. Before he could react, she switched off the engine and pulled the keys from the ignition. "We're going to talk." She jumped out of the truck, slamming the door on his curses, and stalked to her house.

She spun around and glared at him when his foot touched down behind her on the stoop. "You know, you keep growling at me to be honest with you and the second I am you cut me off. I don't know what your problem is, but I'm trying to help you with your investigation. You need to just get over yourself!"

He stared at her, his brown eyes dark and intense on hers. Unbidden, a surge of desire shot through her, awakening the memory of his taste and the feel of his touch. Warmth spread through her,

95

tugging a response deep in her core. She swallowed hard and turned around to unlock the door. She wouldn't allow herself to be distracted by him.

Steven followed her inside as she made her way to the kitchen. She dropped the keys on the countertop and jerked open the refrigerator door, scanning the selection of drinks inside. She pulled a beer from the shelf and twisted the cap off, taking a deep drink. He moved to the refrigerator and pulled out a beer.

"Go ahead, help yourself," she snapped.

His lips quirked. "Thank you."

She rolled her eyes and huffed out a breath, her annoyance dying down. She hated being angry and especially hated that Steven could churn her emotions into a whirlpool of heat with a simple look.

"So, I need to get over myself?" he said, before taking a drink of his beer.

She eyed him, steeling herself with as much patience as she could muster. "Look, you either want my help finding whoever killed those women or you don't."

"Actually, I never asked for your help. You inserted yourself into my investigation," he said, matter-of-factly.

She skimmed her tongue over her teeth. He had a point. "Yeah, well, I was only saving you the trouble of having to ask."

He shook his head with a short laugh.

She sent him a rueful smile. "We didn't get off to a very good start, did we?"

He leaned against the counter, crossing his legs at the ankles. "I'm not usually greeted with a right cross by old friends."

She started to say they were never friends but stopped. They *had* been friends. Good friends. And she'd screwed it up by confusing it with love.

She shook her head, feeling even more contrite, and settled against the edge of the sink. "If it makes you feel any better, I may have bruised my hand." His amused smile made her pulse kick. She bit down on the reaction and gave him an earnest look. "Are you going to let me look in the box we found under Angel's house?"

He closed his eyes and tilted his head back, sighing heavily as if grasping for patience. "Sure." He pushed off the counter and moved into the living room. His overnight bag was sitting on the sofa. He pulled out a pair of dark-purple latex gloves and handed them to her.

"It hasn't been processed into evidence yet, so you need to wear these."

He donned a pair himself before pulling the box from the paper bag. After setting it on the coffee table, he carefully lifted the latch and opened the box. Inside were several items placed atop a black flannel bag. She recognized the bark from a blackthorn tree, leaves from the morning glory plant she'd taken a photo of outside Angel's house, and several dried yellow flowers. This was definitely a spell.

She spread the items around with her finger and removed the flannel bag. Tucked inside the casing was a palm-sized clay molding of a woman, her hands and feet bound behind her. A sprig of black hair was tied to the body, and several copper needles were embedded in the head and torso.

"What is that?" Steven asked.

"I think it's what he used to bind Angel's spirit." She returned it to the box and removed her gloves. "Did you find anything like this with the other victims?"

"Not that I'm aware of. But the bodies were dumped and we were never able to identify the victims, so if he left anything like this at their homes, we won't know."

She frowned and gestured toward the box. "I might be able to unbind Angel with this. But that still gives him at least three other spirits."

"How many would he need?"

"Honestly? I don't know. I'm not familiar with this kind of magic."

Steven stared at the items for several minutes, "For the sake of argument, let's say I believe you. What am I supposed to do about it?"

Sylvia dropped onto the sofa, resting her head back against the cushion. "I don't know. I don't even know for sure if Jerry's behind this or if he's even in town. I'm not sensing him, but it could be because he's not here. Or maybe he is here, and he's found a way to block me." She pressed her fingers to her eyes, pushing against the impending headache.

The sofa shifted with Steven's weight as he sat beside her. "Okay, I'll need some information from Lexie before I can look into him."

"I can give you what you need." She was not going to let Lexie get dragged into this if she could help it.

"Okay. Can I get you something? Do you need some more ibuprofen or something?" he asked, his tone unexpectedly soft.

She opened her eyes to study him. Something was different. He didn't look as angry or annoyed as he usually did when she spoke about magic. In fact, his whole demeanor had changed. He seemed...amiable?

She narrowed her eyes. "What's wrong?"

He frowned at her. "What do you mean?"

"You're different. Like you've flipped a switch. You're less...hostile than you were before. Did something happen?" She thought about their trip. He'd been angry with her to the point of fury when they left Angel's house. But when they arrived at his apartment, he'd changed. He was concerned and cautious and even knew she had a headache. Even on the drive from Austin, his anger had gone from furious, to annoyed, and now resigned. What the hell was going on with him?

She stared at him, waiting for him to answer. He lifted a shoulder with a non-committal shrug.

"You want me to keep an open mind; this is me giving you the benefit of the doubt." He raised his hand to stop her from speaking. "Look, it's been a very long day. I'm exhausted. We'll talk tomorrow." He rose from the sofa and grabbed his overnight bag then headed to her spare room.

"You bet your ass we will," she murmured, as the door closed quietly behind him. "And this time, you're going to tell me what *you're* hiding."

Chapter Eleven

Steven tossed his bag on the bed and sank down on the mattress, rubbing his fingers over his eyes. He wasn't lying when he said he was tired, but he'd escaped the living room and Sylvia's penetrating gaze because he couldn't be in the same room with her. Not after what he saw when they'd arrived at his apartment.

He rose from the bed to pace, locking his fingers behind his neck and stretching the tension from his muscles.

He'd thought she was asleep in the passenger seat until he called out her name to wake her. She was lying still, her breathing so shallow he could barely hear it. Her skin looked ghostly pale and for a brief, terrifying moment, he thought she was dead. Then he touched her, and she shot awake, gulping in air, disoriented, and terrified. She'd composed herself so quickly that, by the time they entered his apartment, he'd convinced himself that what he saw was his imagination. But the image of her lying dead beside him still haunted him.

Beneath the house, the pipes emitted a deep groan, followed seconds later by the heavy rush of water. She was taking a bath.

He left the bedroom and returned to the kitchen. His unfinished beer was still sitting on the counter, but Sylvia's was missing. She probably took it into the bath with her. He picked up his bottle and drank from it, trying to drown out the image of her lean, naked body, stepping into the pool of water.

Outside the window, a flash of light skittered across the sky. He moved to the door and stepped outside onto the slab of concrete that made up the stoop. The security light above the door flashed on. The wind kicked up, swaying the trees lining the backyard. The storm was moving in fast.

He glanced down and noticed a small bowl with bits of kibble still inside. He hadn't seen a cat when he'd been here the day before. Knowing Sylvia, she'd left it out for a stray.

A clay vase the size of a coffee cup was tucked in the space between the house and slab. It resembled the same plant Sylvia had photographed at Angel's house. He picked it up and studied it a moment. It was a simple looking thing, with heart-shaped leaves and violet flowers with a star-shaped center. He moved to the kitchen window where a planter was mounted. The box contained four other vases and left no room for a fifth, so he set the vase on the ground beneath it.

The wind kicked up, howling through the trees, and, for a moment, he thought he saw movement among the trunks. A shiver swept across his neck. He moved his hand to his side, but he didn't have his gun on him.

Lightning flashed, illuminating the yard. He strained his eyes, but he couldn't make out anything except the trees. Shrugging off the sudden discomfort, he returned to the house and locked the door behind him, peeling back the lace curtain to look outside. He rubbed at his neck. He couldn't shake the feeling that someone was watching him.

"What are you doing?"

Sylvia's voice made him jolt. He spun around and glared at her. "Christ, Sylvia, what is it with you and sneaking up on people?"

She crossed her arms and stared at him. She was wearing a thin, satiny robe that barely reached mid-thigh. Her feet were bare, and beads of water clung to her shapely legs. Her mass of hair was clipped atop her head, several loose strands resting against her slender neck. He bit down on the heated rush to his system.

"I could say the same about you," she said. "Why are you skulking around my kitchen?"

"I'm not skulking. I was...." Why did he feel as if he'd been caught doing something he shouldn't be doing? He gestured outside. "Storm's moving in."

As if on cue, lightning flashed, followed by a rumble of thunder.

"Okay." She gave him a look that said she thought he'd lost his mind and made him feel even more foolish.

He nodded toward the floor. "You're getting the floor wet. And, I'm not cleaning it," he added with a smile.

She started to speak then shook her head and left the room. He eased out a breath as fat drops of rain began to pelt the glass. Damn, if he thought he was feeling restless before, the sight of Sylvia in a thin robe with moisture glistening on her skin was definitely going to keep him awake now.

Shaking his head, he returned to the bedroom, closing the door behind him. A burst of lightning briefly lit the room in a pale light. He stripped off his shirt and jeans and climbed into bed, tucking his hands behind his head. Music filtered to him from the bathroom, and he pictured Sylvia relaxing in the tub, frothy water sluicing up her chin, her fingers tapping the porcelain to the rhythm of the music. He scowled and settled more into the pillow, trying to focus his concentration on the sound of the rain. A hint of lavender drifted from the linen pillowcase and he felt his body relax. His eyes slid closed as fatigue washed over him. The memory of their night together awoke in his mind, and he couldn't stop it even if he wanted to.

"This way." Sylvia tugged his hand and led him into the maze of the cornfield. They'd spent the afternoon at the beach, and she still wore the soft pink sundress she'd thrown on over her bikini. Her long black hair glistened under the moonlight and flowed down her back like a waterfall.

She stopped and set the blanket she carried onto the ground. Although they were surrounded by eight-foot-tall stems of corn, she pointed to the north and smiled. "Over there, about half a mile is my parents' house. My father built it for my mother before they got married. It's been closed up since their death, but it'll be Ray's after graduation."

She nodded toward the south end of the field. "And a half mile that way is my grandparents' farm. Right here in the center of the fields, is where my ancestors are the strongest. I like to come out here at night, just to listen. It makes me feel safe. Loved." She looked up at him, a smile softening her lips. Her eyes were extraordinary, like two amber-colored gems. She radiated an energy that drew him like a magnet.

He cupped a hand around her neck and brought her forward. Her breath shuddered out with a sigh when he pressed his mouth to hers. And when he swept his tongue over her lips, tasting, testing, she parted them and invited him in. It was like being in a dream, his perfect fantasy.

He took the kiss deeper as they lowered to their knees. Sylvia reached down to the hem of his shirt, and she slid the fabric up over his head. His pulse raced as she touched her mouth to his chest and up the curve of his neck.

Watching him with a quiet confidence, she pulled her dress off. Though he'd seen her in the bikini most of the afternoon, the sight of her tanned, slender body, closed the air in his lungs. She looked ethereal, unreal in the moonlight.

"God, you're beautiful," he said.

She curled her arms around his neck. "Make love to me."

Taking her in his arms, he pressed his mouth to hers and lowered her to the ground. He'd been with other women over the years, losing his virginity when he was fifteen, so he knew what to do to pleasure a woman. But he'd never felt the jangle of nerves like he did now. This was special. This was Sylvia. And it was as if she'd been meant for him.

Not wanting to allow that wayward thought to plant itself in his head, he left her mouth and followed a trail down her neck. With agile fingers, he untied the spaghetti thin strap behind her neck and slid her top off. He cupped her breast, feeling the weight of it in his hand and stroked a thumb over the hardened tip. She bowed up, a cry of pleasure escaping her throat as he took her in his mouth.

He roamed a hand down her body, stopping to rest between her thighs. Her skin warmed beneath him, her muscles quivering as he dipped a finger inside. She contracted around him, her breaths becoming labored as he stroked her heat.

He traveled down her body, pressing kisses into her flesh; heard her gasp as he caressed his tongue over the bud of her arousal. She bucked with her release, the moan of pleasure fueling his need.

He undressed quickly and moved up the length of her until he reached her mouth, kissing her until her tremors slowed. She opened up to him without hesitation, and he barely noticed her intake of breath as he slid into her.

Her gaze swept up to lock on his. "I always dreamed it would be you. I love you, Steven. Forever."

Steven jolted awake, his heart beating like angry fists. *Christ!* He swung his feet over the edge of the bed and pressed his hands to his face, trying to push the images of Sylvia from his mind and the words she'd whispered as her body let go.

How could he have been so stupid? He'd known she was a virgin and hadn't planned on doing anything other than kiss her. In the back of his mind, he'd known he should have walked away before it continued any further, tell her she should wait for someone else. Someone special.

But when she'd lifted her hand to his face and touched her mouth to his, all thoughts of innocence faded away and all he could do was give her what she wanted. What he needed.

Making love to her had been like a dream, and her words had awoken him with the force of a slap. In that moment, he hadn't known what to say. He didn't even know how he felt about her; love, marriage, a house full of kids was so far off his radar.

So instead of answering her, he'd kissed her again. The equivalent of a pat on the head.

He rose from the bed and paced restlessly around the room. He'd told himself Sylvia had uttered the words in the heat of the moment and she would realize her mistake and regret saying them. And he had to give her an out. So, after he walked her back to the house, he did the only thing he could do. He left. Too ashamed to face Ray, he'd skipped out on the last semester of classes and returned to his home in Donna to help care for his mother. He even tried to break all contact with his friend, afraid Sylvia had told him what happened. But

Ray's appearance at his mother's funeral three months later, and the days that followed told him she hadn't said anything.

If he could go back and do it all over again, he'd walk away and not even kiss her.

"Yeah, right," he muttered. He'd wanted to kiss her since the day he met her. And now, all he could think about was making love to her again.

He stopped at the window and stared out into the blackness. Seeing her again shook him more than he wanted to admit. He'd been in love with her then and he was in love with her now. But, she hated him. How the hell was he supposed to fix that?

With a resigned sigh, he turned to go back to bed and spotted a dim light flickering under his door. He pulled on his jeans and grabbed his gun before stepping out of the room.

He followed the glow of light into the living room and found a petite woman, sitting lotus style on the floor. She wore a pale-blue camisole with thin spaghetti straps and matching shorts, and she was hunched over something in front of her. Black hair curtained her face, and it took him a moment to realize it was Sylvia. Her eyes were closed, her body bent and crooked. She looked more like an eighty-year-old woman than a vibrant twenty-eight-year-old.

Placed on the center of a mirrored platter was the clay figure from the box. White granules that looked like salt encircled the doll, and the needles were missing. Sylvia had surrounded herself with several tea light candles that had melted into liquid pools of wax. The room smelled strongly of sage and several other scents he couldn't place.

Her hand hovered over the circle as she murmured something in Spanish. The tension radiating from her was palpable. As she spoke, she plucked the hair off the sculpture and set it on the flame of a fat candle off to the side. The fire flared white and blue, scorching the hair until it dissolved.

Outside, lightning flashed and the boom of thunder rattled the windows. Sylvia's eyes flew open, and she grabbed the figure and snapped it in half, still chanting in Spanish. The flames on the candles flared, smoke billowing up like a phantom then the candle blew out.

She sat up straight, searching anxiously around her, and he would have sworn her joints had popped as if her bones were resetting. She turned her head in his direction, and his heart stopped. Her eyes were solid white.

She tilted her face up toward the ceiling and murmured something he didn't understand. After a moment, she looked in his direction and blinked at him, confusion turning into surprise as her brown eyes focused. "Steven?"

"What. Was. That?" he asked, his voice surprisingly calm.

She placed her fingers against her temple and shook her head. "That...is very hard to explain." She rolled her neck and shoulders and sighed.

Steven decided he really didn't want to know. He tucked the gun behind him in the waistband of his jeans then stepped forward and held his hands out to help her stand. She hesitated then took his hands and allowed him to help her to her feet. Her legs buckled, and he scooped her up, muttering a curse.

"Just give me a minute," she murmured, resting her head on his shoulder, her breath whispering against his neck. "It's been a while. I forgot how much energy that takes."

"How long have you been doing that?" He tried not to focus on the feel of her in his arms or his body's reaction.

"This morning or in general?"

"Let's stick with this morning."

She inhaled deeply, letting the air out slowly. The warmth of her breath fluttered across his neck and nearly made his own legs buckle.

"What time is it?"

"A little after five."

"Two hours."

He bit down on the thoughts running through his head and carried her into the kitchen. He set her on the counter next to the sink then pulled a carton of orange juice from the refrigerator. "Drink," he said, placing it in her hand.

She did as she was told, her gaze watching him over the rim. She took a swallow and stared at him. "Why are you up so early?"

His dream flashed across his mind, but he pushed the fragmented images back so they wouldn't stick. "Couldn't sleep," he said with a shrug.

She eyed him a moment, and he could tell she didn't believe him. But he couldn't exactly tell her he'd been dreaming of making love to her.

"I can help you do that," she said.

His lips quirked. He picked up a towel to wipe the juice from her chin, skimming her with his gaze. "Oh? What do you have in mind?"

She frowned at him, and her expression chilled.

He mentally kicked himself. "Sorry. I didn't mean to...."

She set the carton aside and eased off the counter. "No problem." She swept her gaze up at him, her expression hooded. "I'm going to go get cleaned up. Why don't you make some coffee?"

He knocked his head against the cabinet as she disappeared from the room. "Smooth, Steven," he murmured. "Real smooth."

Sylvia closed the bathroom door behind her and leaned against it, giving herself a moment to calm. Her legs still felt rubbery, but her body was tingling from scalp to toes as if she'd had way too many double espressos. She wasn't sure if the feeling was from lending her body over to her great-grandmother for two hours or from being in Steven's arms for two minutes.

She moved to the sink and stared at her reflection in the mirror. Her eyes were slightly glazed and dark circles colored the skin beneath. She looked as if she hadn't slept all night—which, of course, she hadn't. So, why did she feel so wired? She'd never come out of a trance with this much energy before.

She turned on the shower and ducked under the cold spray. Bracing her hands on the tile, she closed her eyes and tried to bring back the memories from the cleansing.

It had been an intense battle to free Angel's spirit, but so much of it was blocked that she had to wonder if it was to protect her or keep her in the dark.

"What aren't you letting me see?" she murmured.

The aroma of fresh-brewed coffee drifted under the door, mixed with the savory smell of spices as she stepped from the shower. She dried quickly then pulled on the robe she'd left hanging on the door. She found Steven in the kitchen, scooping chorizo and eggs onto two plates. He'd thrown on a black T-shirt, which molded to the contours of his back and shoulders but left his feet bare.

He turned and held a plate out to her, his gaze drinking her in, and she couldn't stop the flutter in her stomach.

"Peace offering?"

She gave him a friendly smile she didn't quite feel. "Thanks." She took the plate and set it on the counter then moved to grab a mug from the tree next to the coffeemaker. Steven reached out at the same time, brushing his fingers over her hand. She felt the spark, like a surge of energy shooting up her arm, and jerked her hand away.

His eyes narrowed. "Why do you do that?"

"Do what?"

"Recoil whenever we touch."

She blinked at him. Why would he care how she reacted to him? "Maybe I just don't like you touching me," she said, although there was no conviction in her voice.

He wrapped his long fingers around her wrist, his lips curving into a wry smile. "Your pulse is racing. That means you're lying."

She tried to pull her arm back, but he held fast. His gaze dropped to her mouth, and his hand came up to stroke his thumb over her lips.

"You have a great mouth," he murmured. He bent lower, his mouth hovering over hers.

She swallowed hard, her throat suddenly dry. "Don't," she said, unable to control her breathy whisper.

"Are you sure?" His gaze swept up to hers, and her pulse kicked. She didn't realize she'd moistened her lips until his attention shifted to her mouth. "You can punch me later if you want," he said. Before she could react, he tugged her forward and claimed her mouth.

The power of his kiss was explosive and sent shockwaves of heat through her body. Vivid memories of their night together played in her mind, and, instinctively, her body arched toward him.

He caressed his tongue over her lips, challenging her to open up to him. When she did, he wove his hands in her hair and plunged.

She wrapped her arms around him as her knees trembled, threatening to give, and gave herself freely to his kiss. His hands moved to her robe, exposing one shoulder. He lowered his mouth to her neck, burning kisses into her flesh.

"Jesus, Sylvia, I've missed you," he whispered against her neck. "Do you know how much I want you? How much I want to make love to you?"

His words hit her with the force of a cold wave. She pressed her hands against his chest and pushed him back, shaking her head, afraid her voice would break if she spoke.

He blinked at her, and she didn't miss the hunger in his eyes. "What's wrong?"

"This. I can't." She pulled in a shuddering breath. "I don't think I can do this."

He cupped his hands on her face and eased her forward. "Don't think, Sylvia. Just feel." He kissed the corners of her mouth and stroked his tongue over her lips. "Tell me you haven't thought about this, about how much you want to be together. Tell me you want me, too." He tilted her head up, and when her lips parted, he took the kiss deeper.

Desire tugged at her insides, and her defenses weakened. Yes, she wanted him, she'd always wanted him, she couldn't deny that. But was she willing to let him rip out her soul again just to satisfy his own physical desire? It was one of the reasons she hadn't had a physical relationship since Steven. She couldn't bear to go through that pain again.

He grazed along her jaw, nipping her earlobe. She swallowed a moan. Her blood pounded in her brain, her emotions swirling in a whirlpool of confusion. How is it that he is the only man who physically and mentally affects her like this? And why is she so afraid to act on it? For crying out loud, she is an adult. She can have a physical relationship with a man without letting her emotions get in the way. She wanted him, and he wanted her. She just needed to get over herself. She wanted to laugh at the irony. She'd said the same thing to him when they returned from Austin.

Before she could speak, his phone rang. He rested his forehead against hers, his labored breaths matching her own.

"Saved by the bell," he murmured. He straightened her robe and brushed a kiss across her lips before returning to the spare bedroom.

Sylvia pressed a hand to her stomach and turned to stare out the kitchen window. She didn't know if she was relieved or disappointed by the interruption, but she knew one thing for sure—her vow to not get involved with Steven again had shattered the instant he kissed her.

She gave herself a moment to steady her pulse then pushed away from the counter and returned to the living room to gather the items from the cleansing.

Grabbing an old coffee can from under the kitchen sink, she carried everything outside and set it on a patch of ground away from the house. She placed the box and figure halves inside the can then poured lighter fluid over everything and set it on fire. She stood back and watched it burn until it all dissolved to ash. Scooping up some dirt, she poured it over the embers to make sure they were out then set the can on the stoop.

Steven entered the kitchen as she returned into the house. He was fully dressed in black jeans and a white linen shirt with a black jacket and maroon striped tie. Her heart skipped a beat at the sight of him. Then she noticed the overnight bag in his grip.

"Where's the box?" He set his bag on the table and cast a side glance at the spread of Tarot cards she'd laid out the night before, after he went to bed.

She waved toward the door. "Gone. You're leaving?"

"I have to get back to Austin. What do you mean gone?"

"I burned it."

"You burned it? All of it?" He pushed a hand through his hair and scowled at her. "Jesus Christ, Sylvia, that was evidence! What the hell were you thinking?"

She crossed her arms, keeping her expression level. "I was thinking I needed to save Angel's soul."

"Do you have any idea what this could do to my investigation? To my job?" He spun around and paced, his fingers raking through his hair. "Son of a bitch!"

"It's not going to touch you. No one even knew it existed except you and me," she countered. "Besides, now with Angel free, I can reach her in the spirit world–"

He wheeled around and held his hand up to stop her. "Don't even go there," he growled.

She bit down on the hurt and disappointment. She thought they'd reached an understanding about her gifts.

"Look, I'm sorry. I only did what I had to do. The cleansing wouldn't have held otherwise." She turned and filled a mug with coffee, using the time to give herself a moment to calm. After the way he'd just kissed her, she needed to know if he was coming back. "So, how long are you going to be gone?"

He exhaled heavily, his anger no less tangible. "I don't know. There's an issue with another case I'm working on, so I could be gone a while."

She faced him, keeping her expression aloof. She would not allow him to see how much he'd hurt her. "And what about Angel's case?"

"It's nothing I can't handle from Austin."

She straightened and nodded curtly. "Then, we're done."

He took a step forward, frowning when she retreated a step.

"Your cab is here," she said, surprised by the cold inflection in her voice.

He glanced out the window as a green car pulled into the driveway and honked the horn. He turned to her, his expression stoic.

A heaviness centered in her chest, but she gave nothing away. After a brief hesitation, he gave her a short nod.

"Take care of yourself, Sylvia." He grabbed his bag and left the room.

Without realizing she'd moved, she braced her hands on the kitchen table and watched him climb into the back seat of the cab. He didn't even look at the house.

She blinked against the tears stinging her eyes and stared down at the spread of cards on the table, her gaze landing on the *Fool* card. *Yeah, that's me all right.*

Chapter Twelve

Steven's mood hadn't improved during the hour flight into Austin or the fifteen-minute drive downtown, and it only worsened after he'd had to sit through three hours of cross-examination at the Travis county courthouse.

He pulled off his jacket and tie and walked the half mile to the DPS building to get his SUV, hoping the fresh air would put him in a better mood. But with his thoughts still swarming around Sylvia and the way she'd practically kicked him out of her house this morning, he found himself scowling when he reached the vehicle. From where he stood, she had no right to be angry. She was the one who'd destroyed evidence. Granted, he hadn't processed it yet so no one knew it existed. But *he* did.

It was his own fault, he thought as he pulled out of the parking lot and headed toward the interstate. He should never have agreed to let her work with him. She didn't know anything about the law and was too much of what his mother called a "free-spirit"—which, as far as he was concerned, made her too much of a risk to his job. He needed to find a way to get her away from this investigation without completely alienating her.

After a quick stop at his apartment to drop off his overnight bag, he arrived at David's house in Pflugerville in less than fifteen minutes, an advantage to driving a DPS vehicle as most people either slowed down to the approximate speed limit or moved out of his way altogether. David met him at the door, dressed casually in jeans and a navy-colored polo shirt.

"Just in time. Lunch is on the grill," he said, greeting Steven with a handshake.

Steven followed him into the kitchen. "Great, I'm starving." He hadn't eaten anything more than a bagel at the airport, which was part of the reason why he was still in a sour mood.

"How'd the deposition go?" David asked.

"Three hours of the same questions asked and answered. A fucking waste of time. Garza bought himself a new lawyer and he's filed a motion to suppress, claiming we violated his fourth amendment rights."

David pulled a bowl of salad from the refrigerator along with several vegetables. "I think trying to smuggle in three pounds of coke disguised as tennis balls is enough reasonable cause for a search."

"Yeah, well, let's hope the judge agrees." He moved to the refrigerator and pulled the door open.

"How was your stay in Edmondville? You make out okay with Ms. Chavez?"

Steven stopped mid-reach for a water bottle. "Excuse me?"

"Her consult? Has she given you anything to help with Ms. Salazar's case?" David asked as he sliced into a red onion.

Steven wrestled with the thought of telling him about the box they'd found but decided against it. He didn't want David to be placed in a position where he had to lie if the DA found out the evidence had been destroyed. He grabbed a bottle and shrugged. "Not really. Just the hocus-pocus bullshit right now."

"That's too bad. I thought she'd at least have a theory."

Steven took a pull from the bottle and scowled. "She did. She seems to think whoever killed Ms. Salazar is looking for something."

David stopped chopping the vegetables and furrowed his brow.

"Something like what?"

Steven clenched his teeth. "A power."

"A power? Like what? Thor's hammer?" David shook his head and returned to slicing vegetables.

"I didn't ask." It was bad enough she'd destroyed his evidence, now she was making him sound like a fool. "Regardless, her consult is over. I'm not about to turn this into a hunt for witches or warlocks or whatever satanic bullshit these psychos want to throw out there." David slid him a glance but didn't reply.

Steven reined in his anger and decided to change the subject before his mood became any darker. "So, how's Linda doing?"

"Why not ask her yourself?" A woman's voice spoke behind him. He turned and tried to keep the shock from registering on his face. The last time he saw her she'd barely had a bump, and now she looked as if she'd swallowed a person whole. "Wow. You look...."

"Don't say it." She narrowed her eyes at him. "I know how I look."

He grinned and bent to kiss her cheek. "I was going to say beautiful."

"Then I'll take it." She moved beside David and wrapped an arm around his waist. "Anything I can help with?"

He rubbed a hand against her lower back and kissed her cheek. "No. You're supposed to be in bed."

"I've been in bed, now I'm up." She turned to Steven. "Steven, can I get you a drink?"

"He already has a drink," David said before he could answer. "Would you please take her into the living room and make her sit?"

Linda sighed and allowed Steven to lead her out of the room. "Please tell me you've come to take him to work. He's only been here two days and already driving me batty."

119

"I heard that," David said from the kitchen.

"You were supposed to," she called back as they reached the front room.

"Here." Steven pulled several DVDs from his briefcase and handed them to her. "I grabbed a few of my mother's movies for you, to alleviate some of the boredom."

"Thank you." She shuffled through them to look at the titles. "These were some of her favorites. She loved a great romantic comedy. I'll get them back to you, soon."

He shrugged and settled on the sofa with her. "So, how are you feeling, really?"

She set the discs aside and grinned. "Aside from the swollen ankles and frantic husband, wonderful."

"And the babies?"

"*Babies*? Hey, I know I'm as big as Shamu, but I can assure you there is only one kid in here." She rubbed her stomach and furrowed her brow. "Why do you think I have two?"

He took a drink from his water. Sylvia had said *twins* when she'd asked about Linda's due date, and he hadn't even thought to question it.

As if reading his mind, Linda put her hand on his. "David told me about Miss Chavez."

"Yeah, I'm sure he did," he said dryly.

Linda laughed. "Yeah, he mentioned the right cross, too." Her expression sobered. "He mentioned you're working with her right now. Are you okay with that? With her magic?"

Steven shrugged. "I'm managing."

"Steven, I know you better than anyone. Managing isn't exactly your strong suit."

"It's fine, Linda," he said, firmly.

"Okay." She offered him an apologetic smile. "Just...maybe, try to keep an open mind with her."

That was the problem, he thought, taking a drink from the water bottle. He'd kept too open a mind with Sylvia. And, after what she did this morning, he was certain it was going to bite him in the ass.

***

Steven and David spent the remainder of the afternoon working in the kitchen while Linda took the DVD's to her bedroom. As Steven reached for Jane Doe #3's report, the volume from the TV built until it sounded like Meg Ryan was in the room with them, faking her orgasm.

David shook his head at Steven's quizzical expression. "I think she's trying to tell me that from now until eight weeks after the baby is born, that's about all the sex I'm going to get."

Steven gave him a mock shudder. "Thank you for putting that in my head."

David laughed and picked up another file and passed it to him. "Here, this will take it out."

He flipped it open to pull out the pages inside. "You found information on Jerry Kemp already?" On his way to the airport that morning, he'd phone David to let him know he was heading back to town and mentioned Jerry Kemp as a person of interest. But since he didn't have a chance to get any information from Sylvia, he didn't expect to find anything on the man.

"I figured there wouldn't be too many Kemps in our database.

Not a whole lot on him, though. Thirty-four years old. Lives in New Rochelle, New York." David nodded toward the photo Steven pulled out. Jerry Kemp stood against the wall facing the camera, a scowl curling his lips, his eyes dark with fury. A bruise had formed along his jaw, and his black hair was disheveled as if he'd been in a bar brawl. "He has a few complaints against him, but no charges," David continued. "Two years ago, he was questioned in New York for the hit-and-run death of a Christopher Peterson and six months ago for sexual battery against a prostitute. But, there was nothing to tie him to either.

"The only charge against him was the attempted kidnapping of Alejandra Solis here in Texas last year, but that was lessened to aggravated assault, and the charges were subsequently dropped."

"They were dropped?" Steven flipped through the pages. Sylvia didn't mention the charges had been dropped. He wondered if she knew.

"There's a restraining order against him so I called a friend at NYPD and asked if he could check into him. See if he was still in town."

"And?"

"Said he'd look into it. Should get back to me in a couple of days," David replied. "Why the interest in this guy? What's he got to do with our case?"

Steven dropped the file on the table. "That kidnapping last year? That was Sylvia's future sister-in-law. She seems to think Kemp is behind the murders."

David's brow raised to his hairline. "Really? And you believe her?"

Steven looked down at the file and sent David a noncommittal shrug. "Regardless, it doesn't hurt to check him out. See if he has any known associates in the area." He studied the file again. "Who knows? Maybe we'll get lucky and tie him to Garza."

"Yeah, well, I think that's more wishful thinking on your part." David grabbed the file Steven had picked up from the sheriff's department. "Did the sheriff's team find anything useful at Ms. Salazar's house?"

Steven rose from the table and moved to the refrigerator to grab a couple of water bottles. "Nothing we didn't already know. The only prints found were hers. No traces of blood anywhere, which means she wasn't killed at her house." He passed David one of the bottles and sat across the table from him. "Also, her car was a bust. Techs didn't find anything in it, and the impound said it was towed from the Del Mar campus during spring break. I spoke with campus security and asked them to get me copies of the video for the student parking lot. Maybe we can see if she met up with anyone there."

David nodded and looked over the pages in the file. "According to Ms. Salazar's boss, she kept to herself, didn't really have any friends. She was focused on completing her degree." He shook his head and frowned. "She wanted to be a substance abuse counselor. Smart girl, too. She was carrying a 4.0. GPA. Such a shame to see her life end before she had a chance to change it."

Steven pressed his fingers over his lids and rubbed the strain from his eyes. He should really go home, get some sleep, and go back over the files with fresh eyes, but he couldn't help thinking they were running out of time. "We should get with the dean at Del Mar also, see if he can get us a list of students in her classes. Sylvia said Ms. Salazar might have been going on a date. Maybe it was a study date."

"A date? What, did her crystal ball tell her that?" His lips quirked when Steven glared at him. "Sorry. Couldn't resist." He waved a hand at the other folders. "What about our Does? Was your girl able to tell you anything about them? What the symbols on the bodies mean? Or who put them there?"

"We didn't talk about them, and she's not a fucking psychic," Steven snapped.

David shrugged but couldn't quite hide his smile. "Maybe not, but you can't argue she has an insight to the hocus-pocus that we don't. Like it or not, you should stick with her. Keep her as a consult."

Steven gathered the files and stuffed them in his briefcase. He *didn't* like it, but David was right—not about the hocus-pocus, but about keeping Sylvia close. As long as she believed Jerry Kemp was involved in the murders, she would continue to find a way to prove it—which would either screw up his investigation or get her killed.

And he wasn't about to let either of those things happen.

***

The folder with the report for Jane Doe number one was opened, the pages spread across Sylvia's kitchen table. She lifted the second folder, Jane Doe #2, and frowned. She hated that the poor women were being referred to by such anonymous names. They were real people, with real families. Someone's sister, someone's daughter. It was bad enough the bastard who killed them had taken their life, he'd also stripped them of their identity.

She quelled her anger and placed each of the open folders Steven had included in the binder he gave her, side by side. He hadn't taken the book with him when he left, either because he forgot, or he didn't care that she still had it.

She'd been studying the files all morning and couldn't help feeling she was missing something. She wasn't a detective by any stretch of the imagination, but she was good with puzzles, and there were pieces missing from this one.

She braced her arms on the table and leaned forward to scan the diagrams of the bodies from the autopsy reports. Each of the women had the same type of trauma—their heads bashed in, the bodies scarred and bruised from torture.

According to Steven's notes, the women had been dumped in the desert and left to the elements. Much of their flesh had been eaten by whatever predator came upon them, but their internal organs had been removed by whoever killed them, most likely so the killer could complete the spell he was running.

Jerry was capable of working this type of magic *before* they'd stripped him of his power. And it's possible with enough incentive, he'd find a way to get his power back. And revenge against Ray and Lexie is definitely an incentive. But she'd bound his power after they stripped it, so there was just no way he could have taken it without her knowing.

She huffed out a breath and fell against the chair, frustration burning through her. She hated the helplessness, of feeling so uncertain.

She shoved the files into the binder and stood to stretch out the stiffness in her back from sitting at the table too long. The energy she'd had after the cleansing that morning had finally worn off, leaving her tired and cranky.

She grabbed the bottle of Patrón off the counter and poured herself a shot, carrying it to the table. The back door swung open, startling her, and she nearly spilled the glass. Ray stepped into the kitchen, oblivious to the panic he'd caused her.

He cocked his brow and nodded at the shot glass in her hand. "Not even five o'clock and you're already hitting the hard stuff."

"You know what they say, it's five o'clock somewhere," she answered before tossing back the tequila. "What are you doing here?"

"Steven called. Said he was back in Austin, so I came for my truck."

"You walked thirty miles just for your truck?"

Ray laughed. "More like fifteen minutes. I caught a ride with Grandpa. Now, what's wrong?"

She glowered at him. "What makes you think something's wrong?"

"Well, for one, you're more unpleasant than normal," he said with a smirk. He picked up the bottle of tequila and capped it. "And, you're drinking the good stuff. You only do that when something's bothering you."

She bit back her annoyance and moved to the refrigerator to pull out a pitcher of tea. *Great, I'm predictable.* She grabbed two glasses from the cupboard and filled them. "Nothing is bothering me. I just didn't get any sleep last night."

"Is it because of Steven?" he asked, accepting the drink she passed him.

She sipped her tea to give herself a moment to think. She couldn't tell him about what they'd found at Angel's house because she didn't want to worry him, and she sure as hell wasn't going to tell him Steven kissed her.

"So, I take it he isn't going to let you work with him on his investigation," Ray said.

126

She leaned against the counter and crossed her arms. "No, he did. Sort of. He let me look at his files, and I told him about Jerry, or rather a condensed version of Jerry."

"And?"

She shrugged. "He said he'd look into it."

Ray stared at her a moment. "You don't believe him?"

"Do you?" she countered.

"If he said he'll look into it, he will. Steven doesn't say something unless he means it."

Sylvia thought about the way he'd kissed her this morning and the words he'd whispered against her neck. *Do you know how much I want you?* Yet the second things became serious, he booked it out of town. Again.

She shook off the ache and lifted her shoulder with a shrug. "I guess I'll have to take your word for it."

Ray stared thoughtfully at her as she sipped her tea.

She cocked her brow and smiled. "Trying to read me, big brother?"

"I don't need to try, I know you. And I know you're not telling me everything."

"No, I'm not. Call it plausible deniability," she said when he frowned. "If I tell you what I know, then you'll have to tell Lexie, and she doesn't need to worry about Jerry Kemp on top of worrying about your wedding. And neither do you." She held her hand up to stop him from speaking. "Don't fight with me about this. You know I'm right."

He blew out a resigned sigh. "Yes, fine, you're right. But just so you know, if Lexie finds out we've been lying to her, I'm throwing you under the bus."

Sylvia laughed and scooped up his keys from the counter. "I'm not as afraid of Lexie as you are." She tossed him the set. "But, for both our sakes, don't let her find out."

Ray held the keys a moment, his expression sobering. "Just promise me one thing."

"If I can."

"Stick by Steven's side on this." His firm look stopped her from speaking. "Jerry may not have his power anymore, but he's still dangerous. I'll feel better about you going after him if you're working with Steven."

Sylvia paused. How the hell was she supposed to make that promise now that Steven was gone? She'd inserted herself into his investigation earlier because she needed to make sure Jerry wasn't involved. But he'd fired her before they'd even started. *Jerk.*

Okay, so maybe it was her own fault, but she wasn't thinking about evidence or chain of command or whatever police jargon they used when she'd burned the spell box. She just needed to make sure Angel was free and that whatever plans the killer had with her were stopped.

She should probably tell Ray she wasn't working with Steven anymore, but that would only worry him even more. And she couldn't lie to him either because he would know. Like it or not, she was going to have to make amends with Steven, at least until she disproved Jerry was their killer.

Resigned, she nodded. "Okay. I promise. If Jerry is responsible for these murders, I'll stick close to Steven."

***

Steven dropped Jerry Kemp's file on his coffee table and rubbed his fingers over his eyes. He was wasting time looking into Kemp. The man was not his killer.

He shook his head and rested against the sofa. The only reason he'd looked into Kemp was because Sylvia believed he was responsible for the death of Angel Salazar and he wanted to believe her. But Kemp lived in New York and worked as a barista at a small coffeehouse. He was hardly a man with the means to jump on a plane every few months and fly to Texas to kill anyone; unless, of course, he was the powerful witch Sylvia claimed him to be and he rode in on his broomstick. He scowled. Witches, black magic, binding spells. Part of him wondered if she was deliberately trying to make a fool of him.

He stole a glance at the wall clock. Nearly midnight. Another day gone, and he was still nowhere on this case.

He rose from the sofa and went into the kitchen. He poured a shot of Crown Royal, his gaze landing on the fortune cookie, still wrapped in cellophane, on the dining table. He grabbed the cookie and ripped it open. A white strip of paper fluttered out. He picked it up and read: *Do not fear what you do not understand.*

He stared at the words, the memory of his mother's voice saying the same thing to him when he'd questioned her decision to forego chemo in favor of the herbs and incense she'd bought across the border. She'd wasted time and money on a superstition that did nothing to prolong her life.

Sylvia's words from the day before played in his head. *"Why do you find it so hard to believe the magic is out there? You were born and raised in a border town. Hell, even your own mother believed the spirits could help her."*

He'd never told anyone but Linda about his mother's visits to a *curandera* for a cure for her cancer. Not even Ray. So how did Sylvia find out? His gaze shifted to the urn holding his mother's ashes. *No.* He refused to believe the spirit of his dead mother told her.

He tossed back the drink and dropped the fortune on the counter. The paper slid across the surface and onto the floor as if pushed by an invisible hand. *Do not fear what you do not understand.*

"What's to understand?" he snapped. "You're dead because of some stupid belief. I'm not going to make the same mistake."

He grabbed the bottle of Crown Royal and carried it with him to his bedroom as the clock chimed midnight.

Chapter Thirteen

Sylvia placed the tray of letters onto the passenger seat of her Jeep while Lexie lifted the second tray from the cart she'd wheeled onto the loading dock. She stifled a yawn and hoped Lexie didn't notice. She hadn't been able to sleep the past couple of days since Steven left, her mind unable to settle after the promise she'd made to Ray. She'd never gone back on her word before, which is why she never made a promise she couldn't keep. Although, if she really thought about it, she only said she'd stick with Steven if Jerry was the one who killed Angel, so, technically, if Jerry isn't the killer and is really out of their lives for good, then the promise to her brother is null and void. She would be free to hunt down the bastard binding spirits and Steven would be out of her life. Again.

"Sylvia!"

She blinked at Lexie who was standing beside her holding a long tray of letters. "Huh?"

"I said, thanks for taking the back half again today."

"Oh, sure, no problem."

Lexie furrowed her brow and handed Sylvia the tray. "What's with you? You've been acting weird all week. Is anything wrong?"

"No, of course not." She turned to place the tray next to the first one. Lexie had become pretty good at reading her lately, so she didn't want to give her anything to see. "Your sister is coming in later today, right?"

"Yes, tonight," she answered; the smile evident in her tone. "Another reason I'm glad you're letting me off early. I told Ray I'd help him pack. He's staying at your grandparents from now until the wedding."

She turned to look at her future sister-in-law. "Why?"

Lexie's cheeks flushed pink. "Oh, you know, with Rebecca and Robert staying at the house, I didn't want it to be awkward for anyone."

Sylvia relaxed the tension in her shoulders and gave Lexie a knowing grin. "Lexie, you two have been living together for almost a year. I'm pretty sure Rebecca has figured out you and Ray are having sex."

Lexie handed her another tray. "Yes, but I prefer to stay blissfully ignorant about that."

Sylvia shook her head and closed the Jeep door. "Okay. I'm out of here. I told Gabe I'd be back before his lunch break. And, after your shift, you are officially off for the next two weeks."

"Yes, ma'am. Thanks again, Sis."

"Anytime." Sylvia gave her a hug then climbed into her Jeep.

As acting postmaster of the post office, she didn't have an assigned route, but occasionally would pick up a section if a carrier wanted off early. The past few days she'd been taking two hours from Lexie. She'd told her it was to give her extra time to sort things out before the wedding, but, really, she wanted to keep Lexie off the streets as much as possible in case Jerry really was in town. Although she didn't sense him like she had last year, she couldn't shake the feeling that something bad was going to happen. She just hoped the protection spells she'd worked around her family would be enough to keep them all safe.

***

Steven tossed his jacket next to his overnight bag in the back seat of his SUV then set the folder he'd picked up from the San Patricio County coroner onto the passenger seat as he slid behind the steering wheel.

He'd crawled out of bed before dawn after a restless night of sleep and wanted to kiss the gods of fortune when Dave Moser called to let him know the autopsy on Angel Salazar was completed. Since the county office server was down, and he didn't want to wait on the report, he'd jumped into his truck to make the two-hour drive for a hard copy.

A heavy gloom had settled over the town as dark clouds moved in from the gulf with the threat of a storm. He placed his sunglasses next to his travel mug in the cup holder and contemplated stopping at the nearest coffee shop for a refill, but the adrenaline spiking through him told him it wasn't a good idea. Although it wasn't the caffeine making him anxious, he thought as he pulled out of the parking lot and headed toward the highway. It was the dream that had kept him tossing and turning throughout the night and the urgent feeling that Sylvia was in trouble. Normally he wouldn't let his dreams bother him, but something about this one felt so real he couldn't let it go.

He frowned and made an effort to loosen his grip on the steering wheel. "It was just a dream, dammit," he growled. So why did the images of her tied to the ground with a pentagram burned onto her chest feel so real?

The memory flashed across his mind.

He raced through a cornfield, dried leaves slicing at his arms like razorblades. The darkness of night disoriented him in the maze as terrified screams filled the air. He felt as if he'd been pushing through the relentless wall of stalks for hours, searching for Sylvia. He finally found her in a clearing, tied to four stakes on the ground and surrounded by five flaming torches. Her eyes were open and terrified, and streaks of blood colored her arms and torso.

"Sylvia!" His cry grated his throat. She didn't move, didn't acknowledge he was there. Panic gripped him. She wasn't dead. She couldn't be.

Flashes of light sparked behind dark clouds and the wind kicked up, carrying the odor of burning flesh. Two figures wearing long hooded gowns appeared on opposite sides of her. One of the figures stepped toward her, holding a long-blade knife. His head came up and turned in Steven's direction. "You can't stop this."

Though he couldn't see a face beneath the hood, he felt the smile before the figure raised his hand and plunged the knife into the symbol on Sylvia's chest.

The scream of his cell phone jolted him from the images. He pulled in a calming breath and slowed his speed when he realized he was going twenty miles over the limit. Thankfully, traffic was light.

He tapped a button on the steering wheel to access his Bluetooth. "Gonzales."

"Hey," David's voice piped through the speakers of the radio. "Where are you?"

"Just leaving the San Patricio Coroner's office. I have Ms. Salazar's autopsy report."

"Well, if you're heading home, turn around. I think you need to get back to Edmondville. We have another body"

Steven froze as the blood turned to ice in his veins. He swerved to the side of the road and pulled onto the shoulder, his heart battering against his ribcage.

"You still there?"

"Do we know who?" Steven asked, pushing the words out with the air blocking his throat.

"No ID. The vic is male, in his mid-to-late thirties."

Male. Not female. Not Sylvia. It's not Sylvia. Steven repeated the mantra in his head, scrubbing his hands over his face as cold relief washed over him. It took him a moment to find his voice. "Male? Are you sure it's one of ours?"

"I didn't get specifics, but the body appears to have the same markings as our other vics. Cameron County Sheriff's Department is on scene. I texted you the coordinates. Should I tell them you're on your way?"

"Yeah." Steven tapped the phone to access the text and read the numbers. "Let them know I'm about two-and-a-half hours out."

"Will do. Oh, and I spoke to the dean at Del Mar. He has a list of students in Ms. Salazar's classes for us. He also said there are a couple of coffee houses around campus that the students frequent. Linda's mom came in last night, so I'm free to go over and check them out, see if they have video of Ms. Salazar. I'll let you know if anything pans out."

"Thanks." Steven disconnected the call and sagged against his seat to give himself another moment to calm. He'd never been so panicked in his life as when he thought the body was Sylvia's.

He reached for his phone and pulled up her number. For his own peace of mind, he wanted to call her and make sure she was safe. But she would probably hang up on him, the equivalent of a slap in the face.

135

He returned the phone to its holder and shifted the SUV into drive, merging back onto the highway. It'd be better to just go to her. He'd risk the sting of her palm if it meant she was okay.

***

Sylvia pulled her Jeep alongside the curb of the quiet neighborhood and grabbed her bag, already stuffed with the last of the mail, before climbing out.

The street was three blocks long, some of the houses spaced one to two lots apart. Normally, she would drive this end of the route, but she'd made good time with delivery this morning and was in the mood to walk. Walking cleared her head and helped her think, and she had a lot to think about where Steven's investigation was concerned.

She strapped the bag across her chest and adjusted the ball cap on her head before starting toward the first house.

The heat of the early morning sun warmed her skin as she moved past an abandoned lot, the temperature feeling more like summer than early spring. A soft breeze fluttered the newly sprouted leaves on the trees, while a group of pigeons cooed from several rooftops. In the distance, some dogs barked a conversation only they understood. She checked her bag to make sure she had her pepper spray and hoped the dogs were contained.

It took her twenty minutes to complete the delivery. A quick glance at her watch told her it was only ten o'clock. She was going to get an extended lunch break.

She started toward her Jeep as dark clouds gathered in the sky, dimming the daylight. A wave of dizziness washed over her and made her sway. She leaned over, bracing her palms on her thighs, and pulled in a deep breath to quell the sudden nausea churning in her stomach. Maybe she should have had more than a pot of coffee for breakfast.

As she straightened to stand, a low growl rumbled behind her. She whirled around, swinging the mailbag in front of her as a shield and reached for the pepper spray clipped to the side. The neighborhood had vanished, and she was standing in the woods, surrounded by thin reeds of pine trees that stood twenty feet above her. Daytime had turned to night, black clouds blanketing the sky in darkness. The smell of burning wood, mixed with dry earth, filled the air.

"What the hell?"

She turned slowly to gauge her surroundings. At her feet, faceless bodies etched in a cool gray mist rose from the ground, swirling along the base of the trees like children playing hide and seek. The ghostly moans whispering from the spirits prickled the hair on the nape of her neck, but she swallowed the panic before it had a chance to paralyze her.

"Stay calm. You're having a vision," she murmured. *She hoped.* She'd only had one vision in her life, and she'd been five at the time.

Easing out a breath she wandered the forest, her steps guarded. Dried pine needles and fallen bark crunched under her shoes. The mist swirling at her feet seemed to thicken, the specters groaning and pulling at her as if to quicken her pace. "This is definitely creepier than I remember."

A loud crack sounded several feet behind her. She spun around, her pulse kicking in her throat.

"Who's there?"

An ear-piercing screech sounded overhead. She looked up as a large black owl launched from a branch and swooped down toward her. Its eyes shone bright red, like two burning flames.

She ducked, but not in time. The extended talons sliced at her flesh. She gasped a sharp breath, pressing her hand against her arm, the warmth of blood spilling over her fingers.

The bird shot up toward the sky, its shadow spreading across the thicket like a phantom. Sylvia searched the trees, the dried pine needles raining down like confetti. Was it her terrified imagination or did the face look human?

"I'm not here to fight you," she called out.

The owl came at her again, screaming fiercely as it's razor thin talons reached down. She pivoted but not fast enough. The claws burned into her shoulder like three hot pokers.

"Son of a bitch!" Clutching at the wound, she rolled to the base of a tree as the monstrous bird flew into the cover of the branches.

Silvia pulled in a breath then pushed off the tree and ran. Behind her, the trees cracked and splintered like kindling as if someone plowed through them with a chainsaw.

She spotted an abandoned house several yards away near a gap in the trees and ran harder, slapping at the hanging branches to keep from adding to her injuries.

The screams behind her drew closer, the noise battling with her own heart pounding in her ears. She stole a glance behind her as she reached the house. The momentary distraction caused her to lose her footing, and she fell forward, landing inside the doorframe. She threw her arms over her head to shield her from another attack. A heavy gust of hot wind blew past her, pelting the ground with chunks of wood.

When she lowered her arms, she was sitting on the wooden porch of an abandoned house, overgrown dried grass and weeds waving in the breeze, her mailbag at her feet. She pressed her hands to her face and tried to slow her rapid breaths. "What the hell was that?"

The call of a bird sent her heart racing again. Climbing to her feet, she grabbed the mailbag and hurried to her truck.

Whatever it was, she was pretty sure it had to do with Jerry.

Chapter Fourteen

Sylvia flung her mailbag in the corner near her kitchen table and grabbed the bottle of tequila off the refrigerator. She poured a shot and tossed it down quickly, hissing out a breath as the liquid burned her throat. Bracing her hands on the counter, she pulled in a lungful of air to give herself a moment to calm.

She didn't want to chance running into Lexie at the office, so she'd called Gabe to let him know something had come up and she was taking the day off. Gabe, bless him, didn't question her and agreed to stay and close the store.

She carried the bottle to her bedroom, pouring as she walked. The image of the owl with the human face flashed in her mind. It wasn't until she'd calmed down in the Jeep that she realized what she'd seen. A *lechuza*.

According to the stories her *bisabuela* told her, *lechuza* were women who sold their souls to the devil in exchange for magical powers. At night, they would transform into monsters with a bird's body and a woman's face and seek revenge on those who did them wrong. The witch would mark her target, then take their soul, and give it as a contribution to the demon she made the deal with.

Sylvia swallowed the shot and stared at her pale reflection in the dresser mirror. Why would the witch come after her? Jerry Kemp was the only sorcerer she'd ever dealt with, but the owl had the face of a woman.

She thought about the background information she'd found on Jerry Kemp. His great-great-grandmother had been a powerful witch.

Is it possible this was her spirit? And if so, how is she here now?

A part of her wanted to call Steven and ask if he'd learned anything about Jerry, but he'd already made it clear she wasn't welcome on his investigation. Not that it mattered what he thought, this was her family at risk and she was going to do whatever it took to keep them protected.

Her cell phone chirped. She pulled it from her pocket and checked the number. *Vincent.* She hesitated then tapped Ignore to let the voicemail take it.

She moved to her dresser and grabbed a clean shirt. Light glistened off an object beneath the clothes. She reached inside and pulled out a palm-sized crystal ball. Ray had given her the gift as a joke when she was twelve, and she used to keep it on the mantel in her living room.

She turned the globe and studied it. There were tiny imperfections in the glass, bubbles of air trapped inside the sphere. They'd developed after she'd placed Jerry's power inside.

A spark of guilt shimmered through her. She had promised Ray she would get rid of the power, but it wasn't as easy as she let him believe, plus, she just couldn't bring herself to do it. It fascinated her, the strength it carried. She'd tried to touch the energy once and had received a shock so hard she'd felt the tingle for days.

A thought froze in her mind and turned her insides ice cold. Was it possible she made a rip between worlds and released the witch when she touched the magic?

She returned the ball to the drawer and paced the room, biting on her thumbnail. Was the vision this morning a warning that Jerry had found a way to bring his great-great grandmother back? She knew it was possible to pull a spirit from another plane, as long as they found the right human vessel to place it in. But it took a very strong magic to do it. A very dark magic.

She squeezed her arms around her waist and paced some more. Is that why the women were being killed and bound? Was Jerry taking the essence of their souls and using it to open a portal? Did he plan to use Lexie as the vessel as a way of punishing her for leaving him?

She continued pacing, pushing her fingers through her hair. Her gaze slid to the bedside table. The notebook Steven had given her sat closed next to her deck of tarot cards. She'd spent the past few nights trying to get answers from the cards, but none of her attempts had worked. The spirits were barely speaking to her, and she had no freaking clue why.

Stepping to the bed, she picked up the board and sat down on the mattress. She needed answers, and this was the only way she knew to get them. She clutched the planchette in her hand and eased in a breath. "I hope you're there, *bisabuela*. I really need your help."

After lighting a candle and murmuring a prayer, she placed the planchette on the board and closed her eyes.

"Are you there, *bisabuela*? Is anyone there?" She waited, but the planchette stayed in place. "I know you're there. I need your help. Please."

Nothing.

She huffed out a breath and dropped against the headboard. "Dammit, why won't you help me?"

She pressed her fingers over her eyes, causing white spots to dance behind her lids. Memories of the past year flashed in her mind like a movie reel—Lexie telling them about Jerry, Jerry using Ray to assault Lexie, Jerry breaking down Lexie's spirit and pulling her into a pocket dimension, and Ray's fierce determination to get her home.

Sylvia had been so scared for Ray when she realized she'd have to send him on a vision quest to get answers for what he had to do in order to save Lexie. He'd risked his life and his own soul crossing into a world he knew nothing about. But he did it because he loved Lexie.

She opened her eyes and sat up. "That's it!" If she wanted help from the spirit world, then the only way to get it was to go directly to the source. Which meant, she was going on her own vision quest.

After changing into a pair of cutoff shorts and T-shirt, she knelt in front of the chest at the foot of her bed and lifted the lid. Inside were several candles in various sizes, a copper brazier worn with age, and a bag of colored woodchips. She gathered them together along with a vial of Myrrh oil and placed them on the silver tray she'd pulled from the bottom of the chest.

She carried the items into the living room and set them on the coffee table. Normally, she would perform this ritual outside since it took her closer to the elements but, even though her house was well shrouded by trees and her nearest neighbor was half a block away, she would be in a deep meditative state and didn't want to chance anyone coming up and surprising her.

She moved her coffee table closer to the sofa and glanced around the room. In order to go on her quest to the spirit realm, she needed to work in a cherished place. She'd bought the house shortly after her high school graduation with the money her parents had left her. The money had been in trust since she was five, gaining more than enough interest for her to use as a down payment.

Her family thought she'd bought the house in order to show her independence, which wasn't completely untrue. But she'd also bought the house because she had to get away from the farm and the memories of Steven.

She rolled her shoulders to push him from her mind. He was the last person she wanted to think about right now.

She chose the spot in the living room she'd used for Angel's cleansing and placed four candles on small brass plates and set them on the floor, marking north, south, east, and west. Moving into the kitchen, she fished a copper tea kettle and tin canister from the cabinet and set it up to prep her tea. The leaves were a special blend of herbs, including peyote, that would help her go into the trance needed to separate her spirit from her body.

Once the tea was made, she carried the mug into the living room and sat within the center of the candles. She picked up the brazier and a fat, red votive and placed them on the floor in front of her. Apprehension skittered down her spine like icy fingers. She'd never been on a vision quest before. Talking to the spirits through the Ouija board was one thing but going into another plane was something different.

"I need you to be there, *bisabuela*," she murmured.

Exhaling slowly, she scooped out a handful of the wood chips and spread them in the bowl. Lifting the oil, she held it over the brazier and closed her eyes, murmuring a short prayer.

She grabbed the mug of tea and drank until it was empty then she picked up a box of matches and pulled out a stick. White smoke, carrying the floral scent of the chips, wafted into the air as soon as the flame hit the brazier.

Closing her eyes again, Sylvia rested her hands, palms up, on her knees and relaxed her body one muscle at a time. The tea she drank coursed through her veins like a warm current, tingling her skin from her toes to her scalp. Her body felt lightweight as if she were floating among the clouds. The acidic smell of rain mixed with dry earth colored the air around her.

From somewhere in the distance, she heard the steady beat of a drum and the low whistle of a flute. As she relaxed in the contentment of the journey, bright, colorful lights flashed behind her lids. Heat flushed her skin and dizziness overwhelmed her.

She opened her eyes. Panic seized her. The world around her was spinning as if she'd been picked up by a massive funnel cloud, the heavy wind tossing her about like a rag doll. Grotesque images flashed before her like a Quentin Tarantino movie. Then she was standing in a field surrounded by a multitude of dismembered bodies. Bright-red embers rained from the sky as screams of anguish and pain rose from the wounded.

She spotted Steven at the edge of the field. He was kneeling, his hands bound behind him, blood dripping from a wound on his head. Fear and panic squeezed the air from her lungs as a tall figure stepped beside him, carrying a large sword.

"No!" Sylvia rushed forward. She stumbled over a large object on the ground, her hands pressing into something wet and sticky. Bodies frozen in fear and bleeding from open wounds across their necks surrounded her. She looked up to see the man swing the blade up. Before she could get to her feet, he brought the steel down. The scream pealed from her throat. In an instant, the earth crumbled beneath her, opening into a dark pit. Arms flailing, she scraped at the ground, trying to grab onto something solid, but mud and dirt seeped between her fingers.

As she fell into the void, one thought entered her mind—if she died in this world, would she die in hers?

Her body hit something solid, and pain radiated in her head

before the world went black.

Chapter Fifteen

It was after three in the afternoon when Steven arrived at Sylvia's house. He'd spent a couple of hours at the new crime scene, speaking with the deputies from the Cameron County Sheriff's Department and with the medical examiner once she arrived to take control of the body.

Although the only photo he had of Jerry Kemp was a mug shot, there was no doubt in his mind he was the victim. Since Kemp had been a person of interest in his case, the deputies had no qualms about letting him work with them, and now he had the unpleasant task of questioning Sylvia.

He eased out a breath and grabbed his cell phone from the cup holder, shoving it into his coat pocket as he made his way up the front steps. He knocked on the door, waiting several minutes before knocking again. No answer. According to the old man at the post office, she had left work before lunch and wasn't expected to return, so she should be here.

He moved around to the rear of the house. Her Jeep was parked askew in the grass as if she'd been in a hurry to get into the house. He moved toward the back door and found it partially open. A shimmer of anxiety whispered across his neck. He pulled out his gun and moved cautiously into the house. Her bag was sitting on the kitchen table, but nothing was out of place in the room.

"Sylvia?" As he continued toward the living room, a mix of smells, like burning wood and flowers, assaulted his senses. He peered around the doorframe. She was lying on the floor next to the coffee table, four unlit and melted candles surrounding her.

"Sylvia!" Securing his gun, Steven rushed forward and pressed two fingers on her neck to check her pulse. Still strong. He carefully rolled her onto her back. Blood matted her left brow, spilling from a one-inch gash on her forehead.

"Sylvia?" He stroked her cheek. "Wake up, baby."

Sylvia bolted up, her arms flailing and knocking him back. Her chest heaved rapidly, panic and fear etched across her face.

He grabbed her wrists and leaned into her line of sight, holding tighter when she writhed with a strength he'd have never expected from someone so slight. "Hey. It's me. Calm down before you hurt yourself."

She blinked at him, and it took a moment for recognition to set in. "Steven!"

Before he could speak, she threw her arms around him and held on. Her body trembled, and he felt her heart pounding against his own chest.

"It's okay. You're okay." He stroked his hand along her back while she settled her breathing. "What happened? Did someone break in? Were you...?" *Assaulted*? A hard knot settled in his throat and kept him from completing that sentence.

She sat up, her eyes widening with panic. "Break in? Someone broke in?" She shifted as if to stand then winced and pressed her fingers to her brow, pulling them back to stare at the blood. "No. I was.... I fell. I guess I hit my head on the table."

Cold relief washed over him, tamping out the burning anger that someone had hurt her. He rose and took her hands to help her stand. "Come on, let's get you cleaned up." He glanced at the candles on the floor then back at Sylvia. "Then you can tell me what really happened." The expression on her face told him she wasn't sure she wanted to tell him anything.

He took her into the bathroom and pulled a washcloth from the linen closet while she inspected the wound on her head in the medicine cabinet mirror.

"Oh God, I hope I don't need stitches. They will not look good in the wedding pictures."

"I don't think it's deep enough for stitches. Head wounds can look worse than they are because of all the blood." Steven wet the cloth and motioned her to sit on the edge of the tub.

She stared up at him as he dabbed the cloth gently over the wound, her dark-chocolate eyes a mix of gratitude, curiosity, and caution. She didn't flinch when he touched the cut, which told him it was definitely not as bad as it seemed. "So, how about you tell me what happened?" he said.

"What are you doing here?" she asked. "Is it about, Jerry?"

He stopped cleaning the wound. "Why do you say that?"

"Did you find him?"

Steven stared at her firmly. "Only one of us is going to ask questions right now, and it's not you. Where were you two nights ago?"

She pinched her brow, taken aback by his anger or the question, he couldn't be sure which. "Why?"

"Just answer the question."

Her expression cooled. She squared her shoulders and stood, taking the cloth from him to clean her cut in front of the mirror. "Two days ago, I worked from six a.m. until four p.m. I came home at four-fifteen and showered. Vincent picked me up at five, and we went to the Texas Roadhouse in Brownsville for dinner and came back here at seven-thirty."

An ache soured his stomach at the thought of her with the other man. He shook it off and kept his voice professional, watching her reflection in the mirror as she dressed the wound with the antibiotic cream and bandage she'd taken from the medicine cabinet. "And you were here all night?"

"Not that it's any of your business, but yes." After a short pause, she looked at his reflection and said, "Vincent didn't stay. He had to go into work. I was here, *alone*, the rest of the night. Now, enough of your bad-cop routine. What's going on?"

"Jerry Kemp is dead."

Sylvia spun around, her eyes wide. "What? When? How?" Her expression went from shocked to insulted before he could answer her. "You think I had something to do with it? That I killed him?"

"No. I don't. But I have to ask."

She nodded, but her expression stayed hard. "I get it. And before you decide to accuse Ray, he didn't do it either." She pushed past him and left the room.

He followed her into the kitchen. "Do you plan to alibi him?"

"If I have to." She eyed the bottle of Patron on top of the refrigerator then pulled open the door and grabbed a pitcher of tea. "Look, you've known him nearly fifteen years. He's been like a brother to you. Do you really believe he could kill someone?"

"No, but again, I need to question him." He paused, then said, "But it can wait until after the autopsy when we have more information."

She took two glasses from the cupboard and filled them with tea. "So, can I ask what happened? To Jerry, I mean?"

Steven gestured toward the kitchen table and pulled out a chair.

She carried the glasses to the table, and he waited for her to sit before speaking. "He was found early this morning outside Harlingen, off Rio Hondo road. He'd been dead about two days."

"Two days? He's been in town for two days?"

"We don't know how long he's been in town, yet. But decomp and lividity put time of death a little over forty-eight hours ago."

Her tongue slid over her teeth as she processed what he said. "And you're sure it's him?"

"I've only seen his mug shot, but I'm pretty sure. We're waiting on prints to verify."

She shook her head and murmured, "I don't understand. How could I not know he was in town?" She paused then asked, "How was he killed?"

"Hard to say. There's blunt force trauma to the back of the head, but his throat was cut as well. The responding deputy thinks he was either carjacked or meeting someone. They found tire tracks but no car."

"Were there any markings on his body?"

Steven hesitated, not sure if he wanted to show her the body, then pulled out his cell phone and brought up the photo he'd taken at the crime scene and slid it over to her. Using two fingers, she enlarged the photo.

"The 'witches' mark.' Just like Angel." She pointed to Jerry's chest. "They were killed by the same person."

"It's possible. Again, we won't know until the autopsy is completed."

As he reached for his phone, she grabbed his arm and jerked it forward. "Oh my God, is that the time?" Her gaze shifted from his watch to the wall clock. She dropped his arm and jumped from the chair as if it were a hotplate. "Crap! I can't go to dinner looking like this."

Steven ground his teeth. "Under the circumstances, I think you should cancel dinner with your *boyfriend*."

She shook her head, touching the wound on her brow and, thankfully, didn't notice the jealous tone in his voice.

"It's not a date. Dinner with Lexie and her family. Her sister and brother-in-law are coming in tonight, and I'm supposed to meet at her house at five to help her cook. Damn."

"So, why is this a problem?"

She stared at him, bemused. "Because if they see my cut, they're going to ask questions, and they can't know about any of this. Not about Jerry, or Angel, or my vision quest...."

Steven held his hand up. "Whoa. Your what?" He glanced toward the living room. "Is that what you were trying to do in there?"

"It *is* what I did.... I think." She put her hands on the counter and leaned into them. "I'm not really sure. My head is still fuzzy."

She closed her eyes with a deep inhale of breath as if trying to bring the memory back. He thought about how she'd fought him when she woke up and the fear resonating from her body. He didn't know anything about vision quests, but he was pretty sure you didn't come out of them as if you were being attacked.

"Did something happen while you were...during your quest?" he asked.

She looked at him, her expression pensive. "You're right. I need to cancel dinner."

Before he could say anything, she hurried from the room.

Sylvia's cell phone pinged before she could shove it into her pocket. She'd decided to text that she couldn't make it to dinner tonight instead of calling, afraid Lexie would hear the lie in her voice. At least with the text, Lexie wouldn't question her when she said she'd had to work late and was exhausted.

Relief eased some of her tension when she read Lexie's reply: *No problem. Get some rest. We have all weekend.*

She tucked the phone into her pocket and returned to the kitchen. Steven was sitting at the table with the binder he gave her and the folder she'd made on Jerry Kemp, both open in front of him. His expression was unreadable, but she sensed his disapproval.

"You did a lot of research on this guy," he said, his attention still on the folder.

She shrugged and picked up her glass of tea. "I had to know who we were dealing with." His head came up to stare at her. "I was going to tell you," she murmured, feeling chastised.

"Well, it's all pretty moot now." He closed the folder and pushed it aside.

"So, what happens with the case now that Jerry is dead?"

Steven picked up the binder he'd given her and flipped it open. "It doesn't change anything. He was never *my* suspect, he was yours."

Okay, he has a point. She sat across from him at the table. "So, the investigation into Angel's death is still ongoing? What? I watch *Law & Order*," she said when his lips quirked.

"Yes, it's still ongoing."

"Good." She braced her arms on the table and dropped her head into her hands. The wound at her temple pounded, so she rubbed her fingers beneath it to ease the pain.

"Your head hurt?"

"Yeah. Bashing it on the coffee table will do that," she replied.

She shook her head and offered him an apologetic smile. "Sorry. I haven't eaten today. Hunger makes me surly."

"Just hunger?" He grinned at her then rose from the table and moved to the refrigerator. "I saw some color-coded containers in the freezer the other day. I'll heat up one of those for you."

"*Abuela* likes to send me home with food. The blue one has pulled pork. Enough for two," she added as he opened the freezer door.

Steven pulled out the container and opened the lid, sniffing the contents inside. "It smells just as good frozen. I sure have missed your grandmother's cooking." He stepped to the microwave and set the food to cook then reached into the cabinet above the stove and pulled out a bottle of ibuprofen.

"What? Did you snoop through my house when you stayed here?" she said, not sure why it annoyed her that he moved around the room with the familiarity of his own home.

He grinned and winked at her, shooting a battering of butterfly wings to her chest, and handed her the bottle. She focused on removing the cap and hoped he didn't notice her reaction.

She swallowed down the two pills as he moved around the kitchen, gathering plates and bread for sandwiches. She glanced at the binder, open to the notes for Jane Doe #1.

She looked up at him when he sat down. "If you never believed Jerry was the killer, who did you think it was?"

He reached on the floor beside him and picked up a brown satchel. He pulled out his laptop and powered it on. "We've been looking at someone else from the beginning." He opened a folder to several thumbnail photos. Tapping the mousepad, he enlarged what she guessed was a surveillance photo of a casually dressed dark-skinned man sitting at a wrought-iron café table. The man was looking at the camera, a smug smile on his lips as if he knew he was being watched.

"Charming," she said. "Who is he?"

"Caesar Garza, kingpin wannabe. He was our best bet because he has a reputation for doing ritual sacrifices with farm animals. He believes it keeps him and his business *protected*."

She ignored the sarcasm. She'd heard rumors of animal sacrifices for protection but had never run across anyone who did them. It required a type of magic she wanted nothing to do with. "And you think he's moved up to killing people?"

"He's a psychopath, It wouldn't be a stretch."

"But you can't prove he did it."

"No. We haven't been able to identify the first three victims, so we can't connect them to him." He paused, then clicked open several photos. "Do you know these women?"

She pulled the laptop forward to study the photos on the screen. A pang of grief stabbed her chest. The three Jane Does.

The women were young, in their early twenties, and lying on a metal table, their eyes closed. A white sheet covered them up to their necks, a stark contrast against the dull, ashen color of their skin. The marks on their forehead had been stitched shut, but she remembered the drawing the coroner did on the autopsy report. The letter *A* within a circle. She knew the mark but not the women. She shook her head. "No. I've never seen them before."

"You're sure? They aren't *clients*?"

"You don't have to make the word sound so derogatory," she replied. "And, no. They aren't my clients." She looked at him when he sighed and felt the frustration shimmer off him like a wave of electricity. Empathy filled her with remorse. "I'm sorry. I wish I could tell you who killed these poor women. But I can tell you, whoever it is, might not be the same person who killed Angel. Or Jerry."

His gaze came up to meet hers. "How do you know?"

She pointed to the photo of Angel. "Because of this. The witches' mark. Jerry and Angel are the only ones who have it."

Chapter Sixteen

Steven turned the computer toward him to study the marking. "I don't see a difference. They're stars in a circle."

"Do you still have the photo of Angel?"

He reached into his bag and removed a folder and slid out an autopsy photo. The blood and dirt had been cleaned from Angel's face making the burn on her forehead more pronounced. She pointed to the mark.

"Angel and Jerry were branded with a pentagram. The five-pointed star within the circle. The killer burned it into their skin, mostly likely before he killed them, to make the mark permanent. The marks on the other women were carved with a knife or something sharp. And they are actually a letter A within a circle." When he sent her a questioning look, she pulled her binder forward and turned to the autopsy reports, pointing at the drawing. "See? The mark on these women is the symbol for anarchy. The A stands for Asmodeus."

"What is an Asmodeus?"

"*Who*. According to the Old Testament, he's the king of the nine hells. If your Garza was looking for protection, then it's possible he killed these women, and more, as an offering to one of the seven princes of hell."

Steven sat back and scrubbed his hands over his face. "I'm sorry I asked."

The microwave beeped, and he rose and moved to the oven to pull out the food.

"You gave me the benefit of the doubt once," she said, trying to keep the hurt from her voice.

"Yeah, well that was before you put me in the middle of *World of Warcraft*." He hesitated then turned to her and she saw the contrition in his eyes. "Look, whatever you believe about the killer, I can't take it to a grand jury. The case would be dropped faster than you can say broomstick, and I'd be out of a job." He set a plate in front of her. "You should eat something."

She studied him as he sat down. He seemed edgy, more so than usual. There was something on his mind that he didn't want to tell her.

She rested her arms on the table and leaned forward. "Spill it, Gonzales."

His brow rose, a hint of amusement in his eyes.

"I can tell you're hiding something," she said. "So just tell me what it is."

He loosened the knot of his tie as if using the small distraction to avoid answering her. "You're right. I'm not entirely convinced that whoever killed Ms. Salazar or Mr. Kemp is the same person responsible for the first three murders. Especially since the only connection we've made with any of them is—"

"Me." Anger flushed inside her. "I told you I didn't kill Jerry, and I sure as hell wouldn't kill Angel, she was a friend."

He reached out and took her hand, holding tight when she tried to pull it back. "I'm not implying that. Right now, it's only a theory. One of many I've been working on. But for the moment, you're the only link I have to any of the victims, which tells me—"

"You think this is about me," she finished. She shook her head and rose from the chair to pace. "You think someone killed Angel and Jerry because of me? That's crazy! I help people! I don't get them killed!" She locked her arms around her waist, her pulse racing as she moved around the room. From the time she was a child, she'd known her path in life was to help people, and she'd spent all her teenage years working with her grandmother, offering aid to the families in town with everything from colicky children to insomnia. She even taught herself to read Tarot cards and run protection spells so she could help more people. And not once had she ever hurt anyone in the process.

She closed her eyes and inhaled a breath to calm her staggering pulse. Images flashed across her mind in vivid color: fire burning around her, blood pooling on the ground from countless bodies, and the blade of the sword swinging down on Steven's neck.

She pressed a hand to her neck and swallowed against the knot in her throat. No, that's not what she saw during the vision. It couldn't be.

She jolted when Steven moved behind her and placed his hands on her shoulders.

"I told you, it's just a working theory. Now, come sit down before you fall down."

She shook her head. "I'm fine. I just need a moment to think."

"No, you need to eat." He turned her toward the table and ushered her to the seat. "We can figure this all out after."

She sat in the chair and stared up at him. "We? You're still going to let me work on this with you?"

"Yes."

His hesitation was brief, but she saw it. She wanted to question his short answer, but she sensed he didn't want to talk. Fair enough. There was plenty she wasn't ready to talk about, too. For instance, were the images she saw when she was unconscious only a dream or a look at what's to come? And if it was the latter, how the hell was she supposed to stop it from happening?

***

Steven grabbed a bottle of beer from the refrigerator and carried it into the living room, stopping near the threshold of the hallway. The bathroom door was still closed, as it had been for the past half hour. Sylvia had locked herself away in the room after their tensely quiet meal and he decided to give her the time alone since she seemed to need it. He'd heard the water shut off ten minutes ago, but no other noise came from the room. He wrestled with knocking on the door to make sure she was okay but didn't think she'd appreciate the intrusion.

He glanced at the coffee table where he'd set up the files and his laptop, his jacket and tie draped over the arm of the sofa. Although he didn't think she was grieving Jerry Kemp's murder, he could tell it bothered her. Kemp may have been a threat to her family, but he was still a human being who'd lost his life. Sylvia would feel compassion for that.

His gaze slid to the spot on the floor where he'd found her this afternoon. He'd already cleaned up the candles and blood, but the image of her lying lifeless on the floor still made his stomach clench. He couldn't bear it if something happened to her. It was why he'd decided to let her continue working with him. He needed to keep her by his side, not only for her safety but his own peace of mind.

The bathroom door opened, and a sweet and floral smell, like roses and strawberries, wafted from the room. Sylvia stepped into the hall, wrapped in a bath towel, water beading her bare shoulders. She stopped when she saw him but didn't appear surprised he was standing near the entrance.

She shrugged and made a weak gesture toward the bathroom. "Sorry. I used all the hot water, so you're going to have a cold shower."

Her skin was flushed from the heat of her shower, and the ends of her wet hair dripped into the terrycloth. His pulse kicked at the sight of her, his libido coming alive like a lit fuse.

"No problem," he said, surprised his voice even registered since his mouth had gone dirt dry, and he was pretty sure all the blood had been cut off from his brain.

She stared at him a moment then continued to her bedroom, closing the door behind her. Steven blew out a slow breath and took a long pull from the beer. *Damn*. He was going to need more than one cold shower.

He settled on the sofa, dropping his head against the cushion. The memory of their kiss several days ago played in his mind—how she'd opened to him, gliding her tongue over his as he took the kiss deeper. The way her pulse jumped when pressed his lips to her throat. How her fingers made his muscles quiver as she grazed her nails over his chest.

He finished the beer in one hard swallow. He'd promised her they would work together on Angel's investigation, but he didn't know how the hell he could manage that without letting his desire for her get in the way. He wished he could just take her to bed so he could cleanse her from his system. If only it were that easy.

"Okay. I'm ready when you are." Sylvia's voice jolted him from his thoughts, and he bit down on the heated response to his system. She stood beside the sofa dressed in an oversized T-shirt and cutoff jeans. Her feet were bare, and her wet hair was brushed smooth and falling like a glossy black waterfall down her back.

His pulsed kicked up several gears. "For?"

She gestured toward the files. "To get to work."

"Work. Right." He really needed to stop taking everything she said as innuendo. He rose and moved to the kitchen to put the beer bottle away. "There's really not much else we can do right now. And I've read over these files more than a dozen times. There's nothing in them that's going to help us."

She moved into the room with him, her arms crossed, and stared at him. "I thought you weren't giving up."

He set the bottle down with a snap. "I'm not. But I'm not a witch. I can't make something magically appear out of nothing." She flinched slightly. His voice was harder than he'd intended. He rubbed his hands over his face. His sexual frustration and the case were making him cranky. "Sorry."

"Do you blame me?"

He looked at her and furrowed his brow. She stood unmoving, her arms dropped at her sides. "Blame you for what?"

Her gaze shifted to the folders. "Them. Jerry."

"Of course not. Why would you think that?"

She swallowed, and he saw the regret in her eyes. "I blame myself. For Angel, anyway. I promised her I could help her, but I didn't."

He stepped to her and placed a hand on her cheek. "You are not, in any way, responsible for these deaths, and I never, for one second, believed you were." He stroked his thumb over her smooth skin. He loved how touching her made the tips of his fingers tingle. "Whatever the connection to you is, I promise you, I'm going to keep you safe."

She stared at him, her eyes searching his face as if she could read his mind. Her gaze slid down to his mouth, and she scraped her teeth over her bottom lip. Desire, hard and fast, hit him like a punch to the gut. An overwhelming need to be close to her surged through him like a shot of adrenaline. Without giving himself a chance to change his mind, he wove his hands in her hair and pulled her into a kiss.

He half expected her to push him away, but as she had before, she opened up to him, winding her arms around his neck and giving herself easily to the kiss. The taste of mint from her toothpaste, mixed with the scent of roses and strawberries, grabbed onto him with a sensuous grip. His longing became an intense flame in his gut. He'd never wanted anyone like he wanted her. He ached with the need to touch her, to bury himself inside her.

Raising his mouth from hers, he gently cupped her face and rested his forehead against hers. His pulse hammered erratically, his chest heaving with labored breaths, making it difficult to speak. "Sylvia...."

"Me, too," she whispered.

He lowered his gaze to hers. Her brown eyes were dark and intense on his. "You, too?"

"I want you, too." She took his hand and tugged, leading him from the room.

He blinked at her, the air closing in his lungs as his pulse kicked into overdrive. Desire darkened her eyes, a soft smile playing on her lips. "I think we've waited long enough." She continued leading him to her bedroom. When she reached the bed, she pulled off her T-shirt, and his heart nearly stopped. She wasn't wearing a bra.

"Jesus..." was all he could manage as his eyes roamed over her.

"Don't think. Feel." She stepped to him and curled a hand around his neck to bring his mouth down on hers.

The kiss was slow and thoughtful, her tongue caressing his like a promise. Her fingers worked the buttons of his shirt, and she broke the kiss long enough to pull the fabric off his shoulders and drop it to the floor.

He didn't need a piano to fall on him to realize this was happening. Gathering her into his arms, he lifted her from the floor to lay on the bed with her, kissing down the curve of her neck. Her pulse kicked against his lips and her breaths quickened. He locked his fingers with hers and raised her hands above her head as he nipped her earlobe. Her soft moan fueled the fire burning inside him. He wondered if she realized the effect she had on him.

He trailed kisses along her shoulder, continuing his journey down to her breast. His hand came down to cup the soft mound, rolling the taut nipple between his fingers. Taking her in his mouth, he caressed his tongue over her, reveling in her throaty moans of pleasure. His name whispered hoarsely from her lips as he flicked his tongue over the pebbled tip. Longing coursed through him, making him harder than he'd ever been in his life.

He skimmed a hand down the smoothness of her stomach, the need to touch her like a hunger to his soul. Her muscles quivered against his fingers as he roamed his hand down to the silkiness of her thighs.

He unsnapped the button of her cutoffs and slid his hand beneath the fabric. His fingers reached the heat between her legs and his breath caught. She was already wet, and the sudden realization that he didn't have a condom dropped his heart into his stomach.

"Damn," he murmured.

Sylvia tensed. "What? What's wrong?"

He braced himself up and sent her an apologetic frown. "I don't have anything." He glanced at the clock. It was nearly eight. The drugstore would be closed already. One of the downsides to small towns, the stores went to bed early.

She sat up and stared at him. "You don't have a condom? Isn't there a rule that guys are always supposed to carry a condom in their wallet?"

"I haven't carried a condom since high school." He sat back, closing his eyes briefly, and shook his head. And he sure as hell wasn't prepared for this tonight. He cast an expectant look at her. "Are you on the pill?"

She raised her brow at him. "Why would I be on the pill?"

"The obvious reason? You don't want to get pregnant."

"Well, it's not in my immediate plans, but getting pregnant requires having sex, and I haven't exactly done that since...." She stopped, but he didn't need her to finish the sentence.

A smile whispered at the edges of his lips. "Since me? Really?" The thought of no other man ever touching her made his entire body throb with want. She'd made love to only one man in her life, and it had been him. His smile widened. "I think I'm going to be flattered by that."

She shrugged but avoided looking at him. "Don't be. It just means I haven't found anyone I want to have sex with."

"Even more reason to be flattered." Damn, she couldn't make him want her anymore. "When was your last period?"

She blinked at him, her brow furrowing with annoyance. "That's a little personal, and what's it got to do with anything?"

"My ex-wife said she could count the days to know when she was ovulating to avoid pregnancy."

167

Her dark eyes reflected the hurt. "You have an ex-wife?"

Damn, he probably shouldn't have said that. This was turning into the worst foreplay ever.

"Yes, I was married. For a very short time. It didn't mean anything."

Her expression cooled. "It didn't mean anything."

"No, that's not—"

"Don't." She shook her head and climbed off the bed. "I'm not doing this."

Before he could explain, she grabbed his shirt off the floor, shoving her arms into the sleeves and hurried from the room.

He had a wife.

The thought curled in Sylvia's stomach like a sickness as she moved unsteadily into the kitchen. It had never occurred to her that he would ever get married, least of all to someone else. The thought of him saying vows to another woman twisted the grip tighter around her heart.

Tears burned her eyes as she fastened the buttons on Steven's shirt. Clutching the fabric around her, she inhaled heavily. It smelled like him, and her emotions played a vicious game of tug-of-war with her heart.

"Yes, I was married. For a very short time. It didn't mean anything."

She grabbed the Patron from the cabinet and took a pull from the bottle. How could he be so callous about something so important? Marriage was sacred. It should always mean something.

She moved to the kitchen sink and stared out the window facing her backyard. The sun was starting to set, the sky a mix of red and gold, but she couldn't enjoy the beauty of it.

She spotted Steven's reflection in the glass as he entered the room and swallowed the ache in her throat. She knew it was foolish of her to feel betrayed, but she couldn't stop the grief from wrapping around her heart. A part of her wanted to chance reading him, but what if what she saw wasn't what she wanted?

And what did she want?

Their eyes met in the window reflection and a shimmer of awareness settled over her. *Him.* She wanted him. Despite everything, she still loved him.

Before he could speak, she turned to face him, her fingers tightening on the neck of the bottle. He was still in his slacks, but since she was wearing his shirt, his chest was bare. Her gaze landed on the tattoo above his left pec—a sunburst with red and yellow flames licking out. Connecting within the circle was the profile of a man and woman, their gazes locked on each other, their lips touching intimately. Did he get the tattoo for his wife? The thought ripped at her already tattered heart.

She took another pull from the bottle, swallowed then asked, "Did you love her?"

"Yes," he said, and her heart plummeted to her stomach. "But, I wasn't *in love* with her." He moved farther into the room and took the bottle from her and recapped it.

She took the bottle back but didn't open it. "What the hell does that mean?" *How do you marry someone you don't even love?* The words spiraled in her head, making the wound at her temple throb.

"It means, I care a great deal for her, but as a friend."

"You married her. She had to be more than a friend," she said, quietly. She wanted to ask how they met, where they met, how long they dated, but it really wasn't her business. His life was his own, and he owed her nothing.

She shook her head and set the bottle on the counter before stepping around him. "It's none of my business. We should just get back to work."

"She was my mother's live-in nurse," Steven said before she could leave the room. "I met her my junior year of college. She was just finishing up her associate's degree in nursing. As soon as she graduated and passed her state boards, I hired her to help take care of my mother while I finished working on my degree."

Grief clutched Sylvia's heart. She remembered his mother had been battling cancer for many years and that Steven had dropped out of college with only one semester left, to go home and help care for her. It was right after they'd been together. Was that the real reason he'd left her?

Steven leaned against the counter, his hands sliding into the pockets of his slacks. "Near the end, my mother was in a lot of pain and I felt helpless to do anything about it. She kept apologizing for all the mistakes she'd made in her life, how she only wanted me to be happy. It seemed to worry her that I wouldn't find love or settle down.

"Linda and I had...uh...been together, so I didn't think it would hurt to tell my mom we were engaged." He shook his head with a benign smile. "The news was the best medicine I could give her. For a few hours, she completely forgot about the pain. It was as if knowing that I would be okay was all she really needed to let go. We called Father Baptiste from her church to give her last rites, and he agreed to marry us at the house, so she could witness. She held on for another week and passed two days before her forty-first birthday."

Sylvia moved to him and placed her hand on his. "I'm sorry."

"Linda and I knew we weren't right for each other, but we tried to make it work. In the end, we realized we were better friends than lovers, so we filed for a divorce and got an annulment through the church and I moved to Austin."

"Linda? Isn't she married to your partner?"

Steven smiled. "Yeah. The first time I introduced them, I knew they belonged together. That was five years ago, and they've been stupid happy ever since."

"And, now they're having a family."

"And, now they're having a family," he repeated, the pride in his voice brightening his eyes. His expression sobered, and he covered her hand with his. "When I said the marriage didn't mean anything, I meant, it wasn't what my heart wanted because my heart has always belonged to you."

She blinked up at him, the sincerity of his words making her pulse kick. He placed her hand on his chest and tapped the tattoo.

"This. Is me and you."

Sylvia stared at the colored patch and swept her gaze up to his. He laid a hand on her cheek.

"Ten years ago, I was young and stupid and confused. I should have said it then, but I'm saying it now, and I hope to God I'm not too late. I love you, Sylvia, and I don't ever want to lose you again."

The words absorbed into her and sparked like a light to her soul. She'd always known there was only one man in this world for her. She saw it as a child. His image had filled her dreams as a teenager. She knew she'd found him the first time she saw him. And she knew, that night in the cornfield, he would always be hers. And because she knew, she'd jumped into love so fast it made her head spin. She hadn't realized he just needed time to catch up.

"No, it's not too late." Cupping her hands around his face, Sylvia pulled him in and kissed him. "Take me to bed."

Chapter Seventeen

The high-pitched beep of the alarm jolted Sylvia awake. She reached across Steven to turn it off. "Sorry," she whispered. "Go back to sleep."

He rolled her onto her back and kissed her neck. "No, I'm more than awake." He held her hands above her head and nibbled her earlobe, the hardness of his erection through the boxers he still wore pressed heavy against her. "I never thought to set an alarm for early morning sex. What time does the drugstore open?"

Heat pooled in her stomach and shot sparks through her body. Steven wouldn't make love to her last night without a condom, but it hadn't stopped him from doing incredible things to her body with his hands and mouth. She wouldn't mind a repeat performance. If only she had the day off.

She brushed a kiss over his lips and wiggled out from under him. "Sorry, cowboy, not for another five hours. And I have to get ready for work."

He sat up as she climbed out of bed. "Work? You can't seriously think you're going to work today."

She turned to look at him, his profile dark against the beam of moonlight streaming in through the open curtains. "Why wouldn't I go to work?"

"We just determined that whoever killed Angel Salazar and Jerry Kemp might be after you as well. You really want to put yourself in the open so they can finish the job?"

She crossed her arms and stared at him. "First of all, we haven't determined anything. It's a theory, remember? One of many you're working on? Second, I don't carry a route, so I'll be inside all day, and the post office is protected." Even in the moonlight, she saw the muscle in his jaw flick.

She moved to the dresser to grab some clothes, biting down on the twinge of hurt. "The carriers come in at seven, and Gabe comes in at eight, so I won't be alone long. I have to leave soon, so I'm going to go shower." She left the room and closed the door behind her.

She took a quick shower and threw on a pair of jeans and her uniform shirt. Her anger had died down with the shower when she realized Steven's comments stemmed from his concern for her. She'd had the same fight with Lexie last year after Ray rescued her from Jerry.

A smile touched her lips as she remembered the argument at the breakfast table. Lexie hadn't been very happy when Sylvia covered her routes for a week while they awaited word on Jerry, and she wasn't shy about letting them know.

The aroma of fresh coffee and something spicy made her stomach growl as she moved into the hallway. She continued into the kitchen and found Steven at the stove, stirring eggs in a cast iron skillet. He was dressed in the same clothes he'd worn the day before, minus the jacket and tie, and he had his boots on. The thought that he was leaving her again sank her heart to her stomach. She glanced at the sofa but didn't see his overnight bag.

She shoved her hands in her back pockets and kept her voice even. "Are you going somewhere?"

He scooped the eggs onto two plates and carried them to the table. "Yeah. With you." He stepped to her and brushed her lips with a soft kiss. "Eat some breakfast."

She moved to the table as he sat, her annoyance kicking up a notch. "I don't need a babysitter. Or a bodyguard."

He grabbed her hand and tugged her onto his lap. "Humor me, okay?" He nipped at her bottom lip, sending shivers of pleasure shooting to her head. *Damn him.*

She climbed off his lap and shrugged, wondering if he noticed the heat he'd sparked inside her. "Fine, whatever. Come to work with me. But you're going to be bored out of your mind." She took a bite of the eggs and resisted the urge to hum at the flavor. He'd mixed in strips of corn tortillas and the chorizo she'd picked up a few days ago.

"I have plenty of work to keep me busy until your crew shows up."

She cocked a brow and glanced at him. "You're only staying until the carriers show up?"

"I promise. Besides, I have things to do today. But I'll be back by three to take you home."

She sent him a dry look. "The post office is less than three miles away, and I have my Jeep. I don't need you to take me or pick me up."

He covered her hand with his, squeezing lightly. "There's a killer out there. I'm not going to chance anything happening to you."

"Fine." She huffed out a resigned breath and took another bite of the eggs. She knew it wouldn't help to argue with him about the protection spell she kept over the post office since he didn't believe in it.

As Steven ate his breakfast, a dispirited thought flitted across her mind. Was it wise to give her heart to this man if he didn't have any faith in her?

***

After returning to Sylvia's house for a quick shower and change of clothes, Steven arrived at the Valley Baptist Medical Center.

He took the elevator down to the basement where the morgue and Jerry Kemp's body were located. His boots echoed off the tile as he made his way down the quiet hallway. A chill shivered down his spine, raising the hair on his neck. It didn't matter how often he'd attended autopsies or had to accompany a loved one to identify a body, the morgue still creeped him out.

The pungent smell of ammonia hit him when he walked through the door. The room was about the size of his apartment, the stained white walls in need of a fresh coat of paint. In the center of the room were two stainless steel tables, one of them holding a body covered with a white sheet. On the far wall were two large metal doors that looked like walk-in refrigerators.

A woman hunched over a table in the corner turned to smile at him. She was in her mid-forties with curly black hair and light-brown skin. She wore a white lab coat over a burgundy top and black slacks. "You must be Special Agent Gonzales," she said as she moved to meet him in the middle of the room.

"Yes. Doctor Patino?"

"That's me." She gestured toward the table where she'd been working. "Just finishing up the paperwork on the body. I already sent the preliminary to Deputy Hernandez, and he said you might want your own copy."

"Can you fill me in?"

The woman nodded and moved to one of the doors. Steven followed and held his breath as she opened to door, although it didn't help mask the smell of the bodies stored in the room—like raw meat left to rot.

A row of stainless-steel shelves lined the walls, several of the slabs holding long, black body bags. The doctor wheeled out a gurney and closed the door behind her before passing him a set of latex gloves.

"We got a positive ID on the victim." She slid the zipper down on the bag to expose the body. The blood and dirt had been washed away and the flesh looked dull and waxy, like a department store mannequin. A Y incision had been made from the tips of the shoulders and traveled down to the navel. The wound across his neck was sewn closed turning the incision into a distorted smile.

"Jerry Kemp," he said.

"Yep," she returned. "The victim had blunt force trauma to the back of his skull, possibly made by a tire iron. I found rust particles and wheel grease in the wound. But COD was exsanguination caused by the severing of his carotid artery. One swipe of a blade was all it took. He bled out pretty quickly."

Steven noted the raw marks around his wrists. "He was bound."

Dr. Patino nodded. "Wrists and ankles but there are no traces of fiber or adhesive, so it was most likely some sort of wire."

"Was he missing any organs? Kidneys maybe?" Steven asked.

The doctor motioned for him to help her and they rolled the body on his side. "No, nothing missing that I didn't remove. But he has some fresh tattoos on his back."

"How fresh?"

She pointed at the marks. "There's still redness and swelling around them, so within forty-eight hours before his death."

Steven studied the markings. The symbols looked like random geometric shapes blended together. "So, did the killer mark him while he was unconscious?"

"Maybe. His tox screen came back clean, but there are some sedatives that don't show up in our tests."

"Is there anything else? Any foreign DNA?" Steven asked once they lowered the body.

"There was nothing under his nails, but I found a resin in the burn on his forehead. The tests haven't come back on it yet. However, I did find some hotel carpet fibers in the treads of his shoes." She smiled at his questioning look. "He's not the first body I've had who traipsed around in a hotel before he died. Unfortunately, I can't tell you which hotel, but whichever it is, it's probably your crime scene."

"How do you know?"

"His lungs were clear of dirt and dust, which he would have inhaled if he'd been killed in the field where he was found. Plus, there was no blood at the scene and very little left in him, which tells me they dumped him after he bled out."

Steven peeled off the gloves as the ME re-zipped the bag and wheeled it back into the refrigerated room. She returned to her workstation and picked up a file and handed it to him. "Here's your copy. Sorry to cut this short but I have another body to get to."

"Thank you." He pulled a card from his wallet and handed it to her. "If you find anything else, please call me."

She took the card and cocked a smile. "It'd be a pleasure."

Steven waited until he was in his SUV to read the report. Kemp's body didn't show signs of torture like his other victims, or Angel, unless you counted the tattoos. The ligature marks and lack of food in his stomach indicated Jerry Kemp had been held at least twenty-four hours, or more, before he was killed. The killer probably wanted him weak in order to mark the body.

He turned to the photo of the markings. He remembered Sylvia had a book on her shelf about magic symbols, then mentally kicked himself for thinking it.

He tossed the file onto the passenger seat and started the truck. Hopefully, the Cameron County deputies would have something more substantial that would prove Garza was responsible. Although a part of him already knew that was only wishful thinking.

He arrived at the 'sheriff's department a half hour later. After checking in with the officer at the front desk, he made his way into the squad room.

The deputy in charge of the investigation was sitting at a desk speaking on the phone. He spotted Steven and waved him over. Mounted on an easel behind him was a large evidence board with a handful of photos pinned to the surface and each marked with a number.

The deputy hung up the phone and stood, offering his hand. "Agent Gonzales, good to see you again."

Steven returned the greeting. "Deputy Hernandez. Thank you, again, for allowing me access to your case."

"Hey, the more the merrier." The deputy gestured toward the phone. "I just got off the phone with the vic's family. His cousin is flying in to ID the body. Should be here later today."

"Were they able to tell you why Kemp was in town?" Steven asked.

"No. According to Kemp's father, he hasn't spoken to his son in a few weeks and didn't even know he planned to travel."

Steven moved to the board and studied the photos. Most of them were close-ups of the field and road where Kemp's body had been discovered. "Where are you with the investigation so far?"

"Not much further than we were last night. We canvassed the area until it was too dark to do anything, but there wasn't much in the way of evidence." The deputy reached for a folder on his desk and pulled out a photo. "We have the rental car agencies checking their records to see if he rented a car. The tracks we found at the scene were a standard P16 tire used on most passenger vehicles and SUVs. We also found a couple of shoe prints, about two feet from where the body was left. Neither belongs to the vic, though. He's a size thirteen, and the prints are a size eight sneaker, possibly belonging to a woman, and a size twelve boot that could belong to a man."

A cold knot formed in Steven's stomach. *Two sets of prints, belonging to a man and a woman.*

He replayed his conversation with Sylvia from the night before. She'd been genuinely surprised when he told her about Kemp's death, and her alibi sounded believable. But she'd been quick to steer him away from Ray. Is it because she knows he's involved? Or that Lexie is involved?

"We sent a molding of the tread to the crime lab, but it's also pretty common, so it's another needle in the haystack," the deputy said. "I have a few guys out, checking with homes in the area to see if anyone saw anything. In the meantime, I'm heading out to Edmondville to speak to a possible suspect."

Steven's chest tightened. "You have a suspect?"

The deputy sifted through some papers on his desk and picked up a sheet. "Name's Ramon Chavez. Owns a farm a few miles outside of town. Apparently, he and his girlfriend had a bit of trouble with Mr. Kemp last year that resulted in Kemp spending the night in jail. Thought I'd give him a visit, see if he knows anything. You're welcome to join me. You said this Kemp is related to your ritual investigation, right?"

"His name came up as a person of interest, but we haven't found a connection to him or the other victims, yet," Steven answered.

"You ask me, it's a little too coincidental that Kemp just happens to show up here."

Too much, Steven thought. His cellphone chirped. He pulled it out of his pocket and glanced at the number. *David.* "Sorry, I need to take this. What time are you planning to see Mr. Chavez?"

"Heading out now." He handed Steven a slip of paper. "Here's his address. See you there?"

Steven nodded and headed toward the exit as he connected the call. "Hey. What do you have for me?"

"NYPD just got back to me on Kemp. They spoke to his employer at the coffeehouse where he worked, and he said Kemp quit two weeks ago. According to the manager, Kemp said he had big plans in the works."

"Big plans? Like what?"

"The guy didn't know. But I ran down Kemp's financials, and he made a large withdrawal from his bank account the same day, so maybe that will narrow down the timeline of when he arrived in town."

Steven pulled his keys from his pocket and unlocked the SUV. "Maybe. But there aren't any direct flights from New York to Harlingen, everything connects in Houston, so it'll be next to impossible to find which airline he flew in on." He climbed behind the steering wheel but didn't start the engine. "How are you doing with Ms. Salazar's case?"

"I found the coffeeshop Ms. Salazar frequented most, and the dean at Del Mar sent me campus video for the two weeks before she went missing. It's a lot of videos to go through."

"Let me know if you need help."

"Will do."

Steven disconnected the call and glanced at his watch. He still had a few hours before he had to pick up Sylvia. It should be enough time to speak with Ray and, hopefully, clear him as a suspect in Jerry Kemp's murder. Because he sure as hell didn't want to have to tell Sylvia he'd had to arrest her brother for murder.

Chapter Eighteen

Sylvia's phone rang as she pulled the mail truck alongside her house. She pressed her hand against the rumble in her stomach. It was nearly one o'clock, way past her lunch break. She'd spent most of the morning waiting on maintenance to show up on her carrier's route and repair the mail truck that had died an hour into the delivery, and she didn't have time to get lunch.

She tapped Send on her phone as she climbed out of the truck. "Hey, big brother," she said. "What's up?"

"Did you know?" Ray asked.

"I know a lot of things, so you're going to have to be more specific." She pulled her house key out of her pocket and unlocked the front door.

"About Jerry Kemp. He's dead."

Sylvia stopped. "How did you find out?"

"So, you did know. Why didn't you tell me?"

"I just found out last night. How did you find out?" she repeated.

"Steven came by with the deputy sheriff."

She ground her back teeth but kept her voice even. "What for?"

"They told me about Jerry and asked if I had an alibi. Don't worry, I did," Ray said before she could reply.

"Of course, you did. He should never have doubted it." She rubbed the heel of her hand against her forehead. *Damn Steven.* "You didn't tell Lexie, did you? About Jerry?"

"No."

"Good. Don't. After what he put her through, she deserves happy right now." She pushed open the door and continued into her house.

Ray sighed over the phone. "I know there's no love loss, and I'm sorry he's dead, but I, for one, can rest knowing he can't come after us again. Or try to stop the wedding."

"Well, I wouldn't have let either of those things happen."

"Yeah, you're pretty badass," Ray said, humor in his voice.

"And, don't you forget it." She stopped as Steven moved into the living room from the kitchen, his cellphone pressed to his ear. It annoyed her that her body reacted even when she was mad at him. "I gotta run. I'll talk to you later." She disconnected the call and shoved the phone into her back pocket.

Steven returned his phone to his pocket and held up his hand before she could speak. "Before you get mad and yell at me, I was just doing my job. Much like you've been doing today," he said. "You said you don't work a route."

She crossed her arms and stared at him. "You said you weren't going to question Ray."

"Until after the autopsy. It was this morning."

"And?"

"He's cleared as a suspect."

"Told you." She pushed past him to go into the kitchen. Her countertop and kitchen table were cluttered with the pages and pictures from his folders. She glanced at him. "Are you always this messy?"

Steven's lips quirked. "Sorry. I needed more space."

She noted her book on occult symbols was open on the table, in the center of the mess. "Doing some light reading?" she said as she pulled a container from the refrigerator.

He moved to the table and picked up a photo. "Just trying to figure out if these symbols mean anything. They were inked into Kemp's back."

She set the food to cook in the microwave then moved beside him to take the photo. She pursed her lips. "It could be a spell. The killer might be trying to bind Jerry's spirit like he did with Angel."

"Does that mean you're going to destroy more evidence?"

She tossed him a dry look. "Get over it." She pointed to the picture. "These are different, though. Stronger. He's not only binding the spirit, he's imprisoning it. Whoever did this does not want Jerry to ever get out." She chewed her lip in thought. "I feel like I've seen this before, though."

"You've seen it before?" Steven asked as she moved to the table and rooted through the mess to grab the binder she'd made on Jerry Kemp.

She hesitated. She'd seen them in a vision, but she didn't think he'd want to hear that. "I think it might be the same spell that was used on the Galicia Witch...Jerry's great-great-grandmother," she added. "She was a very powerful sorceress a hundred or so years ago and a known descendent of a group called The Order of the Shadows. They were religious fanatics who used their powers to dominate, murder, or torture anyone they considered a threat. The sect had been wiped out during the Christos Rebellion but turns out Jerry's great-great-grandmother managed to get away. It was several years before the townspeople caught up to her. Ironically, they used magic to lock her away in a pocket dimension. I must have left the notes in my bedroom."

Steven followed her out of the kitchen and to her bedroom. She knelt in front of the wood cedar chest stationed at the foot of her bed. "I came across a story about her when I was researching Jerry. The spell to cast her out is the same as the one to call her, but with a few modifications." She lifted the lid and shuffled through the items inside.

"What's wrong?" he asked when she sat back on her heels and paused.

She frowned and looked up at him. "My notes. They're gone."

"Are you sure they were in there?"

"Yes. I put them in here the other day." She pulled out several blankets and the silver tray she'd used during Angel's cleansing. A small black bottle rolled to the side, the cork popping of as the glass hit the wall. She picked up the bottle. It was empty. "Damn."

"What's that?"

"It was myrrh oil, but it's empty. I guess I didn't cap it tight enough when I used it last." She returned it and the blankets to the trunk. "This doesn't make sense." She glanced at her dresser and noticed a piece of fabric caught in the top drawer. Her heart dropped. She jumped from the floor and rushed to the dresser. "No. No. No." Panic tightened her chest as she pulled open the drawer.

"You have a crystal ball?" Steven asked as soon as she took out the glass globe.

"Yes. No. It was a joke from Ray." She turned the ball in her hand to inspect it. It was smooth and clear. No imperfections in the glass. No bubbles of air trapped inside. "No. That can't be possible."

"What?" He stared at the ball as if he thought she could see a vision in it. She wanted to laugh, but panic had replaced any sense of humor she had.

"This isn't mine. I think someone switched them." She set the ball on the dresser, and it rolled to a stop against the mirror frame.

She pressed her fingers to her temple and tried to remember the last time she saw the ball. Yesterday. Before she started her vision quest. She'd been out for several hours, so it's possible someone could have come into her house and taken it. *But who would do such a thing? And why?* Ice prickled her spine as realization set in. *Because they know what's inside.*

Steven stared at her as if she'd lost her mind. "I don't think Ray is going to get upset that his gift was replaced," he said.

"You don't understand. Jerry's power was in there." She looked at his reflection in the mirror when he groaned. "I know you don't believe in this and probably think I'm crazy because I do, but you need to listen to what I'm telling you. If whoever killed Jerry did it because he wanted Jerry's power, then that means he plans to do something really bad with it."

Steven dropped onto the edge of the bed and shook his head. "Okay, I get you believe all this, and I respect that, but regardless, I can't get on board with it. I have five murders to solve which may or may not be by the same person, and the only suspect I have is currently under a grand jury investigation that may possibly turn in his favor. I'm sorry but I can't stop what I'm doing to go on a literal witch hunt."

She turned toward him and tried to keep her tone from sounding too impatient. "I understand your hesitation and your refusal to believe, I really do. But we don't have time for your doubts." She held up her hand before he could speak. "This magic, Jerry's magic, is powerful and dark. Whoever took it knows what it can do.

"You came to me because of the ritualistic nature of the murders, and you heard I was the person to help you understand them. I've been trying to do that, but you refuse to listen or even meet me halfway."

"Christ, Sylvia, because I can't!" he said, with a frustrated huff.

"Not can't. Won't," she tossed back. She pushed down her own frustration and sat next to him on the bed. "I know you have your reasons for not believing in magic, and *I* respect that. But if you want to solve any of these murders, then you're going to have to open your mind to the possibility that the magic is real."

He stared up at her, and she saw the conflict in his eyes. He wanted to believe her but seemed to be at war with his own conscience. She placed her hand on his arm, the contact soothing her with its warmth.

"Look, believing this case is about magic doesn't mean you're giving up your principles. It's just a way of looking at it from another angle. Whether or not *you* believe the magic is real, your killer does, so we have to look at this from his point of view."

"You really do watch a lot of *Law and Order*." He shook his head. "But, you're right. I've been so focused on finding links to Garza I didn't look at these murders through the killer's eyes." He sat a moment longer then rose from the bed and held out his hand. "Okay. You win. We'll do this your way. For now."

She accepted the hand he offered with an inward sigh and stood. It wasn't much of a win, but she'd take it.

"Let me get the truck back to the post office and tell Gabe I'm taking off the rest of the day. Then we can get started."

***

"According to the medical examiner, Jerry Kemp's cause of death was exsanguination, meaning he lost a lot of blood," Steven said as

Sylvia entered the room carrying two glasses of iced tea. They'd moved everything into her living room, and her coffee table and half her sofa were littered with the files of all the victims. "The Cameron County Sheriff's Department has lead on the case, but aside from two sets of shoe prints at the scene, they haven't gotten anywhere with the investigation."

"Two sets of shoe prints?"

"A man's size twelve and a woman's size eight."

She cocked her brow. "I wear a nine."

He winked at her and took the glass from her. "I know. Since Kemp was a person of interest in my case, they promised to keep me up to date on their progress."

She sat on the sofa. "What about Angel's case?"

"Very little there, too." He settled beside her and set the glass on the floor before picking up a file. "Same two shoe prints were at her crime scene, but we'd assumed the woman's print was hers. Your suggestion about her going on a date was helpful. According to her boss at the clothing store, she wasn't seeing anyone, so we're looking at the possibility that it was a study date. We're checking with the students in her class and the local coffee shops she frequented to see who she might have met up with."

"Well, that sounds like more than a little to me." She picked up the autopsy report for Jane Doe number one and scanned the page.

"We know the first three victims were killed by the same person because of the similarities of their deaths," Steven continued. "And we can assume Miss Salazar and Mr. Kemp were both killed by the same person because of the symbols burned on their skin. Both burns had traces of a resin in the mark."

"What kind of resin?"

"I don't know. The ME is still waiting for the results. Right now, we have nothing that links all five victims to one killer."

"Yes, you do," she said. "The blood." She sifted through the pages on the table and laid out each of the autopsy reports. "Look at this. According to each autopsy report, all of the victims, including Jerry, were missing over half their blood."

"Yes. It's not unusual with the amount of trauma they each sustained."

She shook her head earnestly. "Right, but the human body holds over a gallon of blood. The first three victims and Jerry had barely a pint left. Even with the damage to their bodies, they would have still had at least fifty percent of their blood."

Steven sent her a cautious look. "Something tells me you have a theory about what happened to the blood."

She scraped her teeth over her bottom lip then said, "I think the killer took it."

Chapter Nineteen

"Why do you think the killer took their blood? And, please don't tell me I'm looking for a vampire now."

Sylvia tossed a sour look at him. "There is no such thing as vampires, at least not the kind you see in the movies," she said, barely masking the impatience in her voice. She rose from the sofa and moved to the bookshelf to pull out a book. The binding was old and frayed along the edges, the front cover smooth and unmarked.

"I think he is going to use it to perform blood magic. It's an ancient and dark type of magic usually inherited through birth. Since blood is a life force, a blood sorcerer will use it in their spells to enhance their abilities, even make them capable of absorbing another soul's energy so they can control it."

"Control it?"

"Like the binding spell on Angel." She returned to the sofa and laid the large book across her lap. "Now, as far as I know, Jerry wasn't a blood sorcerer. But he did inherit his magic from his great-great-grandmother, who was."

"And that's the magic you took from him."

She blinked at him. Although he said the words matter-of-factly, she sensed his conflict. He was trying, she had to give him that. "Yes."

Steven nodded toward the book. "What's this?"

"It's a grimoire, basically a textbook of magic. I picked it up last year after Jerry came into our lives. It was for research," she added at his raised brow. She carefully opened the flap. The parchment inside was old and yellowed from age. "There are some blood spells that require specific types or amounts of blood in order to be effective. And, if the killer is adding in the organs he took from all of these women, then you can bet he's working on a very dark and powerful spell."

"To do what?"

"I don't know." She bit her bottom lip and sent him a grim frown. "Unless...."

"Unless, what?"

"They know about Jerry's great-great-grandmother and are planning to open the portal to release her."

"Wouldn't he need Kemp alive if he's planning to release his great-great-grandmother?"

"Not if he's found a way to put her spirit into another host. Then all he'd need is Jerry's blood and the sphere he stole from me."

He shifted in his seat, his expression skeptical. "You're talking about demon possession, now, aren't you?"

She shrugged. "In a manner of speaking, yes."

Steven pressed his hands over his face and exhaled heavily. "I need a break." He rose from the sofa and moved into the kitchen and pulled a beer from the refrigerator. He took a long pull from the bottle as Sylvia entered the room.

"Well, I gotta hand it to you. You didn't run screaming from the room," she said, the hint of a smile on her lips.

"Believe me, I was tempted." His gaze slid to the book she'd carried in with her. "What are you planning to use the book for?"

She set it on the counter and smoothed a hand over the front. "I'm hoping there's a spell or something that will help me locate the globe or at least the energy source inside it."

"I thought you didn't do spells."

"I don't. Doesn't mean I can't," she said. "With any luck, whoever has the globe hasn't figured out how to release the power inside."

Steven paused, his expression pensive. "Let's say everything you told me is true. It still doesn't help me with my case."

"But it does. Because now we know why these women were killed and who he's going after next."

"Who?"

"Lexie."

He slowly set the beer down and stared at her. "Lexie? Why do you think she's the next target?"

"It makes sense. Jerry was obsessed with her, even tried to imprison her soul last year. He must have planned to use her as a vessel for his great-great-grandmother, but we stripped him of his power before he could. If she's already been marked, then the killer knows it."

Steven rested against the counter and sent her an earnest look. "If she is the target, then you know you're going to have to tell her and Ray about all of this now."

She shook her head. "No, not just yet. I mean, as long as she's at the farm with Ray and the family, she'll be safe. The wedding is only four days away. Once they say their vows, they'll be spiritually bound, and the killer can't touch her."

"Which means he'll go after someone else."

"Yes. But I'm hoping you'll find him, first."

***

Sylvia eased her foot on the gas pedal and glanced at the rearview mirror and the DPS vehicle following her. Not that she believed Steven would pull her over for speeding, but he seemed to be a bit annoyed with her at the moment. She wasn't sure if it was because she'd demanded she take her Jeep to her grandparents' house or because she didn't want to arrive with him and have everyone question why they were together. She wasn't quite ready to make that announcement, especially since she hadn't yet broken up with Vincent.

She thought about the voicemail he'd left her the day before. He wanted to have dinner on Monday night because he was going out of town for a while. She knew she should call him back, but she wasn't going to break up with him over the phone. He was a nice guy and deserved better.

Red-and-blue lights flashed behind her and made her jolt. A quick look at the speedometer told her she was doing ninety. She eased her foot off the pedal and waved Steven off then turned onto the dirt road leading to her grandparents' house. Ray's truck and a beige Range Rover belonging to Lexie's sister, were parked in the driveway when she pulled alongside the house. She waited for him to park his SUV then climbed out of her Jeep. A mix of spices—onions, peppers, garlic—wafted from the open window in the kitchen.

"Just so you know, Ray hasn't told Lexie about Jerry yet, so keep it under your hat," she said as soon as he moved alongside her.

"Sure. But just so you know, since Kemp was identified this morning, chances are it's going to be on the local news."

"Then I guess we'll have to keep Lexie away from the TV." She put her hand up to stop him before he could move toward the house. "Also, Lexie's brother-in-law, Robert, is a cop and he's very protective of her, so would you mind not saying anything about this to him either?"

He gave her an apologetic shrug. "Too late. He was here when I spoke to Ray."

"You questioned him?"

"He has just as much of a reason to see Kemp gone."

Sylvia glared at him. "Maybe, but he has nothing to do with this either. Are you planning to accuse everyone in my family? Who are you going to question next, my grandparents?"

"If I thought they had anything to do with Kemp's death, then yes."

"Unbelievable," she growled as his phone chirped.

He raised his hand. "Hold that fight." He pulled out his cellphone and tapped the screen. "Gonzales. David, what's up? We do? Just me?" He glanced at his watch. "Yeah, I can be there. Give me a couple of hours. No, we can meet up after and I'll fill you in. Thanks. I'll see you tonight." He disconnected the call and tucked the phone in his pocket. "Sorry, I have to go."

"Everything okay?"

"Yeah. We have a possible witness to Miss Salazar's murder. She's at the San Patricio County Sheriff's Department and said she'd only speak to me, so I need to get to Sinton."

She followed him as he moved back to his truck. "Only you? Isn't that unusual?"

"No. Witnesses can be skittish sometimes and will only speak to whoever is lead on an investigation."

"How long will you be gone?"

"I'm not sure. But I'll be back for the wedding." He took her hand and pulled her closer. "I know you have to work tomorrow, but do me a favor, please? Stay here tonight. I'll feel much better about leaving you alone if you're with your family."

She hesitated then reluctantly nodded. "Fine, but you're going to owe me a tank of gas."

He grinned then leaned in and touched his lips to hers. "Give my apologies to your family. I'll call you later."

A shiver of unease skittered across her chest as she watched him climb into his SUV. She couldn't help the sense that this would be the last time she saw him. A part of her wanted to stop him. Tell him not to leave. Tell him she loved him. Instead, she lifted her hand and waved goodbye.

***

It was nearly midnight when Steven arrived in Austin. He spotted David at the coffee station as he stepped off the elevator onto the third floor of the public safety building. He'd spent nearly two hours at the San Patricio Sheriff's Department, waiting to speak with his witness, finally giving up and returning home when she didn't show up.

David came forward with two cups of coffee. "I wasn't expecting to see you tonight."

"Same to you," Steven said, accepting one of the cups as they moved to a partitioned workstation in the center of the room. There were six units in the room, each the size of a large walk-in closet. A boomerang-shaped desk housing two nineteen-inch computer monitors at opposite ends of the U were set up to accommodate two investigators.

"Linda got tired of me hovering," David said with a laugh. "So, what happened? Did the witness have any reliable information?"

Steven shook his head and set his satchel on the worktable. "She wasn't there." He pulled out one of the two office chairs and sat. "Apparently, she slipped out about ten minutes before I got there. Sheriff said she was there one minute, gone the next. I waited around as long as I could, in case she came back. But no go."

"Too much to ask if she left a name and number?"

He shook his head and tested the coffee. Satisfied it wouldn't singe his tongue, he took a sip. "No, but they have her on video, so we know what she looks like." He removed his laptop from the bag and connected it to the cable plugged into the monitor. He tapped the mouse and pulled up a photo. The image of a woman barely in her twenties filled the screen. She was staring directly at the camera, her expression pensive. Dark circles colored the skin beneath her eyes. Straight brown hair with highlighted tips fell several inches past her shoulders.

David leaned in, his brow furrowed, and studied the picture. "She looks familiar."

"You know her?"

"No, but I've seen her somewhere. Hold on." He pulled out the other chair and sat, then booted up his computer and clicked on a file. Steven waited, sipping his coffee as David sped forward through the video on the screen.

"This is the video from the coffeehouse Ms. Salazar most often went to," he said. "Far as I can tell, she was here about three times a week and an occasional Saturday." On the screen, various people entered and left the coffeehouse, some sitting at tables to read or chat with friends. "She always sat at the same table, reading or doing school work." He slowed the speed down to point at Angel.

He sped up the video, and before he stopped on a clip, Steven saw her. A young woman with dark-brown hair and blonde highlighted tips, sitting in the far corner of the store. She held a book, but her attention appeared to be focused on Angel Salazar who sat two tables away.

"That's her." David tapped the screen. He moved the cursor around to enlarge the photo. It was the witness from the sheriff's department. "She's at this coffee house nearly as much as Ms. Salazar is."

"Another student?"

He shook his head. "I don't think so. The book she's holding? It's the same every time, but she doesn't seem to be reading it."

"Did she ever make contact with Miss Salazar?"

"Only once. But it appeared accidental." David sped forward again. On the video, the woman made her way to a table and appeared to stumble, spilling her drink on Angel's table. The woman grabbed a stack of paper napkins and blotted at the liquid. "The woman apologized, and they spoke for a few minutes then went their own way. They don't interact again except for the occasional acknowledgement when they both enter the coffeehouse."

"Well, now that we know they knew each other, it puts her in the reliable witness camp," Steven said.

"Or a person of interest. I've been going through the campus security videos, and she shows up there, too. This one is from the parking lot." He tapped the mouse and pulled up another clip. The images were in black and white and taken from a distance. Angel moved to a light-colored, older model VW bug parked at the far end of the student parking lot and dropped into the driver's seat. After a moment, she stepped out of the car and opened the hood, leaning over to inspect the engine. A moment later, a dark-red SUV pulled up next to her. A woman climbed out of the passenger seat and moved alongside Angel. After appearing to work on the engine, the woman opened the rear door of the SUV and gestured for Angel to climb in. "It's almost like this woman knew Ms. Salazar was going to have car trouble."

Steven turned to his desk and grabbed a binder from the satchel. He flipped through the pages. "According to the impound lot, the car wouldn't start because the distributor cap was off." Just like Sylvia's Jeep the first day he saw her again. He turned toward David. "How close can you get with that video?"

"Out of my pay grade. We'll have to take it down to tech support. But I'd say chances are pretty good it's the same woman from the coffee shop and the sheriff's video."

"Yes, but there are two people in that SUV. We need to find out who that driver is."

Chapter Twenty

Sylvia slid the tray of letters onto the metal rack and stretched out the stiffness in her shoulders. As she made her way to the front swinging doors, she took her phone from her pocket. She turned it on, frowning when she saw there were no messages. She had hoped to hear from Steven by now.

Gabe was at the counter, weighing a package for an elderly woman and scribbling the information onto a mail order form when she stepped to the front lobby. Lexie pulled open the front door, holding it for the woman to pass through before stepping inside the building.

"Hey," she said, as Lexie moved toward the counter. "What are you doing here? Where's Ray?"

"He's at the drugstore. He dropped me off so I could pick up my check."

"I would have brought it to you if you'd asked."

Lexie shrugged. "I know, but I felt like getting out of the house."

Sylvia sent her an amused grin. "Your sister driving you crazy with the wedding plans?"

Lexie laughed. "Only a little."

"I can go get it for you, Miss Lexie," Gabe said.

"Thanks, Gabe." Sylvia smiled at the elderly man as he moved to the back room. The doorbell chimed, and Lexie turned to glance behind her at the man entering the building. Her body went still, the fear in her stance hitting Sylvia like a whip of icy air. "Lexie?"

"Malcolm." The word whispered from Lexie's lips. She retreated a step, stopping when she hit the edge of the counter.

Sylvia quickly moved around the bar and stood in front of Lexie, her gaze landing hard on the man He was in his late thirties with coarse black hair and a thin gaunt face. His tall, lanky body and the dark shadows under his eyes made him look like a crypt keeper. "Who are you?" she snapped.

"Malcolm? What are you doing here? Where's Jerry?" Lexie moved from behind Sylvia to face the man Sylvia now realized was Jerry's cousin. The same man who'd helped Jerry try to kill Ray and Lexie last year.

Malcolm stared at Lexie a moment, his brow furrowed. "You don't know."

The bell chimed as the door swung open. Ray rushed inside, his forearm coming up and pressing against Malcolm's chest like a battering ram, using the force to push him against the wall.

"What are you doing here?" He spoke in a dangerously low voice.

Malcolm's hands came up, his expression stoic. "I'm not here for trouble. I just needed to know if she...." His gaze moved to Lexie then back to Ray. "If either of you had anything to do with Jerry's death."

"What?" Lexie took a step forward, but Sylvia grabbed onto her arm to stop her.

"Lexie, wait..."

Malcolm straightened from the wall when Ray abruptly let him go. "Jerry is dead."

Lexie blinked at him. "I don't understand. How? When?"

"You didn't know?" Malcolm glanced at Ray then shifted his eyes back to Lexie. "He went missing a couple of weeks ago; his body turned up yesterday. I came in to identify him and bring him home."

"Bring him home?"

"He's at the county morgue."

"Here? He's been here? In town?" Lexie cast a questioning look at Sylvia.

"I didn't know either," she said, choosing to leave out what she did know.

Malcolm took a step forward but stopped when Ray glared at him. "I just needed to see for myself if either of you had anything to do with his murder."

"The police have cleared us of any involvement in your cousin's death," Ray said.

Lexie shifted her gaze to him. "You knew about this?"

"Steven came by yesterday. I was going to tell you." Ray took her hand. "But we thought it best to wait."

"We?" Lexie tossed a glare at Sylvia.

Malcolm moved closer, his expression contrite. "Lexie, about last year. For what it's worth, I'm really sorry. If I'd known what Jerry was planning, I would have tried to stop him. But you know as well as I do…. In any case, it's over." He stole a glance at his watch. "I should get going, I have a meeting with the detective on the case. Hopefully, he can tell me what happened."

"How long are you planning to be in Edmondville?" Sylvia hoped she sounded casual. She wanted to speak to him about Jerry's great-great-grandmother and find out if her theory was correct about the portal, but she couldn't do it in front of Ray and Lexie.

He gave her a scrutinizing look then said, "A few days at most. I'm staying at the Holiday Inn by the airport." He turned to Lexie. "But, don't worry. I won't be causing you any trouble."

"Malcom." Lexie placed her hand on his arm, pulling it away quickly when he turned. "I'm very sorry for your loss. Please give my condolences to his family." She stood still in front of the door and watched him leave.

"Lex? Are you okay?" Sylvia asked.

Lexie pulled in a breath and turned. She didn't look angry, but there was a hint of sadness in her eyes. "I don't know. I'm not sure how I'm supposed to feel. I mean, Jerry wasn't a nice person, but I never wanted to see any harm come to him." She wandered to the counter, her arms wrapped around her waist. "But I feel like that part of my life has finally ended, and I can finally rest easy. Does that make me a horrible person?"

"No. After what he put you through, no one can blame you for wanting to move on." Ray stepped forward and pulled her against him. "But it's okay to grieve as well. He was a big piece of your life once, and there was a part of you that loved him."

"I suppose." Lexie turned and burrowed into his embrace. "Let's go home."

"I'll bring you your check tonight," Sylvia said, as they moved to the door. She stole a glance at the clock behind the counter. She had two hours left of work. Which meant she had two hours to meet with Malcolm before she had to head to her grandparents' house for dinner. With any luck, he'll have the answers they need to stop the killer from releasing Jerry's great-great-grandmother.

***

Sylvia arrived at the Holiday Inn at three-thirty and found a spot next to the airport shuttle van. As she climbed out of the Jeep, it occurred to her that she didn't know Malcolm's last name. She hoped the desk clerk would be willing to look him up with only his first name.

She entered the lobby and spotted Malcolm sitting in the bar area, facing the door as if he'd been expecting her. He had a drink if front of him, and, from the glaze in his eyes, it didn't appear to be his first.

"You knew I was coming," she said.

He answered with a shrug and waved at the waitress by the bar. "Buy you a drink?"

"No. Thank you." She pulled a chair out from the table and sat. The room was empty except for the table Malcolm occupied. A muted basketball game played on the TV mounted in the corner. She waited for the waitress to set down his drink, then said, "I'm sorry for your loss. I know you and your cousin were close."

"What do you want?"

She bit back a sigh. She didn't expect him to be happy to see her, but she didn't want to antagonize him either. He wasn't as powerful as Jerry had been, but he was still dangerous. "I'm hoping you can tell me why your cousin was here."

"Do you mean, was he coming for Lexie?" He shook his head. "No. He promised his father he'd leave her alone. I prefer to believe he would keep that promise."

"If not for Lexie, then why was he here?"

Malcolm paused. "He found a way to get back what was his. What you took from him," he said, gesturing toward her with his glass before swallowing down the liquid.

A chill whispered across Sylvia's neck. Jerry had known she'd taken his power? But how? As far as she knew, Jerry didn't know she existed. "How did he know I had it?"

"He didn't, at least not until a few weeks ago. He received a call from someone who said he could get it for him. At a price." He twirled his glass on the table and frowned. "I thought I had talked him out of coming down here. Told him the guy was just after money, but Jerry said he had proof. Then he showed me a photo of you holding the crystal you put the magic in."

Sylvia swallowed, her throat suddenly dry. Someone had been watching her. How did she not pick up on that? And how did they get through the protection spell she kept around her house to steal the globe?

"You touched it," Malcolm said. Her gaze came up and landed on his. "The power. You touched it. That's how it was found." Malcolm waved to the waitress for another drink. "Not your fault, really. That kind of magic pulls at you, you can't help but want to feel it. And, anyway, Jerry wanted the power back. He was going to find a way." He waited as the waitress set his drink down. He picked it up, swirling the amber liquid. "Whoever has it now found out it belonged to him. And knows how powerful it is."

"I'm sorry. If I'd known—"

Malcolm waved her words away then took a sip of the drink. "What's done is done. Anyway, whoever has it can't do much harm. It's an inherent power, and only blood can wield it."

Sylvia sat up straight. "Blood? Like a great-great-grandmother?"

"Sure, but lucky for us she isn't alive." He stared at her a moment. "Why do you ask that?"

She glanced at the bar. Maybe she should have that drink after all. "What do you know about your great-great-grandmother?" she asked.

He considered her question a moment, then shrugged. "Just what

I was told as a kid. She was a powerful sorceress several hundred years ago. She believed herself to be a God and wanted to enslave the earth. She became so obsessed that even her lover was afraid of her. In the end, he deceived her and helped cast the spell that locked her in a pocket dimension. My uncle, Jerry's father, used to say she's still looking for a way out to seek vengeance on everyone who betrayed her." He swallowed the drink then scoffed. "Your typical boogieman story."

She raised her brow. "You really believe it's only a story?"

He pinned his gaze on her. "How about you get to the point. Why are you asking about my great-great-grandmother?"

She leaned forward, resting her arms on the table. "Because, I think someone took your cousin's power and plans to release your great-great-grandmother from her prison."

Malcolm didn't answer and, again, waved to the waitress for another drink.

She narrowed her gaze. "You don't seem surprised."

"Because it isn't possible." He scoffed at her. "It's not the first time someone has tried. It won't be the last."

"But what if this time is different? Whoever has the sphere also has a spell that can open the portal." When he didn't answer she glared at him. "This is your family's magic. You have to know how to stop someone from calling her through to this world."

He considered her a moment then shrugged. "Maybe. But, what's in it for me?"

She stared at him. "What's in it for you?"

He picked up the glass the waitress set down, his lips quirked. "It doesn't affect me either way, so if you want my help, you give me something in return."

She straightened in the chair and locked her arms across her chest. "What do you want?"

"I want the power back."

She stared at him. If she'd had a drink, she'd have choked on it. "No."

A smile played across his lips. "You really don't have a choice. I'm a direct descendent, just like Jerry, which means I can locate the energy whether it's being used or not."

"If that's true, why haven't you tried to take it back before now?"

Malcolm sighed. "Because I don't have the *right* magic. Not like your brother. I'll need his help."

She shook her head and scoffed. "That's not happening. Ray and Lexie are getting married soon. I won't let him be a part of this."

The hint of anger narrowed his eyes. "He became a part of it last year." He picked up his glass. "You seem to think you have a choice. You don't. If someone is planning to open the portal, they're going to do it during the next lunar eclipse. Which means, the clock is ticking."

The lunar eclipse. It was in two days. How did she not remember that? This year it was happening on the night of the spring equinox during the same time as the new moon. It would be one of the most powerful days for the next hundred years.

Malcolm's lips quirked. "Like it or not, sweetheart, I'm all you got. And I won't help unless you give me what belongs to me."

Dammit, she hated that he was forcing her into a corner. But, he was right. He was the only one who could help them. But, was it wise to involve Ray or give Malcom back the magic when....

"Don't worry. We aren't a threat to your family," he said as if he'd read her mind. "The magic was never intended for the way Jerry used it. He was in over his head. We don't plan to repeat that mistake. And we sure as hell don't want great-great-grandmother released."

She fought the mental war in her head. No matter how she looked at it, he was right. The bottom line was, they couldn't allow the portal to be opened.

"Okay. Fine," she said at length. "I hope I don't regret this, but I'm going to trust you." She glanced at her watch. She had to be at the farm in less than an hour. "I have to go. Meet me tomorrow at three at the post office. We'll go from there."

She pushed out of the chair and headed for the exit. Maybe she should pick up a bottle of Ray's favorite bourbon to lighten the blow that they were going to have to work side by side with Jerry's cousin.

Chapter Twenty-One

Steven dropped the phone onto its base and sat back in his chair, rubbing his hands over his face to push away the fatigue. He glanced at his watch. It was nearly ten o'clock. He'd spent a majority of the day on the phone, chasing leads called into the tip line and speaking with the San Patricio County sheriff and the Cameron Count sheriff offices while David worked with the computer forensics team to enhance the video from the campus parking lot. He was exhausted, hungry, and frustrated.

The conversation he'd had with Sylvia the day before continued to play in his mind, fighting against his sensibility that he agreed to give her the benefit of the doubt. Although, he had to admit some of her theory made sense. At least the part about their killer believing he could perform magic with a human sacrifice.

He tapped his fingers next to the mouse then booted up the laptop. Opening a search engine, he typed in *Order of the Shadows* and waited for the page to load. It didn't surprise him the search showed nearly a million sites dedicated to black magic.

He clicked on a link titled *The Rise of the Galicia Witch*. Distorted images of demons and symbols lined the page next to sectioned paragraphs. He scrolled down to read the passages.

The story was much like Sylvia had mentioned. The sorceress has spent centuries seeking out someone to release her from her prison. She would seek out a powerful witch as an apprentice to help her with the ceremony, deceiving them into believing she would grant them a place of honor in her new world. The apprentice would then seek out the vessel, which the sorceress would mark with three claw-like marks somewhere on her body.

The ceremony, called soul transference, is performed during a lunar eclipse, when magic is at its strongest. If the chosen being has a soul, it may be destroyed or lost by the transference. The process is painful for the recipient and can only be stopped by the blood of another witch before the ritual is complete.

He tapped on the photo tagged 'soul transference'. A hooded figure stood at the head of a stone altar where a woman lay strapped, his hands pressed to each side of her head as if to keep her still. A black mist with fiery red eyes hovered above the woman, claw-like hands piercing her abdomen. Pain and terror filled the woman's eyes and Steven could almost hear her screams of agony.

His thoughts flashed back to his night with Sylvia. He'd noticed three faded scars on her shoulder when he'd taken her to bed. Had they always been there, or were they given to her by the witch?

He dropped his head against his chair and rubbed his fingers over his eyes. Christ. When did he start working for the *X-Files*?

"What are you looking at?"

David's voice made Steven jolt. "Just.... nothing. Letting my imagination get away from me." He quickly closed the page and turned his chair to face David. "We get anywhere with the video?" he asked as David sat at the adjoining chair.

"Maybe. Owens was able to get a decent picture off the other videos campus security sent over. We have a pretty clear photo of the woman, as well as the driver, but it's a profile." He pulled a photo from the file he held. "Owens thinks it might be enough to run through facial recognition."

"Good. In the meantime, let's send the woman's photo to Del Mar and see if she's a student. Maybe it'll get us a name quicker."

David nodded and tucked the photo in the folder. "You look like hell. Why don't you go get a few hours' sleep and I'll call you if anything hits?"

Steven glanced at his laptop. The sketched image of the soul transference flashed in his mind. He exhaled heavily and nodded. "Yeah. I think I will." And maybe he'd call Sylvia, just to be on the safe side.

***

Sylvia twisted off the top of her beer and took a long drink. She pushed her feet against the deck to send the bench swing swaying. The soft scrape of the chains told her they'd recently been oiled.

Across the field she spotted the pinpoint of light from Ray's house. Lexie and her family were safely tucked away there now, shielded by the protection spell Sylvia had placed around the house before arriving at her grandparents for dinner.

She glanced up at the soft glow of the waning crescent moon and frowned. The new moon would be here in two days, along with the lunar eclipse. And somewhere out there, a killer was waiting in the shadows to take advantage of the power it contained. She really hoped to hell Malcolm could help her stop it.

The door creaked open, and Ray stepped onto the porch, carrying his boots. He made it to the steps before she spoke.

"Aren't you a little old to be sneaking out?"

"Jesus, Sylvia," he said, turning to face her. "You scared the hell out of me."

She laughed and pushed the swing moving again. "I seem to do that to a lot of people."

Ray sat on the Adirondack chair tucked against the wall and pulled on his boots. "What are you doing here? I thought you were staying at my place with Lexie."

She shrugged. "I was, but Lexie doesn't get to spend much time with her family, so I thought I'd give her a few more days of alone time with them. I'd sleep here, but my room is filled to the roof with wedding stuff. Who knew there was so much stuff to do for a wedding? If I ever get married, I'm going to elope."

"Believe me, it was a thought," Ray said with a laugh. "You can sleep in my room, you know. I don't mind the sofa."

She waved him off. "Nah, it's okay. Besides, Abuela gave me a list of things to do before the rehearsal dinner, and I can get started earlier if I'm closer to town."

Ray cocked his brow. "Is that really the reason?"

"What do you mean?"

"You've been edgy all night. Something's bothering you."

She took another drink from the bottle to avoid answering him. She hadn't spoken to Ray about her meeting with Malcolm or Malcolm's insistence that they work together. She'd decided whatever help Malcolm needed, he'd have to figure out a way to get it from her. She was not going to let him or anything ruin Ray's wedding.

"Does this have anything to do with Steven?" He shrugged when her gaze came up to his. "We kind of saw you two earlier."

"You guys were spying on me?"

"No, of course not. We heard you drive up, and when we looked out the window, we just happened to see.... So...are you two...?"

Sylvia bit back a smile. "Having sex?" She laughed at Ray's barely

214

suppressed wince.

"That's okay. I really don't want to know about your sex life."

"There's no sex life, exactly. We're just.... I don't know what we are yet." She took a sip from the bottle and frowned. "Don't worry. I won't pursue anything with Steven if it bothers you."

"I didn't say it bothered me."

She waved him off. "Yeah, well, it's probably a moot point, anyway. I mean, I'm dating Vincent. I shouldn't be having an affair with another man."

Ray lifted a brow, his expression doubtful. "Vincent. You mean the boyfriend you've mentioned but never introduced to your family? That, right there, should tell you something." He stood and shifted his feet to settle into the boots. "Little sister, I'm going to give you the same advice you gave me last year. Listen to your heart. If Steven is who you want, then go for it, I'm more than okay with it."

"Sure, the one time you actually listen to me, you throw the words back in my face."

Ray laughed and pulled a phone from his pocket. "By the way, you left your phone on the charger. I was going to leave it in my kitchen for you."

She took the phone and turned it on. A missed call from Steven. It was too late to call him back. "Thanks." She finished her drink and stood. "I guess I'll head on home. Thanks, big brother." She kissed his cheek and moved into the house to retrieve her keys. Letting him believe Steven was the problem on her mind was better than telling him the truth.

Sylvia tossed her keys on the counter as she entered her kitchen from the back door. Her conscience weighed heavily on her. She hated that she'd been dishonest with Ray, but her family's safety had always been her number one priority. She wasn't going to change that now, no matter what.

She pulled open the refrigerator and grabbed a beer before heading toward the living room. A whisper of anxiety fluttered across her neck and stopped her in the center of the room. Something was off.

She cast a look around the dark room. Moonlight filtered in from the front window blinds, a soft breeze fluttering the eyelet curtains. It took her a moment to realize she'd never opened the window.

She sensed the movement behind her. Before she could react, a hand covered her mouth and a bitter smell filled her lungs.

The bottle slipped from her hand and shattered on the floor. The image of a woman shrouded in black flashed across her vision before darkness closed around her.

***

Steven exhaled a contented sigh and reached a hand out to his side. The blanket was empty.

He sat up, taking in the dried stalks surrounding him. "Sylvia?" He grabbed his shirt and put it on as he stood. "Where are you?"

Thick clouds cloaked the sky, and he gave himself a moment to adjust his sight to the darkness. Sylvia had brought him to the center of the field, pointing out her home a half mile away, but with the eight-foot stalks surrounding him, he couldn't tell which end of the field the house was on.

He wove through the stems, the dried leaves crunching beneath his feet, hidden by a cool gray mist swirling around his ankles like coiling snakes. He stepped out of the field into a clearing of dirt and rock. Ahead of him of stood a single-story wood-slat house with a covered porch. Dim yellow light shone behind a thin curtain in the front window.

He made his way forward, a familiarity washing over him. The panel front door was slightly open. Cautiously, he pushed it wider and moved inside. "Hello?"

Soft light from the teardrop ceiling fixture illumined the room, giving life to the tiny dust motes dancing in the air. It was a box-sized space with scuffed hardwood floors that had warped over time. Sitting against the brown-panel wall was a pale, flowered, overstuffed sofa much like the one his mother bought with her first overtime check.

Hanging on the wall above it was a gold-framed painting of *The Last Supper*. Two scarred, oak-colored end tables framed the couch, each housing an hourglass lamp, the lampshades still covered in cellophane.

He closed his eyes and inhaled heavily. The spicy aroma of the food coming from the kitchen teased his senses. His mother's hambone soup. The one meal she always made at the end of the month when the money ran out and she only had the frozen hambone from their New Year's dinner and the meager vegetables from her homegrown garden.

Off to the side of the kitchen was the square wooden table where they ate every meal. The urn that held his mother's ashes sat on the table like a centerpiece.

He moved toward the room and froze. Standing at the stove was a slender woman wearing a turquoise-colored house dress with embroidered flowers along the hem. Her auburn hair was bound in a tight bun at her neck.

She was younger than he remembered. Healthier. The effects of the cancer that had deteriorated her body no longer visible.

"Mom?"

Her eyes lit up with her smile. "Steven." She came forward and wrapped him in a hug. Pain, grief, and guilt burned like acid in his chest. He'd spent so much of his life angry at her for refusing modern medicine to prolong her life that he hadn't allowed himself to miss her.

"You're really here," he said.

She placed her hand on his chest. "I'm always right here." She took his hand and led him to the front room. "Come. You don't have much time."

"For what?"

"If you do not stop her, she will destroy the world."

"Who?" He barely suppressed his groan and let go of her hand. "You're talking about Sylvia's witch, aren't you? Wonderful. Now I'm dreaming about it." What did he expect? The case, Sylvia's obsession with sorcerers and witches, his victims—of course, it was going to plague his sleep.

His mother stopped at the front door and frowned at him. "Do not dismiss something you do not understand."

"Oh good. Fortune cookie wisdom."

Her expression turned earnest. "Your visions will give you your answers. You must believe in what you see. You cannot help Sylvia unless you believe."

The anger Steven held on to over the years surged to his chest. "Believe? Like you did? All the money you spent on spells and potions for your cancer because you *believed*. Do you remember how *that* worked out? You died! At forty-one years old. You fucking died!" He spun around on his heel, pushing his fingers through his hair. Shit. Was he really going to fight with a figment of his dream? Her hand touched down on his shoulder.

"I know you are angry with me. But, it worked out the way it was supposed to."

"What the hell is that supposed to mean? You could have lived a longer life. If you'd just listened to me. If you'd gone to a real doctor instead of a so-called witch—"

"What I did or didn't do is on me. You can be angry, or you can accept." She dropped her hand. "Right now, we don't have time for you to decide. The spell will go through, and there is only one way to save the woman you love."

Panic sent his pulse racing. He faced her. "What are you talking about?"

She opened the front door to reveal a world of gray fog. Dark shapes with hollowed-out eyes filled the mist, their skeletal hands reaching out. Hoarse whispers flowed from the dark. *Free me.* "You will find her in the house of souls. But you must hurry, before it is too late."

He turned to look at his mother, but she was gone.

Free me. Free Me. Free Me.

The fog rolled up the deck and into the house. His skin chilled, and he felt the brush of fingers on his arm pulling him out of the house. Instead of the outside, he found himself in another room. A handful of fat candles were scattered on the floor, blue flames dancing in the wax. At the far end of the room, a woman was chained to a table. A figure in a black cloak stood alongside her, his hands raised above his head and clutching a knife. The woman looked at him, fear and panic rounding her eyes.

"Sylvia!" Before he could rush forward, the man brought the knife down into Sylvia's chest.

The high-pitched ring of his cellphone jolted him awake. Steven sat up on his sofa, his heart beating like a battering ram against his chest. He pulled in a lungful of air and pressed his hands to his face, pushing his breath out on a huff. "Son of a bitch." *It was just a dream. Nightmare*, he corrected. *One nearly realistic nightmare.*

He glanced at his watch. Almost six o'clock.

He gave himself another moment to calm then grabbed his phone off the coffee table and staggered to the kitchen. "Gonzales." He pulled a water bottle from the inside door of the refrigerator.

"Hey, sorry to wake you," David said on the other end. "We got a hit on the driver. You're going to want to see this."

Steven swallowed a gulp of water then grabbed his keys from the counter. "On my way."

He arrived at the station as the sun peeked above the horizon. David was standing hunched over the desk, skimming through a file on his computer monitor. He wore a different suit this morning, which meant he'd gone home sometime during the night as well.

David stared at him a moment then shook his head. "Did you sleep in your clothes?"

Steven ignored the question and handed him one of the cups of coffee he'd picked up on his way in. "Who are the mystery man and woman?"

David took the coffee and passed him several photos. "The woman is Carla Dominguez; last physical address is Harlingen. She's a seasonal migrant worker and occasionally works a farmer's market off Highway 77. We don't have an ID on the man, but I don't think you'll need it."

Steven shuffled through the photos, each a different angle of the man driving the SUV. An enhanced photo of the man standing with Carla Dominguez in front of the coffeeshop made him go cold. He'd seen the man before. At the post office, the first time they'd arrived in Edmondville. It was Sylvia's friend. *What did she call him? Vincent!*

"Send these to Deputy Hernandez at the Cameron County Sheriff Department, tell them to get a BOLO out right away. I'm going to Edmondville." He headed to the stairs, tapping in Sylvia's number as he hurried down the three flights. His dream replayed in his mind. The image of her on the table and the man stabbing her through the chest nearly made him stumble.

It was a dream. It was only a dream. Sylvia's okay. She's safe. That was the only thing he was going to believe in.

***

Sylvia's Jeep was parked behind her house when Steven arrived. According to the clerk at the post office, she had taken off work for the rest of the week to help with Ray's wedding.

He touched the hood. Cold. It hadn't been driven in a while.

He let himself in through the kitchen using the keys Ray gave him that first day he'd arrived. The Jeep keys were laying on the counter, but the house felt empty.

"Sylvia?"

He checked the living room before moving to the hallway. Her bedroom door was open. He peered around the frame then stepped into the room. The bed was made, and the room looked the same as it had the last time he was there. He fought down the panic curling in his stomach. Maybe she was at her grandparents' house. She'd promised him she would stay there while he was gone.

He took out his phone and pulled up Ray's number. He'd tried calling Sylvia during his drive, but the calls went straight to voicemail. He rubbed a hand over the nape of his neck and paced the living room as the phone rang. His stomached soured when he noticed the shattered bottle on the floor. Ray answered after five rings.

"Hey buddy. What's up?"

Steven tried to keep his voice steady. "Hey. I'm looking for your sister. Is she there?"

"No. I think she's at home. Did you try calling her?"

"It's going straight to voicemail. I'm at her house now, but she's not here."

"Oh, well, she said something about running errands for my grandmother today. She probably left her phone in the Jeep."

"Yeah. You're probably right." Steven pushed a hand through his hair as he paced.

Ray's voice lowered. "Is Sylvia in trouble?"

Steven stopped. He'd promised Sylvia he wouldn't involve Ray or Lexie in the investigation. But he wouldn't lie to his friend, especially when it involved his sister.

"I'm not sure."

"I'm on my way." Ray disconnected the phone before Steven could reply.

Chapter Twenty-Two

Sylvia awoke to darkness. She turned her head to look at the clock on the bedside table, but the table was empty. The clank of metal-on-metal rang out when she moved her hand.

"What the hell?" She pulled both her arms, the clanking reverberating in the room. She was chained to a bed.

Panic tightened her chest, squeezing like a vice to her throat. *Calm down. Calm down. Maybe it's just another weird vision.*

She closed her eyes and inhaled to give her eyes a minute to adjust. "Okay, focus, Sylvia," she murmured.

She lifted her head from the pillow and scanned what she could see of the room. A thin strip of light filtered in from the slats of wood covering the window. At the foot of the bed, another light shone beneath the door. It was daytime.

She tried moving her feet. No chains on them. Shifting her weight, she scooted to the head of the bed and sat up. A cool draft and the malodorous smell of decay stained the air. She sensed the presence but couldn't see the spirits.

"Is anyone there?"

The door opened, bright light spilling into the room. She lifted her arm to block the glare. Standing in the doorway was a tall figure, male as far as she could tell.

"Good. You're awake."

Cold relief washed over her at the sound of the voice. "Vincent!" She pulled against her binds, scraping the metal chains. "Thank God! Get me out of here."

"I'm sorry, *mi amor*, I can't do that. Not just yet." Vincent moved into the room, carrying a tray. The aroma of spices steamed from the bowl. He set the tray on the scarred nightstand. "Now, if you promise to be good, I'll unchain you so you can eat."

Sylvia's heart dropped like a brick of ice to her stomach. "You did this to me?" She shook her head. "No. I read you. That first day you asked me out. I read you."

"Of course, you did. I expected no less. I have to say, manipulating what I wanted you to see was tougher than I'd anticipated." Vincent sat beside her on the bed. Lifting a hand, he tucked a strand of hair behind her ear. "I did my research as soon as I learned about you."

"Research?"

"You're not as far under the radar as you'd like to think. But you are stronger than I expected. Breaking through your protection spells was a worthy challenge. Once we began our relationship, getting past your defenses was as simple as a kiss." He stroked his thumb over her lips.

She pulled away and scowled at him. "Don't touch me."

He passed over her words, unoffended. "Of course, getting through your front door didn't quite work out as I'd planned, so I must admit, I had to get a little help to get into your house."

Her bravado shattered. She swallowed hard, the realization of what he did turned her blood cold. "You took the globe. You killed Jerry."

He smiled at her. "And, I have you to thank for Mr. Kemp. I wasn't aware the magic belonged to him or the Galicia witch until I found your journal. Once I learned how much he would pay to get it back, it was like taking candy from a baby."

"Did you kill those other women? And Angel? Did you kill her, too?"

Vincent shrugged. "Like I said, you're strong. I had to get through your magic, and they were my way in. Once I realized you could move through planes, I decided to test you with Angel." He placed his hand on her thigh and squeezed. "And you didn't disappoint."

She couldn't stop the break in her voice. "You son of a bitch."

Vincent flashed a smile then took a key from his pocket and unclasped her left hand. "You really should eat." He tucked the key into his pocket and moved to the door. "I have a little business to attend to, but I'll be back soon."

Sylvia rubbed at her wrist as he left the room. He'd left the door open enough to give her light, but she couldn't see into the next room. She sat back, fighting against the tears burning her eyes. Vincent killed Angel and Jerry and all those other women. And it was all her fault.

***

"Any word?" Ray asked as soon as he entered Sylvia's house.

"No. I spoke to her clerk at the post office and he said she's on leave the rest of the week. She's not answering her phone, and the last couple of calls went straight to voicemail."

"I'll pull up the GPS tracker on her phone." Ray pulled out his phone and tapped on the screen. He frowned. "It's turned off. Dammit. She never turns it off. Not since last year."

"Whoever took her probably tossed the phone anyway."

Ray glanced at the table where Steven had left the open files from the investigation. "I think you'd better tell me exactly what's going on."

Steven nodded. "Maybe you should sit down."

"She should have told me. *You* should have told me," Ray said, after Steven told him about the investigation. "We could have stopped this before he got to her."

"You're right. I'm sorry. Sylvia asked me to keep you and your family out of this. And I agreed because, well...."

Ray shook his head. "I know. My sister knows how to get her way."

"Do you believe her theory? That this has to do with witches and sorcerers?"

Ray looked at him from where he was sitting at the kitchen table. The binder Steven had given to Sylvia was open in front of him. Steven had given him a condensed version of the investigation before sharing Sylvia's theory about the blood magic and Jerry's great-great-grandmother with him.

"If you'd have asked me this a year ago, I'd have said no. But after what Lexie and I went through...." He shrugged. "It's hard not to."

Steven exhaled heavily and pushed up from the counter he was leaning on. "Okay. So, do you know how to find her? Is there some sort of...?" He waved his hand toward the book of spells buried beneath the files.

Ray shook his head. "I don't know. This is Sylvia's field, not mine." He sat back, misery clouding his expression. "We're going to have to tell my grandmother. She's the only person I know who can help us."

"Maybe not. Sylvia doesn't want to involve your family. I think we should keep it that way for now. My investigation has given us a couple of suspects to look at. I'm also working with the local sheriff's department to—." His attention shifted to the window as a shadow moved across the yard.

"What?"

"Someone's here." He lifted his hand to stop Ray when he bolted from his seat, then pulled out his gun. "Stay out of sight."

Steven moved into the living room and positioned himself to the side of the front door, pressing his body against the wall as the knob twisted. The door eased open. Steven rounded the entry as soon as the figure entered the house. He grasped the man by the neck and pushed him up against the wall, holding his gun to the back of his head.

"Police. Don't move."

The man splayed his hands up on the wall. "Hey! I'm just looking for Sylvia. She's expecting me."

Steven spun the man around, keeping him pinned to the wall as Ray came into the room.

"Malcolm."

"You know him?" Steven asked.

"Jerry's cousin. What the hell are you doing here? And what do you mean she's expecting you?"

Malcolm glared over his shoulder at Steven. "Get off me, and I'll tell you."

Steven hesitated then stepped back, holstering his gun.

Malcolm adjusted his shirt and squared his shoulders. "I met with your sister yesterday. At my hotel," he added, casting a knowing smile at Steven.

"Why?" Ray asked.

"Oh, you know. We had a few drinks. Got to know each other."

"Cut the bullshit," Steven growled. "She went to see you about your great-grandmother, didn't she?"

"That's two greats and, yes, my great-great-grandmother came up. Sylvia wanted my help to stop whoever is planning to release the witch before she finds the right vessel. She told me to meet her at the post office, but the old man behind the counter said she was off the rest of the week, so I came here."

"What do you mean, 'right' vessel?" Steven asked.

Malcolm looked at him as if he were speaking to a child. "You can't put that kind of power into just anyone. They have to be special. Powerful. Otherwise, the vessel will die, their soul will die, and there will be nothing left to make the transference with."

Ray's brow furrowed. "Power? Jerry's power? She told me she got rid of that."

Malcolm's lips quirked. "I guess she lied. The power you took from Jerry is energy. It can't be destroyed. It can only be contained."

"The crystal ball you gave her," Steven said to Ray. "She told me she put it in there."

"And now, someone else has it," Malcolm added, his tone accusatory.

Ray's expression turned grim. "And Sylvia."

Malcolm nodded. "She'd be the right vessel. She's strong, powerful, and pretty hot. According to my uncle, great-great-grandmother was obsessed with youth and beauty. She wasn't above killing young women and drinking their blood to keep herself virile. If she's planning to come back, she's going to want to go into a hot, young body." Malcolm crossed his arms and grinned when Steve glared at him. "Look, Sylvia asked for my help, and I agreed to help as long as she kept her end of the deal."

"What deal?" Ray asked.

"I help her find the energy and she gives it back to me."

"Gives it back to you? She'd never agree to that."

"Well, I guess you'll just have to take my word for it. Regardless, the clock's ticking. You have less than forty-eight hours to find your sister and the magic because, once the witch absorbs it, it'll be too late."

Ray turned to Steven. "You mentioned before you had a couple of suspects."

He nodded and moved to the kitchen. "We believe she might be with this man." He picked up his satchel and pulled out the photos David gave him then passed them to Ray.

Ray studied the picture "Who is he?"

"We haven't been able to find anything on him yet, but you might know him as Vincent Rodriguez."

Ray sent him a bewildered look. "Vincent? The guy Sylvia's been seeing?"

"He and a woman named Carla Dominguez are wanted for questioning in Angel Salazar's disappearance."

Ray sifted through the photos, his expression strained. "Jesus. I think Carla is one of Sylvia's clients."

"The county sheriff is helping us try to locate her, but Ms. Dominguez is undocumented, so there's no record of her anywhere."

"Wait. Sylvia keeps a journal with names and addresses of all her clients. It will have Carla's address in it. I know where she keeps it." Ray dropped the photos on the table and rushed from the room.

Malcolm picked up the pictures. "They must be the ones who've been watching her."

"What do you mean watching her?"

"There are pictures on Jerry's phone. The sheriff let me take his belongings." He pulled out a cellphone and tapped the screen. He turned the phone and showed Steven a photo of Sylvia. The angle was taken from outside her bedroom window. She was standing at her dresser, holding the crystal globe she'd shown him earlier. A blue light shone from the globe casting a cone of color over her.

Steven glared at Malcolm. "Maybe you better fill me in on what else you know."

"Sure. As long as we still have a deal. I'll take that as a yes," he said when Steven stayed silent. He tucked the phone in his pocket. "After I met with Sylvia yesterday, I called my uncle Irwin, Jerry's father. He keeps a detailed record of our family history for posterity. You know that whole 'those who cannot remember the past are condemned to repeat it' thing. I gave him a rundown of my meet with Sylvia and of what happened to Jerry, not the full details, of course. It's enough that I know them." He took a piece of paper from his pocket. "He said he's familiar with the ritual to release his great-grandmother. He gave me the spell to counteract it." He pulled it out of Steven's reach before he could take it. "Not so fast. This spell is not going to be a cakewalk. It's going to require a lot of power."

"Meaning?" Steven asked.

"Meaning, like it or not, we have to work together. All three of us," he said as Ray returned to the room.

"I don't have a power," Steven said.

Malcolm smiled at him. "Trust me, you do. Your love for Sylvia is the reason she hasn't already been lost on the spirit plane. You're going to be her anchor."

Chapter Twenty-Three

Sylvia pulled at the chain with two hands, the metal cuffs scraping against her skin. She huffed out a breath and fell against the frame. "Dammit," she murmured.

She narrowed her eyes and took in the dark room around her. The sun had shifted to late afternoon, casting dim light through the boards. She couldn't see much of the house when Vincent opened the door, but she saw enough to realize she was in Angel's home.

She closed her eyes, trying to sense the spirits she'd felt the day she'd come to the house with Steven, but she couldn't feel anything. Whoever had been here before was no longer present. What did that mean?

The door opened, and Vincent stepped inside, holding a halogen lantern. The aroma of something burning filtered into the room—sage, rosemary, she couldn't quite make out the smells. He noticed the tray of untouched food and frowned.

"You didn't eat. Did you think I'd poison you? Or give you something that would make you sick?"

"I don't know what to think of you anymore," she returned.

He smiled at her. "You're looking at this all wrong, *bella*. You should be honored you were chosen to be the vessel."

"Go to hell," she spat.

Vincent laughed and moved toward the table. He stopped short, his lips thinning. "Where's the spoon, Sylvia?"

She swallowed hard, keeping her hand gripped around the worn stainless-steel spoon hidden behind her. She just needed him a little closer. She was pretty sure she could stab him with it if he just came a little closer.

Vincent's expression hardened. "Don't test me, Sylvia. You'll lose. Now, hand me the spoon."

She hesitated then flung the spoon in his direction. Vincent swatted it away and sent the utensil clinking against the floor.

He set the lantern on the end table then grabbed her arm, smiling when she flinched. After clasping the chain on her wrist, he grabbed both of her wrists and pinned them against the frame. He leaned in, his breath warm against her cheek.

"You're lucky she wants to keep you pure. But, I don't mind waiting. Once the transference is complete, you will be mine." He nipped her throat, chuckling when she pulled away.

Pure? She started to tell him she wasn't a virgin but decided against it. Maybe her not being a virgin will keep the spell from working.

"One more thing." Vincent pulled a knife from his pocket. He unclenched her fist and held her fingers flat before slicing the blade across her palm. Sylvia bit her lip against the burning pain as he picked up a brass bowl from the floor and dripped her blood into it.

She sneered at him. "You really think she's going to keep you around once she's free? She'll kill you as soon as she gets the chance. And if there's any part of me alive in her, I'll make sure she does."

He sent her an amused smile. "So much passion. It's what drew her to you. I can't wait to see what she does with it."

Before she could react, he took a syringe from his pocket and plunged the needle into her arm. Her skin chilled, as if he'd shot ice through her veins.

"What is that?"

"Something to help you relax." He stood and moved to the door. "I'll be back soon."

Sylvia swallowed hard against the dryness of her throat. Her palm stung, and blood dripped down her wrist.

He'd left the halogen lamp on the end table. It may not be a weapon, but it would be useful.

She settled against the headboard and closed her eyes. She didn't have much time before whatever drug he gave her kicked in, but, hopefully, it was enough to do what she needed to do.

***

Two Cameron County Sheriff vehicles were parked in front of Carla's house when Steven arrived. He'd called them as soon as he found the address in Sylvia's datebook and had the deputy secure the warrant.

The book Ray had given him was one of many Sylvia kept with a detailed record of every client she'd ever worked with since she was a teenager. The pages were tabbed alphabetically and included an address with driving instructions, a cell phone number, and the type of service she provided—tarot readings, *amparos*, and a few *mal puestas*. He wasn't quite sure how to feel about Sylvia's secret life. Or why she'd never mentioned it to him years ago?

Carla's house was a double-wide trailer set on a spot of land and surrounded by overgrown bushes and mesquite trees. The front yard was a mix of dirt and weed and a failed attempt at a garden alongside the front of the house.

Deputy Hernandez stood beside his car, speaking on his phone, when Steven pulled up. He ended his call and waited for Steven to meet at his vehicle.

"Doesn't look like anyone's here, so we searched the premises first," the deputy said before Steven could ask. "We found something you're going to want to see." He motioned for Steven to follow him to the rear of the house.

Several feet back, concealed by the growth of trees, was a rusted ten-by-ten windowless aluminum shed. The padlock on the front sliding doors had been cut off, but the doors were still closed.

"You might want to use this." The deputy handed him a folded red-and-white paisley bandana.

An officer stood several feet from the building, holding a bolt cutter. After a subtle nod from the deputy, he moved to the shed and slid open the door. A black cloud of flies flew out of the building followed by a strong stench that stopped Steven in his tracks.

"Jesus," he muttered, putting the cloth over his mouth and nose and inhaling the minty smell of vapor rub.

"I don't know what I expected to find, but it wasn't this." Deputy Hernandez turned on the flashlight he'd pulled from his utility belt and lit up the small room.

Pinned upside down on the walls were several animal carcasses—rabbits, goats and chickens. Hanging from the ceiling were rotted red and green peppers. Bolted to the wall beneath the remains were two thick chains with metal cuffs. The dried blood splattering the walls had darkened to near black. Another wall housed a four-legged butcherblock table with more darkened blood staining the countertop. Adjacent to the table sat a large cast-iron vat that looked like something from a Halloween display.

Steven took out his own flashlight and turned it on. Inside the vat was a small pool of black liquid and several human organs, including a brain and a heart.

He swallowed against the pressure in his throat. The condition of the organs in the pot and the dried blood told him the shed hadn't been used for several days. Which meant Sylvia had not been brought here.

"How soon can you get a team out here?"

"I made the call before you got here. CSU is on its way." They stepped out of the building, and the officer standing sentry slid the doors closed. "Our warrant includes the house, but we decided to wait on you before we breach it."

Steven nodded. "Let's do it."

The deputy signaled an officer who moved forward carrying a battering ram. Steven took position on one side of the door while Deputy Hernandez stood on the other side.

The officer connected the ram against the door with one hard swing, splintering the wood. Steven's heart dropped when he rounded the entry.

The house was empty.

***

The sun had nearly set by the time Steven returned to Sylvia's house. He let himself in through the back door and moved to the refrigerator for a bottle of water as Ray rounded the entrance from the living room.

"Sylvia?"

Steven shook his head. "She wasn't there. No one was there. The house had been cleared out."

"What about Carla?"

"Dead." Steven took a long drink of the water to wash the smell of death and vapor rub from his throat. They'd found Carla buried several feet from the shed. Her heart had been cut from her chest, but the ME couldn't, or wouldn't, say if it was the heart they'd found in the shed. Her usefulness to Vincent was done.

Malcolm stepped into the room. "You found something else though, didn't you? I can sense it on you. Something dark, worse than death."

He nodded and took out his phone to pull up the photos he'd taken. "We found a shed that looked like it had been used for rituals. The crime scene unit is processing it, but I'm pretty sure it's where Carla and the other victims were killed." He didn't miss Malcolm's tense reaction. "You know what this is?"

Malcolm hesitated, then said, "It's a *nganga*. A cauldron used for black magic. The magic he's using is called *Palo Mayombe*. It's a type of *Santeria*, except darker. Only a Palero priest has the power to run it."

"Terrific," Steven murmured.

"In a manner of speaking," Malcolm said, "A Palero priest uses a person's essence to feed his power. The more he has the stronger he can be. But there aren't very many who can complete the journey to become a priest. Which means, I may be able to find him."

"How?" Ray asked.

Malcolm grinned and wandered to the stove. "With magic, of course." He rummaged through the cabinets above the stove.

Steven frowned. "What are you doing?"

"Getting the supplies I need." Malcolm pulled out bottles of spices and lined them up on the counter. "While you were gone, I found a brazier and some myrrh oil in the bathroom. If Sylvia has the herbs I need, then I can make a spell that will find the Palero, which—if she's with him—finds Sylvia." He peered out the window above the sink. "Bingo. I wish I'd known sooner she was a witch."

"She's not a witch," Steven and Ray said simultaneously.

Malcolm looked at them, his brow raised. "If you say so." He lifted the window and grabbed several of the potted plants then turned to Ray. "Between the two of us, we should be able to locate the house of the dead. As long as you do as I say."

"The house of the dead?" Ray replied.

"It's where Paleros keep their bound spirits. If he's planning to open a portal to release my great-great-grandmother, then he's harvesting a lot of souls. Most clairvoyants, like myself, like your sister, can sense spirits. If we find them, we find her."

Steven followed as Malcolm returned to the living room and set the items he'd gathered on the floor in the same spot Sylvia had used when she did her ritual. "How are you planning to do that?"

"We're going to ask the dead." Malcolm sat on the floor and motioned Ray to sit.

"You're going to what?" Steven held up a hand and shook his head. "Never mind, I don't want to know."

He returned to the kitchen and sat at the table. The binder Ray had found in the chest at the foot of Sylvia's bed was sitting atop his files. Aside from the date books, she also kept another binder detailing their investigation. The pages were just as thorough as his notes, but more in-depth.

He turned to the report she'd written up after their trip to Angel's house.

There was no sign of Angel in her house. Maybe she hadn't lived there long enough to fill the house with her essence. According to the realtor she'd bought the house from, the house had been vacant for nearly twenty years. It had once been used as a drop house for coyotes until border patrol raided it. I noticed a malodorous smell as soon as I walked in. Steven didn't smell it, of course, but it was strong. As if the house had been used for more than storing bodies. With the amount of souls I felt when I walked inside, it's no wonder her home smelled of death.

He pushed the book aside and covered his face with his hands. "I need some air," he murmured.

A cool breeze whispered over him as he stepped out the back door. Thin, gray clouds had gathered throughout the day, sheening the moon. The rhythmic chirp of tree crickets and katydids cut through the silence of the night.

Sylvia had been gone nearly twenty-four hours, and if Malcolm was to be believed, they were running out of time to find her.

Steven sat on the concrete step and rubbed his hands over his face, pulling in a heavy breath. This was all his fault. He should never have involved her in the investigation. He should never have left her alone. He should have kept her close.

His gut told him she was in danger. If he had just listened to his instincts, she'd be here now instead of.... He stopped the thought before it could visualize in his head. He'd never forgive himself if something happened to her.

He looked absently at the darkened clouds, frustration burning his chest. "Where the hell are you, Sylvia?"

A gust of wind blew through the air, carrying with it the sweet, floral scent of roses and strawberries.

Steven!

His heart jolted at the sound of Sylvia's voice.

Movement in the trees caught his attention. He stood and narrowed his eyes to study the area. "Sylvia?"

A shapeless blur burst from the branches and rushed at him. He braced, waiting for the impact. The specter hit him like a strong gust of wind, but instead of whisking over him, it went through him. His body chilled and tiny spasms trembled his muscles as if he'd been connected to live wires. Images flickered across his mind and he felt as if he were slowly moving through scenes in a movie.

Bolts of electricity slashed against the black sky.

Angel's house, dark and empty on a patch of dirt.

A dimly lit room.

A wood table encircled by various sized candles on the floor.

He stopped at an open doorway. Sylvia sat on a bed with her wrists shackled to the frame. Her terrified brown eyes locked onto his.

Steven! I'm here!

A tall, lean, figure wearing a red cloak appeared across the room. Crimson eyes locked onto him from beneath the hood.

Before Steven's mind could register the movement, the figure charged at him. The specter slammed into him with the force of a three-hundred-pound linebacker and knocked the wind from his lungs. His knees buckled and dropped him to the ground on his hands and knees.

Steven gasped in air, trying to catch his breath. His arms quivered, and a headache pounded against his temples. He eased himself onto the steps and waited for his pulse to steady.

"Son of a bitch." What the hell was that? He rubbed a hand on his chest and tried to focus on what he'd seen during his...hallucination was the only word he could come up with, but he couldn't get the images to form.

"Steven," Ray's voice sounded from the doorway and made him jolt. "Malcolm said he has something."

He gave himself another moment to make sure he was steady then followed Ray into the kitchen. Malcolm sat at the table, holding a photo from Steven's files.

"Here." Malcolm passed the photo across the table. "This is the house of the dead. It's where the Palero is."

Steven took the photo. The image of Sylvia chained to a bed flashed across his mind. *I'm here.* "What makes you think they're here?"

Malcolm cocked his head with a knowing look, his lips curved. "Same reason you do."

"You know this place?" Ray asked.

"It's Angel Salazar's house. It's about two miles outside of Mathis."

Ray grabbed his keys from the counter. "Let's go."

Steven pulled out his cellphone. "I'm going to call the San Patricio County sheriff and have him meet us there."

"I wouldn't do that if I were you," Malcolm said. "Do you really want to explain to the sheriff what he could be walking into?"

Ray frowned and looked at Steven. "I hate to agree with him, but he's right."

"Regardless what you two believe, I'm not going in without backup."

"You're not. I'm going with you," Ray said.

"Ray, you're getting married in two days—"

"And Sylvia is going to be there," Ray said firmly. "You can argue all you want, but that's my sister this bastard has. Nothing is going to stop me from helping her."

Steven nodded toward Malcolm. "What about him?"

"I'm going, too." Malcolm stood. "I'm not about to let you screw me out of getting my family's power back." He looked toward at the living room. "I'm going to need some things from my hotel room before we go."

Steven checked the time on his watch. It would be midnight before they reached Angel's house, which meant they would have the element of surprise. He just hoped to hell they weren't wrong about Sylvia being there.

Chapter Twenty-Four

"Steven!" Sylvia awoke with a start. The house was gone, and so were her shackles. Like her vision the week before, she was surrounded by a thicket of tall dry trees. A gray fog swirled along the ground, withered bodies moaning softly, reaching up as if begging for nourishment.

She took a step forward, kicking up the mist and strained her eyes to see beyond the trees. Light flickered behind dark clouds, offering dim light to the woods.

A shape appeared in the distance and sent a chill skittering across her neck.

"Hello? *Bisabuela*, is that you?"

In an instant, the figure materialized in front of her. It was dressed in a red, hooded cloak, its face a grotesque mask of rotting flesh.

Before Sylvia could get away, the figure grabbed her by the throat and yanked her forward. Fear, shock, and panic collided like a wrecking ball in her chest. She grabbed on to the figure's arms in a weak attempt to loosen the hold, rising to her toes for support as the demon lifted her from the ground. Sharp pain lanced her chest, but she couldn't cry out. Her lungs constricted as if the life were being pulled from her.

As quickly as it appeared, the figure vanished into a black cloud. Sylvia fell to the ground on her hands and knees, coughing and gasping to fill her lungs with air.

"Drink this, quickly." A woman appeared beside her and handed

Sylvia a small goblet, her warm-brown eyes offering comfort. "It will help."

Sylvia hesitated then swallowed the liquid. It was syrupy and tart like a lemon drop and soothed the rawness of her throat. "Thank you."

The woman curled an arm around her waist to help her stand. "Can you walk?"

Sylvia nodded, but the woman had already started ushering her forward.

The bodies on the ground groaned and wailed, reaching out with bony fingers as they wove through the trees. The mist thickened, rising from the ground until they were cloaked by gray fog.

"Hold on to me." Within seconds the fog vanished and they were standing in the middle of a cornfield, fresh green stalks waving in the breeze.

The woman held Sylvia at arm's length to look her over. "Are you okay?"

"Yes, I think so. Thank you." Sylvia did her own inspection of the woman. She was in her late twenties with dark-brown hair that fell in waves to her shoulder. She wore a cream-colored gown that flowed above bare feet.

"Who are you?" Sylvia asked. Overhead an eagle screamed, its great shadow moving across the corn. She swallowed her panic and glanced around. "Where are we?"

"My name is Soledad. I was sent to help. We're between worlds right now. I was able to get you here, but I don't know for how long."

"Get me here from where? How?" Sylvia followed the woman through the maze. The last thing she remembered was Vincent injecting her with a drug and her attempt to project her spirit to

Steven.

"The man who imprisoned you is a Palero priest. He is using a blood spell to bind your spirit, so he can transfer it to the Galicia witch during the lunar eclipse."

Sylvia touched a finger to her palm where Vincent had cut her and swallowed her unease. Vincent had already told her his plan, but it didn't make it any less terrifying. "We have twelve hours, right? We can reverse this. Get me back before the eclipse."

Soledad's grim expression froze Sylvia in her steps. Has she been gone longer than she thought?

"It's started already, hasn't it?"

"Which means time is running out. The witch can move between planes and has been doing this for many years to gather her strength."

Sylvia glanced toward the field, the image of the ghostly mist flashing across her mind. "The souls on the ground. She's already drained them?"

Soledad nodded.

"So, how many more souls will she need before she can leave her prison?

"It is not the amount of souls she needs, but the one she wants. The essence of a powerful witch. You're cloaked right now, but I don't know for how much longer. Come on. We need to move." The woman started walking again, moving through the corn with purpose.

"I'm cloaked? Hold on a minute." Sylvia grabbed the woman's arm and stopped her. "I am not a witch."

The woman frowned. "Being a witch is not a bad thing."

"No, of course not. I didn't mean to imply that. It's just...is that why she wants to use me as a vessel? Because she thinks I'm a witch?"

The woman cocked her head with a puzzled expression. "Because you are a witch. It's in your blood. The first daughter of the first daughter for many generations were powerful witches. You should have been taught this as a child. Didn't your mother—?

"My parents died when I was a child," Sylvia said.

"I'm sorry." The woman frowned and resumed walking. "I wish I could explain all of this to you now, but like I said, we don't have much time."

They reached the edge of the trees and stepped out to a vacant patch of land. A mile away stood a dilapidated wooden shack.

"What is that place?" Sylvia asked.

"It's the house of souls. It has what you need to make a spell that will open the portal and return you to your body. You must get through before the sun passes over the moon." She turned to Sylvia. "Do you know how to run a spell?"

"Sure. More or less," she said. "What happens if I don't make it out before the eclipse is finished?"

The woman frowned. "You can never go home."

Sylvia thought of her family—her grandparents, her brother, and Lexie. She thought of Steven and the life they could have. She cast a firm look at the woman and shook her head. "That's not going to happen." She quickened her steps and headed for the house. Behind them, the sky darkened with black clouds, causing the hair at the nape of her neck to bristle.

The shack looked even older up close. It was a square, wooden building with a porch that extended from one end of the house to the other. The steps were warped, the deck worn and splintered in several places. Dust and grime covered the pane glass windows where thin, eyelet lace curtains were hanging inside.

Sylvia pushed the front door open, the wood scrapping against the floor. It took her a moment longer to get it closed as the floorboards were also warped.

The inside of the house was as old as the outside and smelled of dirt and must. The meager furniture consisted of an old wooden rocker, a pedestal coffee table and a loveseat with metal springs sticking out of the fabric.

"The kitchen is this way. I will stay and help you as long as I can." As she spoke, the woman moved to the kitchen and pulled open cabinets to gather small mason jars. "There is a wardrobe mirror in the bedroom. Bring it in here and set it up on that wall."

Sylvia hurried to the adjoining room. The iron frame bed with the thin mattress made her pause. She spotted an oval wardrobe mirror stationed in the corner of the room. She stepped forward and stroked a finger over the tarnished, silver frame. Mirrors were often used as conduits to other dimensions. Spirits could also be contained and imprisoned within the glass. She hoped to hell she made it home before it happened to her.

The light in the living room dimmed as the clouds moved in closer. Sylvia positioned the mirror in the center of the room. "I have the mirror. What now?"

The woman stood at the kitchen table, pouring the contents of several mason jars into a bowl. "This mixture will help you to move into the mirror world. Once you are through, find the shack much like this one. The mirror is there. You will need to repeat the mix and the incantation to open the portal." Soledad handed her a knife, her expression grave. "I warded this to help you, in case you run into trouble. Do whatever it takes to stop her from finding the other mirror. All of our souls depend on it."

Sylvia weighed the blade in her hand then tucked it into her pocket. "I will."

She took the bowl and drank the contents. The light dimmed in the room, the world outside turning black. She repeated the words Soledad murmured in Spanish. The room chilled as if she'd walked into a large refrigerator. She opened her eyes. The house was gone, and she stood in the middle of a thicket of dead trees.

A cold chill iced its way down her spine. She spun around, fighting against the panic tightening her chest.

The witch stood before her, a feral smile curving her lips. "I've been waiting for you." Her hand struck out and gripped around Sylvia's neck, yanking her forward.

Her lungs closed as she fought for air. Pain stabbed her chest, her body weakening as the ache increased. Reaching behind her, she pulled out the knife and sliced it across the witch's cheek. The woman howled out a scream and staggered back, dropping Sylvia to the ground. When she glanced up, the witch was gone.

Sylvia staggered to her feet and ran for the edge of the woods, her chest heaving painfully with each step. Thankfully, whatever Soledad did to the knife, it worked.

She stopped at the edge of the thicket to catch her breath and spotted the wooden shack in the distance. She pressed a fist against the ache in her chest. The witch had ripped out a piece of her essence but, thankfully, not all of it. Unfortunately, what little she took was enough to see into Sylvia's mind.

Which meant the witch knew where the portal was located.

***

David's truck was parked along the shoulder of the road when they arrived. Since David was part of the investigation, Steven called him for backup.

"Why are we stopping here?" Ray asked as soon as he climbed out of his truck.

"The road is filled with ruts and loose gravel. I don't want to chance him hearing us coming. We'll have to walk. And no flashlights," he said when Ray turned on the light he held. "We'll have to make our way using the light from the moon." Footsteps crunching on the gravel sounded behind them. Steven pivoted and withdrew his gun. "Jesus," he muttered when David appeared out of the dark.

David lifted his hands. "Woah, it's just me." He moved forward as Steven tucked his gun away. "I went down to check out the house. See what we were up against."

"And?"

"Far as I could tell, only one in the front room of the house. The windows are boarded up, so I couldn't see into any of the other rooms."

Malcolm came forward, adjusting a backpack on his shoulder. "Could you see what was happening?"

David gave him a scrutinizing look. "No, but I heard chanting."

"That means he's starting the ritual." Malcolm handed each man a small canvas bag. "Here. Put these in your pocket."

Steven weighed the bag in his palm. "What is this?"

"It's angelica root. I found it in Sylvia's pantry. It's for protection." Malcolm glanced toward the road. "There's some strong magic down there. You're going to need all the help you can get."

Steven tucked the bag in the front pocket of his jeans. At this point, he wasn't going to argue. He moved with David to his SUV and pulled out two Kevlar vests.

"What's the plan?" Ray asked.

"David and I will go in. You two stay out of the way until I give you the clear to come in." He turned to David as he finished strapping on the vest. "Let's go."

***

Sylvia staggered up the steps to the house, fatigue weakening her muscles. She pushed her body as hard as she could against the door. Wood scraped against wood as the door finally gave. She noted everything in the room was the same as the other house, except it was backward.

"Like looking in a mirror," she murmured. Behind her, thunder rumbled as dark clouds rolled toward the shack. She leaned against the door, using her weight to push it closed.

She hurried to the kitchen, flinging open cabinet doors until she found the mason jars. The wind kicked up outside, dirt and rocks pelting the building. She scooped up the supplies and a wooden bowl and carried them into the bedroom. A sheet had been draped over the mirror. She pulled it off and froze. Vincent stood on the other side, wearing a black cloak and surrounded by candles. A body covered in blood lay unconscious on a table beside him. It took her a moment to realize it was her.

Thunder boomed like an explosion, rattling the building. She spun around as the door burst open, splinters of wood flying across the room. The witch stepped inside.

"Thank you for your help. You belong to me now."

***

Steven led the way down the narrow road, staying close to edge where the ground was more stable. Dim light from the moon filtered through the canopy of trees, giving just enough light to make out the road.

When they reached the edge of the woods, they veered to the left of the house to where the only window faced the living room. A gust of hot air blew through the trees. Dark clouds bunched in the sky, streaks of lightning zigzagging over them, the static raising the hair on his arms.

Steven pressed against the side of the house and peered through the slats of wood covering the window. Angel's meager furniture was gone, the empty house seeming larger without the pieces. Several black candles were placed on the floor, the dancing flames casting large shadows along the walls.

A tall figure wearing a black, hooded cloak, stood with his back to the window. Across from him was a full-length mirror. In the reflection, Steven recognized Vincent. He stood beside a long table and held a wide-mouthed goblet. His eyes were closed, and his lips were moving as he murmured something Steven couldn't hear. When Vincent shifted, Steven saw another reflection that set his blood cold. Sylvia lay prone atop the table, each wrist locked by her side in iron cuffs that were bolted into the wood.

He swallowed hard and bit down on his panic. She was alive. He had to believe she was alive.

"What do you see?" David asked.

"Looks like only one suspect, but Sylvia is inside. She's chained on a table at the far side of the room."

"Any weapons?"

"Not that I could see," Steven said. "It looks like he's meditating or something. I don't think he'll hear us breach."

"Let's do it."

Steven took out his gun and moved onto the porch and waited for David to move to the opposite side of the door. The light of the moon dimmed. He looked up to see the black spot moving across the moon. The eclipse had started.

He lifted a hand and slowly turned the doorknob. It wasn't locked.

He nodded to David then swung the door open and rounded the frame. "Police! Put your hands where I can see them!"

Vincent spun around, one hand raised and blood dripping from his fingers. Steven's gaze landed on Sylvia, and every cell in his body froze. She was dressed in a cream-colored sleeveless gown, the bodice opened to form a V. Blood covered her chest and arms and spilled down her temple. It took him a moment to realize Vincent had smeared the blood onto her.

The momentary distraction blinded him to the movement in the room. Before he could react, a hard punch rammed his chest. He slammed against the far wall, his gun falling to the floor with a clatter.

Through the ringing in his ears, he heard David's voice and the unmistakable pop of a gun. He glanced up to see David aiming his gun and Vincent jerking back as the bullet hit him in the upper shoulder. With a sweep of his hand Vincent sent David sailing through the door and tumbling off the porch.

Steven shook off his daze and searched for his gun.

Heavy footsteps sounded on the wood, and the room filled with a bright light.

Malcolm charged into the room, calling out in a language Steven didn't understand. Before Vincent could react, Malcolm barreled into him, throwing him against the wall. He pulled a knife from the waist of his pants and plunged it into Vincent's stomach. Vincent's eyes widened, his hands coming up in a weak attempt to push Malcolm away. His breath hitched then his eyes went flat. Malcolm stepped back and let Vincent slide down to the floor, blood smearing the wall behind him.

"Sylvia!" Ray charged into the room and rushed to his sister. He placed two fingers on her throat then took her hand in his. "It's okay, little sister. It's me. It's Ray. Wake up, honey." He turned to Malcolm. "We need to get these cuffs off."

Malcolm grabbed the backpack he'd dropped on the floor when he'd come into the house. "I can take care of her. You go help your friend. Looks like he took a pretty hard hit."

Ray paused then glanced at Steven as he braced his hand on the wall to stand. He rushed forward and wrapped an arm around Steven's waist to help him stand. "Hey, buddy. You okay?"

"Sylvia?"

"She's okay. I think. The blood.... it's not hers. He must have used a drug or something to knock her out, but she's breathing."

Steven rubbed the back of his head and winced when he felt the knot. "David?"

"Got the wind knocked out of him, too, but I'll go check make sure he's all right. You sure you're okay?"

Steven nodded, regretting the movement when his head started to pound. "I'm good. Have him call in for backup."

Steven picked up his gun then moved toward the front room as Ray headed out. Malcolm was facing the table where his backpack sat open on the floor.

Steven glanced at Malcolm's mirrored reflection. He was holding the globe from Sylvia's dresser in one hand and a knife in the other. His eyes were closed, and he was murmuring something much like Vincent had been doing.

Steven lifted his gun and pointed. "Drop it!" Malcolm continued his chant. "Don't think I won't shoot you. Drop the knife!"

Malcolm met his eyes in the mirror. "You don't understand. It's the only way." He swung his hand up. Steven fired.

"Son of a bitch!" Malcolm dropped the knife and clutched a hand over his biceps.

Steven rushed forward and kicked the knife away, keeping his gun trained on Malcolm. "It's a flesh wound. You'll live. Turn around." He pressed Malcolm's face against the wall and snapped the handcuffs on his wrists as Ray ran into the room.

"I heard shots. What happened?"

Steven picked up the knife. The blade was about six inches long and set in a wood handle that was carved with intricate designs. "He was planning to kill her. With this."

Ray lunged for Malcolm, but Steven grabbed onto him before he could strike. "You son of a bitch! I knew we couldn't trust you!"

"You don't understand. It's the only way to save her!"

Steven spun Malcolm around and pinned him against the wall. "What are you talking about?"

"Ray? Let me out." Sylvia writhed on the table, the iron on her wrists knocking against the wood. "They hurt. Get them off me!"

Ray moved to the table. "Hold on. I'll find the key."

"No key. It's just a pin. Take out the pin."

Malcolm tried to pull away from Steven. "Don't do it! It's not her! That's not Sylvia!"

Ray pulled the pin from one cuff and moved around the table to open the other side. As soon as he opened the second cuff, Sylvia jumped from the table and grabbed him by the throat. She pinned him to the wall, her gaze roaming over him. "Power. You have power." Her voice sounded deep and gravelly.

Ray grabbed her wrists, her name choking from his lips as he tried to loosen her hold.

Steven rushed forward and tried to pull her away as Ray gasped for air. "Sylvia!"

She turned her head and glared at him. Her eyes beamed red and fierce. A force pushed against him and knocked him to the ground at Malcolm's feet.

"The knife," Malcolm whispered. "You have to stab her with the knife. Trust me. That isn't Sylvia. Sylvia is in there!" He gestured toward the mirror.

Steven looked at the full-length mirror in the corner. Mist swirled around on the other side of the glass. Sylvia materialized in the fog, her hands flat against the pane. She threw a glance over her shoulder then turned, terror filling her eyes, and begin to frantically hit the glass.

Although he couldn't hear her, he saw her lips moving, calling out his name.

"The knife! Stab her with the knife," Malcolm hissed. "Before the eclipse is over!"

Steven grabbed the knife and rushed up behind Sylvia. He curled an arm around her waist and yanked hard, but her grip stayed wrapped around Ray's neck.

Tears burned Steven's throat as he readied the knife. "I'm sorry. I'm so sorry, baby. I love you." He plunged the knife into her lower back praying with everything he had that he didn't hit any major organs. The handle of the blade warmed against his palm, a current shooting up his arm as if he'd touched a live wire.

Sylvia screamed, her hand falling away from Ray. He fell to the floor, coughing and wheezing as he tried to fill his lungs with air.

"Hold her tight. The blade has to stay in until it's done!" Malcolm said.

Steven wrapped both arms around Sylvia and dropped with her to the floor. He gripped the knife and held Sylvia tight against him. She bucked, fighting to get away, and howling like a wounded animal.

Outside lightening flashed like a strobe light and thunder boomed, shuddering the house. A black mist filled the room, the malodorous smell of death coming with it. The mirror shattered, sending shards of glass flying. Steven tucked Sylvia against him and shielded her with his body as pelts of glass struck his vest.

Sylvia's hand came up and touched his arm. "Steven." Her voice sounded weak.

He shifted and cradled her in the crook of his arm. "Sylvia, baby, you're okay. You're going to be okay."

"H...hurts."

"I know, just hold on. You've been stabbed. I'm going to remove the knife. I just need you to stay still." He pulled in a calming breath then he curled his fingers around the sheath and slid the knife free. She cried out. He kissed her forehead and pressed his hand over the wound. Blood, warm and sticky, spilled between his fingers and spread over the fabric of her clothes. "I'm sorry, baby. But it's out now. Hey, keep your eyes open. Stay with me." He brushed a kiss over her cheek and fought to slow his racing pulse. "You're going to be fine. Stay with me, Syl."

Her eyes opened and locked on to his. Her lips moved as if she wanted to speak.

Then her body went limp.

"Sylvia? Sylvia!" He shook her gently then pressed his fingers to her throat. "No. No. Please...baby, no..." He tilted her head back, placing his lips on hers to blow a breath into her. "Come, on. Breath. Don't do this." He blew in several more puffs, touching two fingers to her neck to check for a pulse. With a choked sob, he pulled her against him. "I'm sorry. I'm so sorry."

Ray crawled forward and took his sister's hand in his. "Sylvia?"

Steven looked at Ray as his heart shattered. "She's dead."

Chapter Twenty-Five

Ray scrambled up and lunged at Malcolm. "You son of a bitch! You planned this! You knew this was going to happen!" He landed a punch to Malcolm's jaw before Malcolm was able to kick out and knock him away.

"I couldn't tell you. But I can help her. Take these off me and let me help her." He sent Steven a beseeching look. "You have to believe me. I can help her."

Steven reached into his jacket and pulled out the keys then quickly unlocked one cuff.

Malcolm scurried to the side of the table and grabbed his backpack. "Set her on the table."

As Steven lifted Sylvia onto the table, Malcolm plucked another knife out of the bag along with some gauze pads and a small black container the size of baby food jar.

"Give me your hand," he said, reaching out to Steven.

"What?"

"Your hand. Give me your hand!" Malcolm grabbed Steven's wrist and yanked it forward. "Trust me," he said when Steven tried to pull it away.

He slid the blade across Steven's palm, cutting a six-inch gash into his flesh. Before he could react, Malcolm opened the jar and scooped out a black tar-like substance and spread it over the wound. The mixture smelled sweet and floral and warmed his skin on contact.

"Press it to the wound. To her wound and press it tight!" Malcolm said.

As Steven did what he was told, Malcolm cut the blade across his own palm and squeezed, dripping the blood into the brazier he'd taken from Sylvia's house. He pulled a small pouch from his pocket with his free hand and poured the contents into the bowl. Then, he grabbed one of the candles and touched the flame to the mixture. Smoke billowed up from the bowl, a rancid odor floating into the air. Malcolm waved the smoke over Sylvia's body and murmured in a language Steven didn't understand.

He looked down at Sylvia, blinking against the blur of tears. He stroked his hand over her cheek then lowered his forehead to hers, willing her to come back to him. Her skin felt cold. So cold.

His pulse thundered in his ears, pieces of his heart chipping away with each beat. She couldn't be gone. This couldn't be their end.

He pressed a kiss to her lips. "Come back to me, baby. Please, God, come back to me. I love you, Sylvia. I need you." He straightened as David ran into the room.

"Steven! Backup's on its way. I have an ambulance in route." David stopped short when he saw Sylvia. "Is she—"

Sylvia bolted up with a sharp intake of air, knocking Steven back a step.

"Steven!"

He grabbed on to her and held her tightly against him. "You came back to me. Oh God, I thought I'd lost you." She threw her arms around him and burrowed into him. He couldn't tell which of them was trembling more.

When he was sure he could speak, he pulled back and looked into her eyes. "It's you, right?"

Sylvia gave him a short laugh and nodded. "Yeah. It's me." She winced when Malcolm stepped beside her and taped gauze to her wound. "Ouch."

"Sorry," Malcolm said as she twisted to inspect her injury. "Your boyfriend stabbed you."

She locked her gaze on Steven and smiled. "He saved me."

Ray moved to the table and pulled Sylvia into a hug. "Sorry," he said, when she winced.

She touched his throat. "I'd say we're even. I'm sorry, too."

He shook his head. "It wasn't you. You scared the shit out of me, little sister. I thought we'd lost you."

"You can't get rid of me that easily." She pulled him into a hug. "I love you, big brother."

"Sounds like the sheriff's almost here," David said as the sirens wailed in the distance.

"That would be my cue to leave." Malcolm grabbed his pack and shoved the supplies back inside. He searched the floor then looked at Steven and held out his hand. "My knife, please?"

Steven glared at him. "You killed a man. It's evidence."

Malcolm glanced at Vincent's body and shrugged. "Better him than us."

"The power is in the knife," Sylvia said.

"It is," Malcolm answered. "The Palero had to absorb it into you first, instead of her, in order to complete the transference, because you aren't a virgin." He looked at Steven with a wry smile. "Good job on that one."

Sylvia spoke before Steven could comment. "So, what happened to your great-great-grandmother?"

Malcolm glanced at the broken mirror frame. "Tossed back in the portal, for now. She'll be someone else's problem in about a hundred and fifty years. Now, if you don't mind?" He held his hand out again.

Sylvia took hold of Steven's hand. "I promised him." She turned to Malcolm. "A deal's a deal."

Steven lifted their joined hands to his lips and placed a kiss on her fingers. "Okay," he said. He nodded toward where he'd left the knife. Malcolm moved around him and picked up the blade. He held it in his hand a moment, as if checking the weight then smiled and placed it in his backpack.

"Malcolm?" Sylvia spoke before he could leave. "Thank you."

Malcolm winked at her then hitched the bag on his shoulder and walked out into the night.

***

Sylvia awoke with a start and a hint of panic. She gave herself a moment to steady her pulse then sat up. Soft light filtered in through the miniblinds and a chorus of birds, who'd made their home in the tree next to her bedroom window, chirped their morning greeting.

She was home, in her own bed—she glanced to the left side of the bed—and alone.

As if she'd willed Steven to her, the bedroom door opened. She tried not to show her disappointment when Ray walked in

"You're awake." He closed the door behind him and moved to sit on the bed.

"How long have I been out?"

He glanced at his watch. "About five hours. How's the wound?" He turned her and peeled back the fresh bandage, so he could inspect the cut. He nodded. "Looks like it's healing well."

"It's fine. Doesn't hurt...much. How'd I get here? I mean, when?

Last thing I remember is going to the hospital and them sewing me up."

"You told them you weren't going to stay so they released you. I knew you'd prefer to be in your own bed, so I brought you home. I stayed over and took the guestroom."

She didn't want to ask but she did. "Where's Steven?"

"He headed back to Austin."

"Of course, he did," she murmured.

He took her hand and squeezed. "Hey, he'll be back."

"I know. For your wedding."

"For you. He loves you, Sis. I heard him tell you, and I saw how much it tore him up when we almost lost you." He closed his eyes as if to give himself a moment to steady himself. "You scared the hell out of me, Sylvia. I don't know what I would have done if...."

She placed her hand over his. "I know. I'm sorry. But I'm fine. I'm here." She waited a moment then said, "I'm a witch, Ray."

He gave her a half smile. "Well, you can be difficult and opinionated, definitely stubborn, but I wouldn't call you a bitch."

She slapped at his arm. "I said witch. When I was in the portal, or between worlds, there was a woman there. I don't know who she was, but she said I was a witch. That the women in our family are witches."

He gave her a thoughtful look. "Well, it would certainly explain a lot."

She frowned. "Steven is not going to want to come back to that."

"Look, after what happened, what Steven saw, I don't think you need to worry about how he feels toward magic, anymore. But I'll be happy to kick his ass for you if he hurts you."

She smiled at him since she knew he was both kidding and serious.

"You should speak to Grandma about the witch thing, though," he said. "She would know. She's...uh...making lunch right now."

A hint of panic sparked inside her. "You called them?" She glanced at the door. "How upset are they with me?"

"On a scale of one to ten?" He sent her a commiserating smile. "They're just happy you're here and safe."

Lexie's voice outside the door made her brace. She didn't sound angry, but she didn't sound pleased either. Sylvia pulled in a breath and exhaled slowly. "I guess I should get it over with."

"I love you, little sister." Ray pressed a kiss to her forehead, lingering a moment before standing. "I'll let them know you're awake."

Sylvia stole a look at the empty side of the bed and fought back the tears. She knew Steven loved her and he promised to return, at least for the wedding. But she couldn't shake the feeling that he didn't plan to stay.

***

Sylvia smoothed her skirt and checked herself in the wardrobe mirror. The bridesmaid dress Lexie had chosen was a stylish, short, and chic sleeveless mesh dress with a round neckline. It cascaded on one side and had a pleated back shaped like a diamond. Thankfully, it covered the flesh tone bandage on her wound. Although Sylvia had balked at the color, she decided the mint green wasn't so bad.

Lexie's sister walked into the dressing room the church had designated for the bridal party. She was ten years older than Lexie, petite, with short black hair that fringed her shoulder. She wore the same type of dress as Sylvia except in soft pink.

"The guests are still arriving, the photographer is set up, and the groom is looking super-hot. We have twenty minutes to liftoff." Rebecca lifted a bottle and beamed. "And we have champagne."

Sylvia turned and smiled. "I won't say no to champagne."

Rebecca held the bottle and narrowed her eyes. "Are you okay to drink?"

"I think that question is redundant," Lexie said as she entered the room. She went still, her expression panicked when they turned to look at her. "What? What's wrong?"

Sylvia blinked against her tears. The dress was a light cream-colored A-line gown, with a lace bodice and a pleated waistband. Lexie had left her hair down, the sides pinned up with silver clips. She'd decided not to wear a veil. "Oh, Lexie. You're beautiful. My mother would be so proud to see you in her dress."

"Don't." Lexie waved her hand in front of her face. "Don't make me cry. It took forever to get my makeup right."

A knock sounded on the door as Rebecca filled their glasses.

"I'll get it." Sylvia moved to the door. "Ray, this better not be you trying to get a peek," she said as she opened the door. She froze. Her pulse kicked into warp speed and took her breath with it.

Steven stood in front of her. He wore a fitted black tuxedo with satin edges and a black bowtie. A red rose was pinned to his lapel.

Before she could speak he pulled her forward and into a kiss. She felt the emotion in it; the fear, the love, the want. Her pulse raced, throbbing the wound on her back. A short cry escaped her lips when his arm circled her waist to pull her closer. He loosened his hold and eased back.

"I'm sorry. Your wound. How is it?" He gently ran a hand over the bandage.

"It's fine. Abuela put some salve on it. It's just a little tender."

He cupped her face and kissed he again. "I missed you"

She looked at him through the blur of tears. "I didn't think you were coming back."

He brushed a tear from her cheek. "I'm sorry. I wanted to call, but I've had a lot to take care of before I could come back." He stopped, his gaze shifting to the door as it swung open. "Lexie." He stared at her a moment then said, "Wow. You look beautiful."

Lexie stepped to him and pulled him into a fierce hug. "Thank you," she said through a choked sob. "Thank you for bringing my family home safely."

Steven glanced at Sylvia as if unsure how to answer.

"Makeup, Lex," Sylvia said.

Lexie moved back with a laugh and gently wiped at her eyes. "Right. But it's worth it. I'll leave you two alone." She took his hand and gently squeezed. "Steven, thank you."

Steven kissed her hand then waited until she'd returned to the room before turning his gaze to Sylvia. "We need to talk."

The four words sent a cold chill of dread skittering through her body. They never meant anything good.

He took her hand and led her to a bench seat at the end of the hall.

"Did you get into a lot of trouble because of what happened at Angel's house?" she asked.

"Nothing I can't handle. It's going to take a while to get it situated but it'll be fine. I have to head back first thing tomorrow." He placed a finger under her chin and lifter her face up to look at him. "I want you to come with me. I called your supervisor, and he said you have the

266

next two weeks off," he said before she could reply.

She blinked at him. "Two weeks? I can't take off two weeks. With Lexie on her honeymoon, I have to cover her shift, and Gabe is already working overtime because we're short a carrier and—"

He kissed her to stop her talking. "It's covered." He closed his hands over hers and held as if he thought she would vanish. "Sylvia, when you died....my world crumbled. I could already feel myself shut down; my mind, my heart, my very soul. I'd never felt so lost, so broken as I did when you...."

She reached up and stroked the tear that had spilled down his cheek. "Steven. I'm here now. Everything is fine. It's all okay."

He kissed their joined hands and locked his gaze on hers. "I lost ten years with you because I was a fool. I didn't want to admit I was in love with you then because I didn't think I deserved you.

"But I did love you. I do love you. With everything inside me, I love you. I don't think I'll ever be deserving of you, but I want to spend the rest of my life trying."

She lifted a brow and studied him. "The rest of your life? That's a pretty long time to commit."

"Not long enough. Marry me."

She stared at him then took the chance and read him. She saw it, inside him, inside his heart. Love and need colored his emotions like golden sparks of sunburst.

His fingers tightened around hers, as if he thought she'd say no. She sent him a wry smile then gripped his jacket and pulled him forward.

"Took you long enough," she said, then crushed her mouth to his.

Also by Terri Molina
An Excerpt from Forget Me Not

Chapter One

The suits gave them away. Standard black linen. Crisp white shirt. Dependable black tie. FBI agents. At her front door. At eight o'clock in the morning.

This can't be good.

Casey adjusted the thin robe covering her even thinner teddy and pasted on a bright smile. "Good morning," she said, resisting the urge to cringe at the overly perky tone in her voice.

"Casey Martinez?" The older of the two men spoke, his gaze looking her over as if committing her to memory.

"Yes, I'm Casey Martinez." Although there was nothing sexual in his perusal, she rechecked her robe to make sure it was closed.

"I'm Special Agent John Simms. This is Special Agent Darryl Hawthorne." In unison they removed their wallets and opened them to reveal a gold badge and picture ID.

She blinked at the stoic men blocking her doorway, her mind spinning with reasons for their visit. Her latest novel had been set at the FBI academy in Quantico, Virginia, but she was sure she didn't write anything in the book that would offend the government. It was romance fiction, not a tell-all.

"May we come in, please?" Agent Simms asked, though it sounded more like an order than a request.

"Oh. Of course. I'm sorry." She stepped back, motioning them through the door. She wished she'd taken the time to get dressed. Or at least brushed her teeth.

The agents stepped into her apartment, scrutinizing the layout with keen eyes. It was a moderate sized room, sparsely furnished with an overstuffed sofa and matching loveseat that had come with the lease. A roll-top desk sat tucked against the wall next to the terrace, the surface hidden by a computer, several piles of paper and an overflowing ashtray. A week's worth of empty pizza boxes and cartons of Chinese food contributed to more of the clutter. Stacked against the plain white walls were various-sized packing boxes, most of which contained books. A few of the cartons were opened and rummaged through, while the others remained sealed. She had never placed any pictures on the walls, even the mantel above the fireplace sat bare. Looking at the apartment through their eyes, Casey realized she had never tried to make it a home.

After another check of her belt, she waved toward the couch. "Please, have a seat." She scooped up a basket of clothes from the sofa and placed it on the floor, mentally chastising herself for not cleaning the room sooner.

The younger agent, Hawthorne, nodded and sat on the rust-colored sofa while his partner wandered to the terrace doors and studied the skyline with feigned interest. A soft breeze drifted in, rippling the drapes into a delicate dance around him.

Casey skirted around the sofa and sat in the loveseat. "So, what can I do for you?"

"We have a few questions we need to ask you. Don't worry, you won't need a lawyer," Agent Hawthorne said offering her a reassuring smile.

"Sure, okay. What is it you need to know?" She settled back in the loveseat and tried to make herself comfortable. "Oh, wait. This doesn't have anything to do with the packages I've been getting, does it? I mean, I didn't think the FBI looked into that sort of thing."

"Packages?" Agent Simms asked. He turned away from the city view to face her.

"Every now and then I'll get some sermonizing rants and Bibles from a holier-than-thou fanatic who thinks I need to repent for my sinful lifestyle or something ridiculous like that. I guess they don't like my love scenes," she said with a smile.

They both gave her a blank stare.

She swallowed her sigh and added, "They're just harmless books and a few notes. After the third one came in, Jo insisted I turn them over to the police."

"Joe? And he would be...?" Agent Hawthorne took a small notepad from his jacket and scribbled the name on the page.

"*She*, actually. Josephine Landry. She's my agent." At the continued blank looks, she added, "I'm a writer. Paranormal romances. But not your typical vampire or werewolf story, more like witches and demons, which, I guess annoys enough of the zealots out there that they want to try and save my soul. Hence the Bibles. I'll admit when the first one came in all highlighted and dog-eared, it made me nervous because some of my readers are incarcerated, which isn't surprising since a small number of romance fans are convicted felons because our novels are mostly what the prison libraries are sent." Casey stopped and mentally kicked herself. She was babbling. *Geez.* She didn't intimidate easy, but there was something disconcerting about the men in her living room. She offered them a smile and shrugged. "Anyway, they really weren't threatening, but Jo wanted the police to look into it."

"How long ago did you get your first package?" Agent Hawthorne asked. He continued to scribble in his notebook as if he were writing his own great American novel.

"The first one came about six years ago, after my first book came out then another one two years later. I ended up donating them to a used bookstore. The third one came in a year after that, and Jo gave it to the police. But, like I said, since they weren't the least bit threatening, they decided it didn't warrant looking into." She shrugged. "These things just come with the territory. Sometimes readers will confuse the characters with the author or the author with the story. Believe me, the Bibles are the last thing I have to worry about from a fan."

"Have you received any of these notes or packages recently?" Agent Simms asked.

Casey heard the annoyance in his voice and looked at each of the men, fighting against the sudden knot of anxiety coiling up to her chest.

"I don't know. I keep a box at the post office and only picked up my mail yesterday. I haven't had a chance to go through it yet." She waited. Then, because Agent Simms seemed to expect it, she rose from her chair and moved to the desk and the mound of papers on top. She moved the stacks aside, trying not to make the mess any worse.

"So, did you find out who the guy is? Did he do something?" Although she wasn't really sure she wanted to know the answer. If the Feds were at her home this early, it couldn't be good.

"We just want to cover all our bases, ma'am," Agent Hawthorne said. He rose from the sofa and stepped forward to join her at the desk.

Before she could ask him what he meant, Agent Simms grabbed her attention.

"Do you do a lot of traveling, Ms. Martinez?" He stole a look at her Simpson's desk calendar. She hadn't changed the date in over a month.

"Yes, some. I do the occasional book tour or writing conference. I also tend to relocate when I'm writing. But something tells me you already know that, Agent Simms." She sent him a sidelong glance. He stood just over six feet tall with a broad chest and wide shoulders that filled his dark suit. His once-black hair was nearly taken over by gray, and she guessed him to be in his mid-fifties. Hard lines etched his face, giving him a gruff look. Piercing dark-brown eyes watched her with a tense patience that told her she didn't move fast enough for him. If they were planning to do the 'good cop-bad cop' game, she would have no problem determining who was who.

"Do you generally travel alone or do you have an assistant or ...someone?" Agent Simms asked.

Casey slowed her search and looked up, arching her brow. "Sometimes I travel with Jo, but most of the time I'm alone. But I haven't traveled in a while. My last few book signings were local."

"Did you have one of these signings recently?"

Casey grabbed a handful of letters and sifted through them. "Yes. A couple of nights ago in Manhattan. Why?"

"Do you generally get a lot of people at these? Men, perhaps?" Agent Hawthorne asked.

"There are always a few men, yes. They claim they're getting signatures for their wives or girlfriends. I guess no man would admit to reading romances, even if they are suspenseful," she said with short laugh. When they didn't respond, she stopped sifting and placed the mail back on the table. "I'm sorry, gentlemen, but I'm a little pressed for time this morning. If you're not here about the notes or Bibles, then could you please tell me what this is all about?"

"A young woman was found murdered in her apartment last week," Agent Simms said.

The words hit Casey like a sledgehammer and made her heart stop. "Oh my God. Who?" Her mind raced with names. She didn't have many close friends, but she knew a lot of people in the writing community. The fact that the agents were at her house told her she must know the victim.

"Her name was Catherine Flores. She was a school teacher from New Rochelle."

Casey blinked, processing the name in her mind. The weight eased slightly from her chest. "I'm sorry. I don't know her."

"No ma'am, we didn't think you would," Agent Hawthorne said.

"You didn't? Then why—? I don't understand."

Agent Hawthorne tucked his notebook in his jacket and motioned toward the desk. "May I?"

She nodded and stepped back, shoving her hands in her pockets while the agent rooted through her chaos.

"The person who murdered Ms. Flores left one of your books next to the body," Agent Simms said. "Initially, we thought the woman was you because of the picture on the back cover. We couldn't be sure because the guy did quite a number on her face. Until the dental records confirmed her ID, we believed the victim to be you."

Casey looked at the agent as if he had just sprouted wings. "So, what exactly are you saying? You think this guy was after *me*?" She shook her head, as if she could erase the words from her mind. They couldn't be serious. Sure, she was an up and coming name in the romance business, but she was hardly a big enough celebrity for someone to fixate on, much less want to kill.

"It's something we aren't ruling out at the moment," Agent Hawthorne said with a subtle shake of his head at his partner. He motioned Casey back to the armchair and returned to his place on the sofa. "Do the months April or June have any significance for you?" he asked as she returned to her chair.

"No," she said, her voice harder than she'd intended. She shrugged. "My birthday is April twenty-first. But there's nothing about the month of June I find important." She rolled her shoulders to ease the tension in her muscles. She was not going to think about *him*. She shifted in her seat and tried to relax. "Why do you think this has anything to do with me? I mean, I didn't know Ms. Flores, so why would anyone want to kill her if they were after me?"

Agent Simms joined his partner on the sofa, his expression stoic. "Maybe he made a mistake."

Casey glared at him. "Made a mistake? A woman is murdered and

275

you want to call it a mistake?"

There was a slight shift in the agent's expression, as if he'd been pleased by her anger. Maybe it made his job easier if he didn't have to control a hysterical female. Not that she'd ever been hysterical about anything, at least, not in the last twenty years.

"If you've been getting unwanted mail then you may have a stalker. He could be anyone," Agent Hawthorne cut in, shooting a look at his partner. "Maybe he's a crazed fan or a jilted lover. We were hoping you could tell us. Is there anyone you can think of who has any hostilities toward you?"

"No, of course not."

"Have you dated anyone recently or in the past that maybe didn't like how the relationship ended?"

"Not really. Well, there was Aaron. But our breakup was ...fairly amicable," she said.

"What do you mean?" Agent Hawthorne asked.

She sent him a direct look. "He was cheating on me, so I dumped him. But Aaron is no woman killer. He loves them entirely too much."

"Just the same, we'd like to speak with him," Agent Simms countered.

Casey shot him a look that he returned with more authority. She mentally shook her head and rose from the chair. "Fine. I think I still have his number somewhere."

Returning to the desk, she inhaled a calming breath before sliding the top drawer open. It was pointless to get angry with the agents. They were only trying to find a killer and believed she could help. But they had to be off the mark if they thought she was the intended target. She'd been invisible her whole life and didn't attract attention from anyone, much less a psychotic killer.

The doorbell chimed as she grabbed her address book. Agent Simms stood, his hand shooting into his jacket as if he planned to pull out his gun. Casey sent him a dry look and moved to the door. "Don't shoot. It's just the messenger."

A young man in faded jeans and a red T-shirt stood at the door, his hand resting on the worn satchel strapped across his chest. "Good morning, Ms. Martinez. Sorry, I'm late. Do you have a pick-up for me?" he asked with a toothy grin. His smile wavered when he noticed the two men inside her living room.

"Good morning, Tommy. Hold on a minute. I have it right here."

She stepped back to the desk and grabbed a large padded envelope. Beside her laptop was a mug in the shape of a frog. She dug her hand inside and pulled out some money and handed it to Tommy along with the package.

"Thank you, Ms. Martinez," he said, shoving the money in his pocket with a wide smile. "Oh, wait. I have a package for you, too. Mr. DeAngelo said it was left in the mailroom and asked me to bring it up." He withdrew a manila envelope from his bag and handed it to her.

"Thanks. You be careful out there." She tucked the envelope under her arm and closed the door behind him before turning back to the men. "These are just the copy edits for my next book. Sometimes the letter carrier can't fit them in my mailbox so he gives them to the landlord for me," she said to ease their visible concern over the envelope. She grabbed her cigarettes from the desk and lit one up, dropping the pack into the pocket of her robe.

"Ms. Martinez," Agent Simms said, his voice strained with impatience. "Is there anyone else you can think of? An ex-husband, maybe?"

Casey paced to the terrace and blew out the first lungful of smoke through the open doors. The sky was overcast, the temperature unseasonably warm for the beginning of May. In the distance a school bell rang, the laughter of children catching on the breeze. She closed her eyes and tried to focus on someone, anyone that she'd had contact with over the years. But the sad truth was she didn't have any jilted lovers or a husband. In fact, she didn't have any lovers at all—not since Aaron—and that was three years ago. She preferred to spend her time working on her books instead of working on a relationship. It was much less exhausting, and she didn't risk losing more than her heart. As far as she was concerned, love was beyond the bottom of her list of priorities.

She turned back to the men and shook her head. "I'm sorry, Agent Simms. There's no one, really. I've never been married, and I don't date much. My work takes up most of my time." She tamped her cigarette out in the ashtray on the desk and set the stick in the groove before moving back to the armchair. "I really wish I could help you, but I just don't think this has anything to do with me."

Sliding a finger under the seal, she opened the envelope and poured the contents onto her lap. Several photographs of a bloodied, nude body spilled out. The eyes of the victim had been scratched out and thick red streaks were smeared across her image like rivers of blood. Casey's new book, *Unholy Alliance—Dancing with the Devil*, had been placed in the extended, bloodstained hand of the poor woman, as if showing who was responsible. The letters had been intricately edited out of the title to read *U Die*.

She shot up from the chair, her chest expanding with the sharp intake of air. Her stomach pitched. The pictures scattered onto the floor.

Agent Simms vaulted from his seat, breaking the stunned silence. "Get that messenger back in here, now!" He pulled a handkerchief from his pocket and covered the pictures as Agent Hawthorne ran from the room.

"I'm sorry you had to see those," he said through clenched teeth, using a pen he'd pulled from his inside pocket to push the photos back in the envelope.

Casey pressed a hand to her chest, working to slow her rapid breaths. She staggered back to the open terrace and gulped in the warm spring air. At least she could be grateful she hadn't eaten breakfast yet. Gripping the sliding door, she closed her eyes and tried to erase the pictures from her mind. In most of the photos the features were unrecognizable. But in one,*her* face had been pasted onto the picture.

Casey filled her lungs with air and squeezed her eyes tighter, biting into her bottom lip. Her heart pounded against her breastbone as the unwanted memory of another murder filled her mind. The eerie silence of the bedroom. The rich copper odor of blood. Her mother's butchered body draped over the bed. The lifeless eyes staring at Casey, accusing. She pushed it all away and focused on breathing. Emotions rained down on her like ice water, but she wasn't sure what she was supposed to feel. Fear? Panic? Guilt? She closed her arms around her waist and stared blindly at the still waters of the Hudson River.

It had to be a mistake. Why would someone want to kill her? She never did anything to anyone. She didn't have any friends and rarely socialized outside of the writing community. The pictures were just a joke. A very horrible joke. They had to be. Catherine Flores' murder has nothing to do with her. *But the agents think it does.* She mentally shook herself. *No, they have to be wrong! They're reaching and trying to find a connection because they're desperate. Ms. Flores was killed because she was at the wrong place at the wrong time.* It was New York, after all. People were murdered every day with no rhyme or reason to it. Okay, so maybe there was a resemblance between her and the murdered woman, but that was a coincidence, too. *Everyone has a twin or two in the world, it doesn't mean anything!*

She pressed her fingers to her eyes and saw the picture again. *U die.*

Forcing the image from her mind, she swallowed hard. Determined to keep her panic in check, she turned around to face Agent Simms. He stood at the foot of the sofa, waiting and watching with the same blank expression all federal agents seemed to master. "Okay. You have my attention. What is it you aren't telling me?"

The agent motioned her back to the sofa and waited for her to sit. "We believe we have a serial killer on our hands, Ms. Martinez, and we think he may have fixated on you." He paused as if waiting to see if she would react. When she didn't, he continued. "Three years ago I was assigned a case involving the murder of a young woman named Michelle Castillo. She was the only daughter of an attorney in Manhattan. She'd been raped, her body mutilated. Within a week several more cases with the same MO started pouring in. Each of the women was between the ages of twenty and twenty-five. All Hispanic and all who ...all who looked a lot like you."

Casey swallowed. He'd spoken the words gently but she couldn't help feeling as if he blamed her. "How long has this been happening?" she asked, her voice barely audible.

"As far as we can tell, the first murder happened five years ago."

"Five years?" Casey stared at him. The words struck her like a punch. "You've let this happen for five years? How could you have let this go on for so long?"

"It's a bit more complicated than that," Agent Simms said, his voice tight. "The first two murders were two months apart and in two different states. The trails on both went cold fast, and the local officials pushed them to the back burner. The third murder didn't occur until ten months after that. No connections were made to any of the victims until Ms. Castillo's case landed on my desk three years ago. It wasn't until then that we realized we had a serial killer on our hands, and I've been playing catch-up ever since."

Casey paused. A part of her wanted to apologize for offending him, but she knew he wasn't telling her everything and would keep her as much in the dark as the rest of the public.

"How many?" she asked. "How many has he killed?"

"The murder of Ms. Flores makes thirteen." The annoyance in his voice eased, but his expression stayed grim. "So far the only connection we had was that each of the victims was found with shredded pages of a book. We're still trying to piece together enough of the pages to know what type of book they are, but we're almost certain they were all written by you."

Casey took the pack of cigarettes from her pocket and tapped one out. Her hand shook as she lit it, and she inhaled deeply. The smoke tightened the air in her already constricted chest. She'd spent the last twenty years trying to forget everything she'd come from, everything she'd been. But now, because of her, women were being murdered. Just like her mother.

Her gaze moved to the spot where the pictures had fallen. She could still see them there.

"Are you okay, Ms. Martinez?" Agent Simms asked. "Is there

something I can get you?"

Casey blew out a slow stream of smoke and fixed her eyes on him. "I'm fine. Please finish. I know there's more." She'd managed to keep her voice cool and calm, showing no trace of the shock or panic racing through her. She would not be that hysterical female; no matter how much she wanted to scream.

"You asked us before if we thought this man was going to come after you." Agent Simms paused and returned her steady gaze. "We think that answer is yes, Ms. Martinez. This last murder, the one in those pictures you just received, leads us to believe he's coming for you next."

www.ingramcontent.com/pod-product-compliance
Lightning Source LLC
Chambersburg PA
CBHW020304200626
46814CB00006BA/2070